THE RIDGE

THE RIDGE

ELEANOR
TOMBS

iUniverse, Inc.
Bloomington

The Ridge

iUniverse books may be ordered through booksellers or by contacting:

iUniverse
1663 Liberty Drive
Bloomington, IN 47403
www.iuniverse.com
1-800-Authors (1-800-288-4677)

ISBN: 978-1-4759-8961-8 (sc)
ISBN: 978-1-4759-8962-5 (ebk)

Printed in the United States of America

iUniverse rev. date: 05/06/2013

This book is dedicated to all the readers who can sympathize with any of these character's tragedies, just know you are never alone. Also I would like to dedicate this book to those in my past. Thank you for giving me insight into a darker world to inspire this book. Thank you to my Mo grá, without your nagging, this book never would have seen the light of day. Last but not least, thank you to my children, for giving me inspiration to leave a legacy.

CHAPTER 1

Ruth's Place. I had made it. It was a long, drawn out drive. Throwing the old Chevy in park, I took a deep breath. I commanded my body to calm down. I met people everyday. Today would be no different. Still, that deep breath didn't make me feel any better. It still felt like I was being followed, stalked, something. I'm going nuts I thought to myself. Paris to here was a good hour and a half away. Two hours if you drove like a Grandma! Besides, I hadn't seen any suspicious vehicles. Pull yourself together. With that I drew another demanding breath.

To my right, my daughter sat looking out her window. She had light brown hair with sunny highlights that danced over her shoulders when she moved her head. She was babbling over the flowers, birds, or trees. I'm not sure which. She does this on a regular basis. On and on about nothing. I contribute this to her age of six. Her sapphire eyes flashed at me, perhaps wondering why I was still frozen in my seat and not getting out. I adjusted the rear view mirror so I could see my face. Every hair in place, make-up flawless. I flashed a smile to my reflection. I was ready. I slipped on my sandals, opened my truck door, stepped out, and slammed it. With these old trucks there's no other way to shut them.

I brushed my hands down the back of my sundress trying to flatten out the wrinkles. Kera, still talking, came to my side. I took her small hand and headed towards the porch that wrapped around the small store. Two huge maple trees created enormous shade in front. To the left of the porch was a wooden chair and rocker. Two other chairs and a table, made out of white wicker, sat to the right. The porch was painted hunter green. The trim around the windows was a brick red, matching the frame of the screen door. I opened it as it let out a screech from the coil spring that had held it closed.

Opening the front door, I noticed a sign stuck in the window that read 'Yes, We're Open.' A jingle rang out from the string of bells wrapped around the door handle and the scent of pine danced in the air. It was a homey sight. Photos of families were posted all over the walls. Plastic coated, red and white checkered table-cloths draped over the tables, the kind you would use at picnic sites. An old cigarette dispenser hung over a wooden counter with an old cash register off to one side. White Christmas lights outlined the ceiling in a continuous glow.

To the right of the store was a cooler with filled milk, soda pop, and eggs. An isle, perpendicular to the back wall, was packed with your essentials such as bread, beans, snack cakes, and dog food.

The radio was playing a country song that the lady at the counter was humming to, while she poured a tall glass of ice tea. She was a cheery lady with strawberry blonde hair, more strawberry than blonde. She smiled at me for a moment or two before she looked down at my little girl still holding my hand.

"Well, Hi y'all!" she said with an earthy country draw. "How are y'all today?" She was an older lady about fifty to fifty-five. She wore a t-shirt and long denim shorts just above her knees.

Without skipping a beat, Kera smiled back at her and answered, "Good. We're gonna live here now." My cheeks filled up with warmth.

"Glad to have ya!" She responded with a hearty laugh that was so contagious that I found myself snickering.

I cleared my throat. "My name is Ivy Colvin, and this is my daughter, Kera. We were told to meet someone here named Ethan Blackburn. We're a little early." My voice flowed over the words effortlessly.

She smiled and extended her hand out over the counter. "I'm Ruth and this is my store." I took her hand in mine and couldn't help but noticed her hands were soft, probably from being submerged in hot, soapy water. "That your truck, Hun?" she asked, peering over my shoulder and out the door.

"Yes, it is. She's a good truck. Dented but keeps us safe." I smiled. "Do you mind if we had something to drink while we wait?"

She placed her hand on the side of her cheek. "My goodness, where's my manners? What can I getcha? Tea?"

"Tea's fine, thank you." I just want to meet Ethan and get this introduction stuff over with.

She grabbed two glasses and dunked them in her ice bin. She looked up at me and I noticed a smile dancing on the corners of her lips. She took the tall pitcher off the counter and poured the tea in one cup and then the other. "I guess you're the one movin' in."

"Huh? Yeah," I said. Her smile was puzzling me. She had it on her face too long, like a someone with inside knowledge waiting to see how long it would take someone else to figure it out. What was it for? Was Ethan a good landlord? Was he mean or something worse? Doesn't matter. I've lived my whole life wrestling men. I could handle anything Ethan could dish out.

Ruth led the way to a table right next to the window. Good. I could look out and watch for Ethan, but unfortunately I had no idea what he looked like.

"It's nice havin' new folks movin' in," she said. Ruth turned to Kera, sitting across the table from me, and placed the back of her hand on her hip. "How old are ya? Six? Seven?"

"Six." Kera answered in between sips.

"Well, Ethan's gotta boy that's seven." Ruth winked at her and laughed that contagious laugh again. She turned to me. "His name is Zachary. Sweetest little boy. Hops on that four wheeler and comes down almost everyday. Gets a Dr. Pepper, that's his favorite. Of course y'all be neighbors cause he owns all that!"

Following her finger, I looked out the window across the highway. Green grass, tall trees, and in the distance I saw a mountain ridge. "All that?" I was very impressed since I had just moved out of what I refer to as filing cabinets. Apartment life. No yards. No pets. No space. No privacy.

"Yup. All that," she said.

Peering out the window, still trying to wrap my mind around all that greenery, a red Dodge extended cab blocked my view. I turned my eyes back into the small store and down at my glass. Ruth giggled. Again I observed her, wondering why she was so giddy. Poor old lady must be losing her mind.

The bells sounded when the door was opened. A man walked through the doorway and lifted his sunglasses to his forehead. He was six foot tall. He had broad muscular shoulders and arms. As a matter of fact, his thighs and calves were nothing to snub about. His khakis shorts and blue t-shirt fit nicely around his physique. The smile he wore on his face was like a beacon. Bright white teeth and pink lips. His nose and ears were evenly proportionate for his head, which was nice because most people fail in that area. He had dark brown hair, short, but boyish. He stepped in our direction when I noticed he had a shadow. A little boy about seven. His blonde hair draped down his forehead with blue eyes that twinkled above that same luminous smile.

Ruth spoke up immediately. "Hey Ethan. Look what the cat drug in!" She held out her hands like a showcase lady showing off a prize you could win.

I slid out of my seat and stretched out my hand. "Hello. I'm Ivy, and this is my daughter, Kera." He took my hand, firmly shook and released it. He was quite gentle, but formal.

"Hi, I'm Ethan and this is Zachary, my boy."

"Nice to meet you, Zachary," I said.

"Yes Ma'am," Zachary replied. "Hi Kera."

"My name is Ivy, if you want to call me that."

"Yes Miss Ivy," Zachary said after he had gotten a silent approval from his fathers' face.

"Y'all wanna drink?" Ruth asked.

"No thanks Ruth. I wanna get these ladies up to the house. Daylight's a burnin'. Hopefully we'll get 'em all unpacked before dark."

"That would be nice," I said.

Ethan made his way to the door. "Are you ready?"

"Yes, but, Mrs. Ruth how much do I owe you for the teas?"

Ruth winked. "Don't worry 'bout it. We'll be seein' lots of each other." She threw one more smile at me and went over to the counter. Ethan opened the door and jingles once more rang out.

We all piled outside single file. It was warmer out, more humid than a half an hour ago. Kera stopped in her tracks in front of me. Her mouth was gaping wide and her eyes taking long blinks. Three big dogs were perched in the back of the red Dodge, their front paws hanging over the side. Ethan stood next to me chuckling.

"Oh, those are my boys. You like dogs Kera?" he asked.

"Those aren't dogs are they? They look like horses!" she blurted out.

"Those are Great Danes Sweetie." He walked to his truck and placed his hand on the first dog's head. "This one's name is Blue." Blue was a smoky gray with white speckled patches on his coat. His eyes were different colors, one ice blue the other dark brown almost black. Ethan moved to the next dog. "This one is Sampson." He was jet black with a white patch on his chest. He had dark chocolate eyes. Ethan then went to the final dog and scratched behind its ear. "This one's Isis." Isis was pure white. On her floppy ears, the end of her tail, and the end of each toe was black. Ethan stroked them affectionately and gave them kisses. They seemed like well mannered dogs with massive tongues. I wondered how they got them back in their mouths.

Zachary climbed in the bed of the truck and was quickly covered by dogs. They were all happy to see him, as if he had been gone for years. Kera gravitated to the truck and asked if she could get in too. Ethan looked at me and before I could get the breath in to answer he said "I don't care," shrugging.

Watching Kera's excitement, I just nodded. I didn't want to be a kill joy. I grabbed the handle on my truck and got in. I watched Ethan say something to the kids before getting into his truck.

We got on the highway and a half mile down the road we turned off on a back road. It dipped down and then slowly crept in a zig zag crawl upwards. Wild flowers of yellow, purple, blue, and orange grew on the sides of the road. There were pine trees, Silver Leaf maples, oak trees, cedar trees, and cotton wood trees mixed with bushes of a wide variety. It was beautiful. Something out of a fairy tale. All we needed now are fairies flying around.

I settled in my seat, relieved the meet and greet was over and we were finally going to the new house. This will do fine. Even if this house is a shack, I'll do just fine. The hum drum life of people scrambling to and fro like ants can't touch me here. The people that walk in a trance, thumbing their phones like the world would end if their 'OMG' wouldn't 'SEND.' The ones in their cars so stuck in their mundane lives that the two second slow reaction to a green light would make their lives spiral out of control.

"Pathetic," I said aloud. They made me sick. Self absorbent ants. Building buildings, tearing down beautiful places like this for more filing cabinets. They are so predictable and easily manipulated. It wasn't hard to do. Know your enemy, how it acts and thinks, and then just blend. That thought brought a smile to my face.

Three miles from the highway, the green veil lifted abruptly to yield a cut lawn and a tear drop shaped driveway. An oak tree with a tire tied to a limb stood in the middle. The house before me was pretty. It had a small front porch with two windows and a dormer above the front door. There was white trim on dark wood logs with white chink. The roof was silver metal. Ethan's Dodge quieted and the kids and dogs jumped out. Kera and Zachary headed for the tire swing, racing.

"Well, here it is." Ethan strolled to me, arms out at his sides.

I scanned the tree line then looked back to the house. "Wow. This is great."

"I cut the grass yesterday and did a walk through. The house has been empty for five years. I have a little bit of work to do, painting and plumbing stuff. You just came quicker than I expected."

"I'm sorry. I was in a hurry to leave. I can help you paint if you want." I didn't want him upset or feel rushed. That would be the wrong foot to begin on.

Ethan walked to the porch and stopped abruptly. He took a deep breath and went for the doorknob. It was unlocked and when he opened it, the hinges creaked. He called over his shoulder, "Comin'?"

I looked to the kids swinging on the tire, laughing and playing. The huge, panting dogs were spread out all over the lawn. Ethan held the door open for me and I stepped inside. An old musky smell lingered in the air. It looked much bigger inside. Oak wood flooring ran the entire length of the house. There was a gray stoned fireplace in the living room along with furniture, two couches and a chair, covered by floral sheets. To the side of the living room before the kitchen, was a stairwell leading upstairs.

A kitchen table was tucked in the corner of the kitchen. Two long atrium windows lit up and draped sun rays over it. Wood planks made up the ceiling and walls. They were painted white, which were now yellowing slightly. The dark oak flooring stood out in contrast. The kitchen had all your necessities: range, oven, microwave, and refrigerator. I spun in the kitchen to go to the stairs when I noticed Ethan still at the door. His eyes were on the floor and his hand on the doorknob.

"You okay?" I asked walking towards him.

Still looking down, he slowly answered. "Yeah, sure." He climbed the wall with his eyes and then to the stairs. "Your bedrooms and bathroom are upstairs. I hope you like it. It's the best I could do. Jack said you were in a hurry."

"Yes. Thank you. It's perfect." I turned and hurried up the stairs. I wasn't sure if I wanted to pry. He was a stranger to me yet I was curious to what was bothering him. The beauty of the house pulled my thoughts away from Ethan. The stairs were built of the same dark oak that the downstairs displayed. When I got to the top, to my right was the master bedroom, directly in front of me was the bathroom, and to my left was the smaller bedroom.

The master bedroom was furnished with a four post, king sized bed. The wood of the bed was lighter than the floor. A desk and chair was on the opposite side of the room, offset from the bed. Two rounded beams protruded from the vaulted ceiling which had a black, long necked fan hanging from it.

The bathroom was all tile. The floors, counter, shower, shower seat, everything, white tile. Easier to clean, I thought. The smaller bedroom had the same vaulted ceiling and a twin sized bed. Also, fit snugly under the dormer window, was a wooden toy chest. It looked old and loved. It reminded me of a treasure box from a very well-to-do pirate.

This will do fine I thought. Jack did just fine. I peered out the window not really seeing anything, just thinking. Jack was one of the very few people that I valued as far as people go. He wasn't an ant. He never lied to me that I know of. Believe me, it's hard to lie to me. He was straight forward and I liked that. He was a regular customer at the last job I had and we struck up a friendship. He became one of my few closest friends. I could talk to him about anything easily. Whenever I needed anything, he was there for me. Being poor and orphaned, charity, in a way, becomes a part of you.

I started telling him about some weird things that were happening to me one night. He listened intently. He acted as if we were having an everyday conversation, such as things being misplaced inside my home. Furniture being moved slightly around my apartment. My truck keys found themselves in my cabinet inside my bowls. My purse that I always put on the table next to the front door, was under my bed. Kera knew better and would never do things like that. Many more things moving around or being lost all together. The last straw that made me confide in Jack in the first place, was my truck was moved clear across the parking lot at my apartment complex.

I told him that I felt like I was being stalked. My feminine intuition was telling me I was in danger, life and death danger. I felt eyes following me when I was out in public. Shivers when I was alone covered my body. I told him I was probably crazy and just being silly.

Jack told me I should never dismiss my intuition telling me something. That's why I have it, to warn me. He asked my permission to follow me for a couple of days. It was just to make me feel safer, or so I thought. In three days he was trying to convince me to move.

I felt there was more to the story than Jack was telling me and the tone he used when he talked about me moving to the country, I knew there was. One night I overheard a conversation Jack was having with someone on the phone and all I caught was him saying "the situation is bad." Jack arranged this move, gave me the gas money, called in a favor to Ethan, and helped me pack up. So here I am. I really wonder what he meant by "the situation is bad."

I jumped back into reality and my knees and ankles hurt. I guess I had been standing there awhile thinking. I walked down the stairs and outside. Zachary and Kera were playing hide and seek in the trees. Zachary was counting with his face buried in his hands. Ethan was by the oak tree in the driveway. His eyes fixed on a dark patch of trees. He didn't move. As my feet touched the shale driveway, it made a crunching sound under my sandal. Ethan's head snapped towards me, his yellow-green eyes fixed on me.

He relaxed his shoulder muscles and released his fists. "Sorry. I was paying attention to the kids. Are you ready to get your things inside?"

"Yeah, thanks," I said slowly. I was shaken by that glare. Did I show outwardly how unsettled it made me?

With Ethan's help, we got the truck unpacked in no time. I didn't have much, but they were all I had other than my daughter. Boxes of clothes, trash bags with more clothes, Kera's toys, our toiletries, blankets, pillows, a radio, and other small things.

Ethan told me he would be back in the morning to get started on the plumbing. He needed to do some touch-up painting on the yellow spots around the house also. The first thing I did when they left, was open all the windows and let out that musky smell. The outside breeze swirled in the house, revitalizing it along with me.

CHAPTER 2

Early in the morning I found myself spread out all over the king sized bed. Surprisingly I slept soundly. My sleep had always been broken up my whole life. I never slept straight through before. Maybe it was this house? It was so comfortable. Throughout my years I have just existed in my cage. I moved from here to there never staying in one place for too long. Rage is the only constant in my life. It's the only thing that has lasted. Rage towards my father, mother, siblings, friends, everyone. My so called friends that all turn out to be back stabbing, two faced, good for nothing liars.

This place was foreign to me but, I feel as if I have been here before. Some distant dream perhaps. It's really not the house or location though. It's the feelings I'm feeling. I've never had feelings before. Well not like other people do I'm sure. I do cry watching sad movies, but not for reasons others do. I cry because I can't feel that loss. I can't feel that love. I can't feel anything outside my lonely painful world. I am hateful.

My skin is a jail. Being pretty is a curse. No one looks past the aqua blue eyes, red full lips, the black spiral curls that frame my face, or the tall, slim frame of my body. If they did, they would avoid me like the plague. My silver serpent tongue wouldn't be able to soothe or deceive them. The devastation to those I have touched is fatal. I destroy lives. In a way, I feel sorry for them for being so weak. They deserved it. They shouldn't be so blind.

Man, I'm Miss Negativity this morning. I'm just trying to dodge this peaceful calm feeling. To make matters worse, I'm attracted to Ethan. That doesn't help me at all. I have impulse issues. At Ruth's, Ethan's smile penetrated my stone heart. I hope I didn't show it externally. My heart has only had enough room for my daughter. I would fight and kill for her in a heartbeat, without a second's thought. I tried to refocus my thoughts. So why does Ethan keep coming to the front of them? He was a mystery to me. He was so strong, enticing, scrumptious. I can't read him. That drove me nuts. I could get anyone's number after a few minutes. Their vulnerabilities, dislikes, those sort of things. Not Ethan. After all he was just a man. Why was he so intriguing?

"Put him out of your mind!" I demanded swiping my face with my hands hard. I got out of bed and slapped my bare feet on the oak floor. I went to check on Kera. Anything to change the subject. She was laying on her side with a pillow over her head and one between her knees snoring. "Silly girl," I whispered. I walked quietly down the stairs to the kitchen for a glass of water. Nursing it, I walked to the front door. I found my mind on Ethan again looking out the window.

I realized I was not the only one looking down the driveway. On the porch was a dark chocolate dog with its back to me. It was sitting like one of those lions or gargoyles rich people have to welcome you at their large gates. The only signs of life to it was the ribcage expanding.

I was standing there a minute when the dogs floppy ears perked up on top of its head. The sound of tires smashing rock got louder as they approached. I took a breath in and forgot to exhale when I saw the red Dodge. He had a train of dogs following him as he parked behind my old truck. The doors opened up and Zachary and Ethan got out.

Ethan had a black muscle shirt with cut off shorts on. His defined, tanned biceps and shoulder muscles glistened in the early morning sun. Zachary, wearing a tie dyed t-shirt and cargo shorts, waited at the truck as his dad walked around the front and towards me. The chocolate dog greeted Ethan with its tail beating its sides with each wag. White fur was splattered on its belly and chest. On its face was also white around its nose with a thin line running up between the eyes.

Ethan slapped the dogs cheeks back and forth playing. His attention drew to me as I opened the front door. I repeated in my head, "He's just a man, he's just a man, he's just a man." Ethan looked at me smiling that glowing warmth at me. The words I just said evaporated. All I could do was smile back. Damn it.

"Good morning. Did you sleep well?" Ethan asked. He took a step up on the porch.

I crossed my arms over my chest, "Yes. As a matter of fact I did. How was your night?"

"Good. Zachary wants to know if Kera can go for a walk. There's a creek behind the house pretty close he wants to show her." Ethan stopped arms length away from me.

Please Lord don't let me blush. I could feel his breath floating in the air touching my shoulders. It was warm but comfortable outside. The air was moist filled with the fragrance of fresh tree and earth. I pulled a quick breath in, "She's still sleeping, but I have to get her up anyway." I turned back to the house feeling flush. I only got three steps inside before Kera bolted down the stairs and almost ran me over. I snagged her elbow as she passed me. "Wow! Good morning to you too!" I bent down and kissed her forehead.

"Morning Momma. Can I go with Zachary?"

Ethan laughed. "I got some donuts." I let go of her elbow and she skipped out the door.

"Get the bag of donuts for y'all and bring me my food." Ethan told Zachary. His arms were crossed over his chest which made them look delicious. He was leaning on the porch post looking at me.

If I didn't know any better I'd say he was looking through me peering at my soul. It scared me. Not another human being ever looked at me so intensely. I wonder what he saw. Maybe it was my mind examining this to the extreme, as always.

"Come on!" Zachary's voice was fading as they ran off with a white bag and dogs in tow prancing behind them. Ethan was holding a bag and petting the only dog that stayed, the chocolate dog. Its coat was silky shiny.

Ethan said to me in a soft voice, "This is Nomad." As if by some weird notion the dog knew Ethan was introducing him to me, he turned his head and looked right at me. "He's a Stafford Shire Pit bull. He has razor's edge in him.".

I dropped to one knee and made kissing noises with my mouth. "He's beautiful." I said. Nomad walked over to me and sat inches from my face. His eyes were deep pools of comfort. "Razor's Edge? Is that a bloodline?"

"Yeah. Since the other dogs went with the kids, they won't hear me say this." Ethan whispered, "Nomad's my favorite. He's the leader of all my dogs. He's the best dog I've ever had." Ethan knelt down in front of me. "Are you alright?" His face full of concern.

I straightened my posture and relaxed my facial features so I was blank. My stone facade was failing me. He was going to see through me and fast. My heartbeat picked up. I don't want to be labeled the silly girl that fell for her landlord. The image I get from that belongs in an "X" rated film. I swallowed and it was louder than I wanted it to be. "Yeah, why?"

"You seem preoccupied." He shrugged.

I smiled, I couldn't help it. I'm just glad he couldn't read my mind.

After a short pause Ethan changed the subject thankfully. "You ready to make a mess in there?"

"Ready."

"I have some tools to grab, but first, are you hungry? I made breakfast burritos." He held up the bag.

"I'm starving." We walked into the house to the kitchen. I took a seat at the head of the table after Ethan sat down. "I would offer you something to drink, but all I have is water."

"Have you looked in your fridge or cabinets?"

"No, I planned on hitting Ruth's today."

"Well," he sat back in his chair, "Jack called after you hit the road in Paris. He helped you pack up your truck and saw your lack of groceries and asked if I would pick some things up."

"Great!" I interrupted. "How would Jack know that I didn't stop at a store and do that for myself?" I felt irritated. The thought of Jack thinking that I couldn't feed my daughter enraged me. If he thought that, how did that conversation go? 'Hi Ethan. Jack here. I'm so sorry to bother you, but Ivy is so irresponsible that she didn't pack a single thing for her daughter to eat. Can you be a pal and help her out? If you don't do it, I don't know what will happen. Put it on my tab ol' buddy, ol' pal?' I was furious. Here comes the rage, I grit my teeth.

Ethan responded in a calm voice. "He didn't know. He was just worried. He wanted you to have a few days to adjust and relax before you had to run all over town."

I took a long inhale, in through my nose and then out through my mouth. Calm down, I thought. "I'm sorry. Thank you." It was all I could come up with. I needed to keep that animal in its cage and not let Ethan see it. Deep breaths and clearing my thoughts was the only thing I knew how to get that switch to turn off. Finally the monster was retuning to it's cage.

Ethan pulled thick burritos out of the bag and placed one in front of me. "That's alright. I would take a glass of milk though," he chuckled.

I got out of my seat as controlled as I could. I didn't want another outburst to happen. I walked over to the refrigerator and slowly opened it. The light lit up the cold compartment. I had a gallon of milk, lunch meat, butter, eggs, jug of water, hotdogs, and condiments. I quit looking and gabbed the milk. "You call this some things?" I asked turning my back to him and setting the gallon on the counter.

"You never know what those midnight cravings are gonna be like!" He said.

"Are the cabinets just as stocked?" I shot a look at him over my shoulder then turned my attention back to the milk.

"Look. When it comes to kids I don't hold back. You needed some food. I gotcha some. End of discussion. Where's the problem?" He held his hands out palms up.

"I don't want to feel like I owe you anything other than rent." I said without thinking, looking down at the counter. Damn. Not the most intelligent thing I've ever said.

"You don't," he snapped. I stood at the counter afraid to turn around and see anger on his face. I opened the cabinet and pulled out two cups. I filled them and returned to the table.

He sighed and smiled slightly. "You need to understand that you're in the country now. We take care of our own here." His voice was sweetly ringing in my ears soothing my thoughts. He was right. I had to adjust but he was surely not the man to get me in check.

"So, what do we do first?" I changed the subject.

"We eat, then we'll start upstairs."

I took a bite of the burrito and the taste danced on the tip of my tongue. Bacon, eggs, salsa, and pepper jack cheese. My eyes widened. "Wow, this is great!"

"Thank you." We ate the burritos quietly. I ate all of mine and didn't even leave a scrap of shredded cheese on the paper towel. I chugged my milk and went to the sink. Ethan followed and his arm brushed mine while he put his cup down. We both simultaneously froze for a moment. A jolt, current if you will, rippled and glided over my skin and made goosebumps all over me. They were oddly warm goosebumps, like the ones you get in the shower when the water is too hot. It jerked me back to that distant dream feeling. It wasn't this house or location I realized, it's Ethan! Our skin touching made my body react instinctively. I turned to look at him when I saw that the front door was open.

Did he feel it? Was this in my head? How do I ask him if he felt it? Why did I feel anything at all? "Go away" I growled to myself. I can't think straight when I'm experiencing feelings. I forced myself into the living room as Ethan came back in.

He had brushes and a gallon of paint. "Did you say something?" I was close enough to him I noticed his eyes were a different color. They were a yellow-green earlier. Right now the green had cleared out of the iris and lingered on the outside edge. An eery yellow invaded the center I stepped in front of him as he was headed for the stairs. I looked right into his eyes.

"It was nothing, just talking to myself. Your eyes are-." I hesitated.

"Yeah," he whispered. We were so close together I would have jumped if he had spoke it.

"Yellow." I whispered back. My eyes shot down to his mouth. How soft were his lips? What did they taste like? I imagined my mouth caressing his. Reality came calling. What was I doing? I stepped aside and glared out the window. He's just a man Ivy, control yourself.

Ethan cleared his throat. "Let's go upstairs and start on the small room first." He walked to the first step and hesitated. He gripped the paint brushes and began up the stairs. I stood in the middle of the living room for a minute and centered myself. When I finally got up stairs in Kera's room, Ethan handed me a paint brush, and went back to work. We painted the small room in silence. I had two more planks to finish when Ethan left the room. I waited a few minutes and I sat my brush on the edge of the paint can. I left the room and saw Ethan in the bathroom leaning on the sink staring off at the floor.

"What's wrong?" I asked from the doorway.

"This used to be my home. I shared it with my wife and son. We were in the process of finishing the house I live in now when my wife died." His voice strained as he spoke of her.

"I'm sorry. I could finish painting and you could check the plumbing tomorrow if you want?"

He lifted his head. "No. I have to face my demons someday. It just happens to be today. I'll be okay. If we do the rest of the house together it'll get done quicker." He rolled the paintbrush in his hands for a moment and then began to paint again.

I think doing the rooms together was his way of saying he didn't, or couldn't, go into the master bedroom alone. How many memories were locked in the walls of his old bedroom? Good? Bad? Memories that could bring things to the surface that maybe he hadn't dealt with? Or maybe he wanted to spend more time with me in the same room? That would be dangerous. I couldn't help but grin.

Painting is not a hard job. I rather enjoy painting. After a few hours of Ethan and I glancing back and forth at each other, Kera and Zachary came into the house and wanted to help paint. That is when painting does become a hard job. The kids got more paint on their clothes and body than the walls.

It was wonderful to see Kera interacting with an adult male. Her father left me when I was eight months pregnant. She never had another male in her life due to my inability to trust. The only one that was there in regular intervals was Jack.

It was cute to see Ethan and Kera whispering and laughing. The powers little girls have over adult men are amusing. It didn't take us long to get most of the painting done. Ethan kept looking over at me while we cleaned up as if he wanted to ask something.

When we were done cleaning the paint brushes I asked, "What is it?"

"I have to come back tomorrow, if that's alright? I need to get under the house and work on the plumbin'. You can use your toilet but your shower needs some fixin'." Ethan explained.

"Alright. Around about what time?" I was drawn into his eyes again as we were talking. The swirls of dark green outlined lighter green and in the middle a thick yellow vein. I could get lost in them so I tried to look away.

"Early. If ya want, I can take ya to town and show you around after I'm done."

"Sure. That would be nice." I walked him to the front door and out to his truck. The children came running from the trees followed by all those dogs. They were out of breath and giggling. There was an uncomfortable awkward silence before Zachary and Ethan got into his truck.

"Tomorrow then." Ethan said as he glared into my eyes. A warm rippling tossed in my stomach.

I swallowed quickly and replied. "Tomorrow." I turned and walked to the porch without looking back. I needed to reset. I needed to put him at arms length, away from me.

Nothing good can come out of getting physical with him. I knew he felt something for me, but this was strictly fleshy. I had enough of that in my life. I am not going to start that way with him, if anything starts in the first place.

It was a long night of unpacking and thinking. I'm not any good at tidying up and all the clothes had no dresser to be put in. I piled the clothes up on the closet floors. I was happy with this house and where it was. This was just far enough out of the way to give me breathing room. I would miss Jack though. I talked with him for hours. I had no phone here and no way of getting a hold of him. I really didn't want to get wrapped up in all the new technology. I didn't have a cell phone, or internet access, or even a computer. I was not up to date, so to speak. How was I to get a hold of Jack now? I would have to talk to Ethan about getting a land line hooked up.

Kera was in her room reading one of her books, "There's a Wocket in my Pocket" by Dr. Seuss. She had all the books by him. I loved reading them to her. Listening to her read through the wall was entertaining. She mimicked silly sounds that I made when I read it to her. I sat on my bed beginning to feel lonelier than ever. This was about the time I would see or talk to Jack. It has only been two days or so but I never understood our relationship until now. He would always make me feel better or put things in perspective for me. I remember one time we were talking late one night after I got off of work. He was waiting by my truck in the parking lot. He could never sneak up on me. He tried anyway though. It was a cloudy night and I was done with people and their stupidity. I was also done with the cold icy chills up and down my spine that were there all day. I walked to my truck on sore feet and knees. The closer I got to my truck, the warmer I got. A sense of calm came over me. I assumed it was my way of winding down from a ten hour shift. I knew it was over by the sight of my truck. Jack was leaning on the front fender of my dented Chevy.

He was smiling and holding out his arms. "Nice night huh?"

I gave him a bear hug and inhaled the fresh air in relief. "Yes. Nicer now that I'm off of work. So many idiots came in today."

"I had to pick up Kera from Tabby's," he sighed. "She really is not the best babysitter."

I rolled my eyes. "What happened this time?"

"Her boyfriend got put in jail . . . again." He held the door open for me and I sat in the seat feeling the blood work its way into my swollen feet.

"Will she ever learn?" I hollered out the windshield watching Jack walk around the truck and open the passenger door.

"Nope. Not her kind." Jack said sitting down. "Kera's sleeping in my car. I'll follow you home." Jack kissed my cheek and got out.

I lived only ten minutes away from the gas station I worked at, so it was a quick ride. Jack carried Kera, snoring, into my apartment on the second floor. I plopped down on my couch and exhaled a long breath. Jack turned Kera's light off and came down the hallway. He placed his butt right next to me. I slid off the back of the couch and my head landed on his shoulder.

He chuckled. "That bad huh?"

"Stupid people. They just keep breeding! One guy came into the store and asked if we had a bathroom. Not that the big neon yellow sign that says 'Restrooms' didn't give it away. Later some woman came into the store with a truck that used diesel fuel, and she tried to put the big rigs nozzle in hers. It took her ten dollars worth of gas before she realized it wasn't going into her tank. Then she proceeded to gripe me out because she got gas all over herself and the side of her truck. Like that's my fault she's a moron!" Jack laughed and petted my hair. "Man how idiotic people are." I yawned and processed the night. Jacks fingers felt good in my hair. "Well, how was your day?"

"Same ol', same ol'. I talked to my friend Ethan again today. I haven't talked to him in a year or so." My head had slid down off of his shoulder and onto his chest. Jack's heart was beating strong and hard.

"How's he?" I remember him talking about him quite fondly.

"He's doing well. Him and his son have, since I left, moved into their new house and are adjusting. Someone moved into my house shortly after I left. A husband and wife with three children. They have a nice view of the mountains where the house is and it sits on forty acres. They should be happy there. Town's only a few minutes away." Jack said with a somber voice.

"Why did you move here from that place if you loved it so much?" I asked.

"Ethan and I are so much alike in many ways that . . . well, the mountain side wasn't big enough for the both of us. When you're around someone that is so much like you, it's neat at first. You have a lot to talk about, but after a while, the things that make you so similar, drives you both nuts." He laughed. I yawned again. I wasn't being rude by any means. I was just exhausted. Jack turned the television on and flipped through the channels as I began to fall asleep.

"Good night my little Bambino," he whispered in my hair.

When I awoke in the morning, he was gone. He had always been in and out of my house. He was very good at popping in to check on us when the worst, it seemed, rained down. He picked up Kera and watched her at a moment's notice. He was lucky. He had tons of money and had the luxury of not having to break his back for a living. I did love him deeply. I just couldn't shake the feeling, even though I knew better, that he was helping me and being in my life out of pity.

Kera's voice has toned down from reading, and she had probably fallen asleep. I stretched out on the king sized bed and spread my arms out beside me. The cool blankets felt good on my sore arms from painting. I slid my head up on the pillow, faced the doorway, and a haunting memory came scratching to the surface. I couldn't ever sleep with my back to the door. I remember when I was a child having to be aware of the monster that crept into my room late at night. Always having to pretend like I was sleeping so maybe he wouldn't hurt me that night. That was far and few in between. Sleeping like this never went away. Here I am, an adult, and still scared he will come snaking his way to my room.

CHAPTER 3

In the morning Ethan and Zachary were knocking on my door at five o'clock. I hadn't even been asleep three hours yet. I was up all night thinking and unpacking. I was wearing a pair of black laced hip hugging panties and a bright yellow half top. I jumped out of bed grumbling, "Just a second!" I threw on a small pair of black shorts, ran down the stairs, and cracked the front door just enough to pop my head out.

"Morning." Ethan smiled. "You need a few minutes? We're early risers. Sorry. We could come back in a couple of hours if you want." He held his thumb up over his shoulder. His face turning a dark shade of pink

"No. That's alright. I'm going to get dressed and get Kera up. We'll be just a minute." I shut the door and rubbed the sleep out of my eyes. Shaking the warm shell of sleep off my brain, I continued up the stairs to Kera's room. She had tossed in the sheets so much last night that all she had on the bed with her was a pillow and it was between her knees. I gently rubbed her shoulder and woke her up.

"No, Momma. Five more minutes," she said pulling the pillow up over her head.

"Zachary's here." I whispered.

"Really?" She popped her head out slowly. I winked at her and she took a minute to look around and then a spark came to her eyes. "Okay. I got to pee." She climbed out of bed and stumbled into the bathroom. I went to my room and pulled the curtains back letting the new morning sunshine in. I jumped up on the bed and bounced off the other side. I landed a few feet away from the closet. I rummaged through the piles of clothes, knocking them over in the process, to get a pair of cut off shorts and a tank top. Simple, yet nice looking. I passed the bathroom and ran into Kera as she pushed passed me to get into her room. She was peeling off her nightgown in the middle of the room. I pulled a cute outfit out for her, a pair of shorts and a pink t-shirt. I ran a comb through my hair and put some make-up on my face. I brushed my teeth with Kera, who was now trying to see herself in the mirror. I grabbed my purse off of the end table and I shut the front door behind us.

"You look nice Kera." Ethan said.

"Thanks." Kera said running after Zachary that was playing on the tire swing.

Ethan's eyes climbed up my body to my face. "So does your Momma." he said quietly.

"Why thank you." I flashed a smile at him and curtseyed. Please don't blush, I thought, think of something quick before you get caught. "How far away is town?"

"It's about twenty, twenty-five minutes away. Would you two like to join us for breakfast? There's a really good restaurant there in town. They have the best southern cookin' 'round."

"That sounds great. I could go for a cup of coffee." I sighed trying to drag my eyes away from his arms being hugged tightly by the sleeves on a black 'v' neck shirt.

I walked towards my truck, breathing in and out slowly. And wouldn't you know it? Ethan had to get my attention. "Would you like to ride with me?" He paused. "It would save ya some gas," he added.

"I guess that would be fine." I smirked. Today is going to be one big mistake. Ethan opened the door for me smiling. I called for Kera and she climbed in the back with Zachary. Ethan opened his door and got in and away we went. His dogs followed us halfway down the road. We left them behind in a cloud of dirt. Ethan hit the highway taking a right. The children were playing a game Zachary called 'spot that'.

I felt butterflies in my stomach. I was sitting in the front seat trying not to look over at Ethan so, I pushed my focus to around me instead. His truck was tidy and smelled like apple cinnamon. He had nothing hanging on his rear view mirror. There was dust on his dash but I suppose living on the road he lives on, there is nothing you can really do about that. His radio was playing a country tune, of course. The song was about a man that lost his love and she was getting married to someone else today. Poor man. You could hear the agony in his voice. I am glad that I don't feel things like that. Ethan was humming along with the chorus. His sunglasses didn't help any with trying not to find him so attractive this morning. They finished that gorgeous package like a bow on a present. I tried to look out the window and focus on the endless landscape of trees, cows, green grass and the occasional rusted tin roofed, falling down barns.

We had only been in the truck for eight or nine minutes before there was a fork in the road. You could go straight, which bent left, or to the right. Ethan pointed to the right, "That way is Zachary's school. And this way is town." His strong hand pointed right in front of my face. It was attached to his big forearm and bicep. I just couldn't help myself but to run my eyes over them again. My mouth began to water and I threw my attention out the window for I was only torturing myself. I could feel, every so often, him looking at my legs and the side of my face. I tried to ignore him. Doesn't he know what he does to a woman?

About five minutes from there, he pointed to the left of the road. "There's the lake we go swimmin' at on the weekends." I really couldn't see anything through the pine trees that layered the ground. They were like a fortress hiding the lake. A sign was the only thing giving it away which read 'Clayton Lake' on a faded white sign with pale red letters. As he drove closer to town, homes began to surface. They were spread out nicely. Some were trailers and others were beautifully built two story homes. The mountainous terrain put some homes on small cliffs over looking the curvy road that climbed and fell. The closer we got to town, the smaller the hills.

The speed limit changed from sixty-five on the highway, to twenty-five gradually. It was only a few more miles until we arrived in Clayton. A single street named 'Main street' ran through the heart of the town. Go figure. As you drove into town there was a gas station/grocery store to the left.

"This store was owned by one of the oldest residents here. They settled here before the town was Clayton." Ethan began. "Obviously they are dead now so they passed it down through the generations." It had a light blue metal roof and siding with white bricks along the lower half of it. Diesel fuel pumps were off to the side and at least ten other gas pumps in front of the store. They had just opened for business and not many cars were in the parking lot.

To the right was a beauty shop. It had big windows in the front with letters on them. 'Angel's Beautiful Oasis'. Ivy plants outlined the window ledge inside and women walked about the shop getting things ready for opening. One lady, by the front door, had her head tilted to the side holding a phone between her ear and shoulder talking.

Right next to her shop was the post office, a brick building with a wooden awning over the front that had bird nests tucked into the big letters. An old man in his sixties was walking to the front door and began swinging his cane trying to fend off the mother birds as they dive bombed his head. I laughed and shook my head. Down the road was the old downtown buildings decorated in old, faded, and chipping paint still on the walls of the outsides. There was an insurance company, a newspaper office, a police station and other stores. Some people were about and going into some of the places. We continued to the end of the town. to a restaurant that was called 'The Kettle'. The restaurant was a ranch style building. Dark blue metal siding and a white gutter/spout. Several trucks were parked in the light gray, gravel lot.

Ethan put his truck in park and looked over at me. "Ready?"

"Yes. I am. Are you kids?" I looked in the back seat and Kera and Zachary were already unbuckled and getting their doors opened. "I guess so." I laughed as we all got out of the truck. He gathered the children and walked to the front door, opened it for us, and we went inside.

The walls were painted in a country blue and white style with the little ducks with ribbons around their necks bordering the walls. There was a counter in front of the door, set back some. An old cash register and a bell to ring for service sat on the counter. The floor was made of sand color tiles. I could see the cook looking up at written orders on paper slips hanging on the metallic round holder. She was an older lady with curly gray hair and blueish gray eyes with dark circles underneath them. She was short and could barely see over the square cut hole in the wall to dish out the plates for the waitress. She smiled at us and her face softened.

"Come on in. Have a seat anywhere. Ethan, what you got there?" A small grin replaced the smile.

"Mornin' Jane. This is Ivy and Kera. They just moved here from Texas." Ethan said laughing.

"Hi Ivy. Hi Kera. I'm Jane and I'll make ya anythin' you wanna eat. Ethan, I'll send Wanda out to ya." She winked at Ethan and moved out of the window. The sound of sizzling and metal utensils clanking on a grill filled the restaurant while I followed Ethan.

He took us to a table in the corner of the room. He sat with his back to the wall. Great! I needed to sit facing the room. I needed to see what was coming and going around me so I could be aware of everything. I stood talking to myself and noticed Ethan was looking at me puzzled. I took the seat next to him. No need to go into all my weird quarks with him. He would undoubtedly think I'm crazy. I heard it all my life. An assault of words like tidal waves against the fortress I live in. Crushing, rippling away from thick iron clad walls I'm suffocated by. No one gets in. No one.

Kera's silverware clacked loudly on the hard floor jerking me away from my thoughts. I immediately grabbed them up. Zachary was giggling and I took a strong steady breath clearing away my unsteadiness. I glanced around me. The table was rounded and before anyone could say anything a woman came out of the double swinging doors with a round hole in each, to our table, and locked eyes on Ethan. She smiled from ear to ear with menus in hand. She was tall and slim. She had thick brown hair with subtle highlights. Her eyes were big brown doe eyes and the light blue company shirt fit snug on her torso. She had a small cute nose, light pink lipstick on, and the rest of her makeup was done modestly. Her waitress apron was spot free. It matched her black slacks that were snug as well. She had a black and white pen stuck in the pony tail that held some of her hair on the top back while the rest draped over her shoulders.

"Good morning Ethan. How ya doin' this pretty morning?" Her voice was soft, shy and she was fidgeting with her order pad.

"Good. Wanda, this is Kera and Ivy." He pointed to each of us smiling.

"Good mornin'." Wanda shot a look at me. I think she spoke a little flatter. It might be my imagination, but I am pretty sure of it. She looked at my Kera. "My, you're beautiful."

Kera just laughed and innocently said, "I know." I kicked her leg under the table. She quickly added, "Thank you."

"Hey Zach. How are ya?" Wanda squatted down next to Zachary's seat.

"Fine Miss Wanda."

"Did ya get any of those dinosaur skeletons put together I gotcha?"

"Yeah, two of 'em. The T-Rex and the one with big plates on its back."

Wanda stood up. "I'll have to see them all done someday if it's alright with your Dad." She flashed a smile at Ethan while she passed out the menus.

"Well, someday. That would be nice." Ethan said. "But for right now, how about a coffee for Ivy and me. The kids would like some chocolate milk. Alright Kera?"

"Sure." Kera said looking at the menu like she knew what she was reading. She really was imitating Zachary.

"Okay. Be right back." She smiled ear to ear again at Ethan as she left the table.

"Well. She seems nice and friendly." I said straightening my posture.

"Yes." Ethan said picking up his menu. "She is."

"I'm starving." I changed the subject. "Do you have any preferences?"

"I love their southwestern omelets. Jane's a wonderful cook. Zachary loves her pancakes. She draws smiley faces with whipped cream and raisins," he laughed.

"Hmm. Kera what do you want to eat?"

"I want what Zachary's having."

Wanda appeared out of the swinging doors carrying a tray full of our drinks. She placed each of our cups in front of us and pulled her pen out of her pony tail. She immediately made eye contact with Ethan blushing. She saved his coffee cup for last so she could stand right next to him I bet.

"Y'all ready to order?"

"I'll have the usual and Zachary will too." Ethan said, handing her the menus.

"And you two?" Wanda wasn't as smooth as she thought she was. I caught her fingers lingering on Ethan's as he gave them to her.

"I'll have the southwestern omelet with light toast and hash browns. Kera will have the pancakes with bacon." I looked over my menu and saw Wanda glancing up at Ethan between writing the orders down. I felt vexed all of the sudden at her. She really needed to stop eyeballing him. "Do you have creamer and sugar? I need it for my coffee." I interrupted her glassy, twitterpated eyes. I think she is too wrapped up in Ethan's eyes to do her job properly.

"Oh sure. Sorry 'bout that." Wanda swept up our menus and went off with our orders to the kitchen.

"I think someone has a crush." I winked at him.

"No. She's a real nice lady and likes Zachary. She has a little boy 'round his age."

"Whatever you say." Seems Ethan is oblivious to the flirtatious Wanda.

She returned with the sugar in a glass container with a silver lid and some milk in a little metal gravy boat. She, not surprisingly, glanced up at Ethan before she left our table and went over to welcome another couple coming in the door. They were an older couple with silver hair and holding hands. Wanda called them by name and sat them at a table. She then went to the kitchen and returned with a soapy rag and wiped the table down. Must be their usual table. I offered Ethan some sugar and creamer but he liked his coffee black.

"I have to get under the house today and check out the plumbin' and that's 'bout all I gotta do to it I think."

"Okay. Hey, just curious, how hard would it be to get a land line hooked up?" I stirred my coffee watching the color lighten up.

"Not hard at all. I could call the company tomorrow and get it set up for sometime next week. I would have it on for ya now, but they have to come out and look at the old wiring. The house has been sittin' awhile. They'd have to set up an appointment for ya."

"No. That's fine. How much is the deposit do you think?" I mumbled. I hate talking bills.

"Not sure. I just transferred my phone from that house to my new one. I haven't paid a deposit for anything in forever," he chuckled.

"Great." Never having to pay deposits. Not having to worry about money. Just the type of person that would have to run, and I mean run, from me. I could have all he owns by morning. Damn it, I can't think like that. I need to stop myself from destroying everything, everyone. "Keep yourself in check Poison," I thought.

"Ya know, if ya want to, I could put the phone in my name and just have the bill come in with mine." Well! He's not going to make this easy on me is he? I just sat there keeping my mouth shut. I will not have an outburst here in this restaurant with little miss doe eyes watching.

Ethan moved his coffee to the side of the table for Wanda to place his food. She came out of nowhere. His plate was full with an omelet that barely fit, a three cheese blend melted on the top and salsa underneath it. The toast, hash browns, a huge helping of bacon, and sausage almost didn't fit on the plate it sat on. I have no idea how he is going to eat all that.

The kids plates were cute as could be. Three large pancakes with whipped cream smiles and groups of raisins for eyes. Butter sat right in the middle for the nose. Wanda sat three small glass pitchers in the middle of the table with syrup in them. They all had labels in white naming the contents. Maple, Strawberry, and Raspberry.

"Jane told me to tell y'all she has freshly made blueberry syrup in the back. She just made it from her blueberry patch at home this mornin', if y'all want some." Wanda, though enthusiastic, was of course looking at Ethan while she talked.

I spoke up. "Thank you." I was wondering where my food was but Wanda didn't have it on her tray. She politely smiled at me, if you could call that thin lipped smile polite, and left the table to the kitchen. She came back in minutes with my food. It was not as full as Ethan's but, I couldn't eat that much food anyway. All of it was cooked just the way I asked and it did taste wonderful just like Ethan said it would. To my surprise, he did eat all of his food and to my amazement, Zachary left a few bites on his plate, and he ate those too.

Wanda popped in now and then to check on us and fill up our coffee cups. The kids ran to the front counter with quarters in hand to buy some of the prizes from the machines shortly after they ate their food. Ethan and I went to the counter after we were finished with our coffee, and of course, being a nice person that Ethan is, he paid for all the food.

"That was great. Thank you for buying our's." I got in the truck with Ethan holding it open.

"You're welcome. It was my pleasure." He winked at me and his lips curled into a grin. Instantaneously, butterflies flew in my stomach. I quickly looked out over the dash and breathed in to try and flatten them. It took some effort because Ethan crossed my view to get to his side of the truck and I saw those strong muscles under his sleeves. My mouth watered.

We talked about nothing really on the way home and the children played in the back seat. It's nice Kera has some one so close in age to play with now. We pulled into my drive and Ethan jumped right in and worked on the plumbing. The children played out in the front yard and I tried to keep myself busy with folding and refolding my clothes upstairs. Ethan ran in and out most of the day and I cooked frozen pizzas for the kids for lunch. Ethan and I had sandwiches. Turkey, lettuce, tomatoes, and all that. Thank goodness I had that in the house. Ethan would see what a bad cook I was if I were to have to cook something. Hamburger helpers and frozen dinners are the extent of my cooking abilities. The day then flew by. They were done in no time and were packing up to head home. Ethan said he would call the phone company later tomorrow and get the guys out as soon as possible.

Over the next few days, Ethan had got the phone on and was over everyday. We ate lunch, some breakfasts together, and Kera had also gone over to his house to pick out some toys Ethan had made. We were spending a lot of time together. This made me nervous. He was getting in my circle and I have issues. He is a good guy and I am attracted to him, but I also know me. I will hurt him. Men seem, underneath, so fragile. It was only when Ethan stopped over about a week after I had been moved in, that he really appeared to have a mission to the visit.

It was in the evening hours after Kera and I had finished up supper. Ethan knocked, smiling through the white laced curtain in the lemon shaped window of the door. I strolled to it trying to control every move so he wouldn't see the excitement in me. I opened the door.

"Hello." I said controlled.

"Hi."

"Do you want to come in?" I stepped aside opening the door more.

"No." He just stood there staring at a spot across the room.

"Okay." I broke the weird silence and then waited a few more seconds.

"Ivy? Would you like to come over to my house for a cook out?" His words blurted out of his mouth.

"Umm . . . I guess." I wonder why he took so long to ask or why it was even difficult to ask.

"Just to let you know, I have other people coming as well. So you wouldn't be the only one there if you feel uncomfortable. Just some steaks and stuff." Those words came stumbling out fast. Could he be nervous? Why would he be? It's not like he was asking me out on a date. He was fidgeting with his pockets. Poor guy.

I felt girly. His movements were making me blush. "Alright. That's fine."

His face lit up I and swear his eyes sparkled. "I'll send Zachary down to getcha."

"Sure."

"About five?"

"Okay." I held a giggle back watching him as he walked backward to the door of his truck smiling and almost tripping over his white and black horse of a dog.

"Alright then." He regained his composure and opened his door. "Tomorrow."

"Tomorrow." I was doing everything I could not to bust up laughing. That would be very bad.

His truck roared to life. He drove around the tree and for a moment I thought he would have stopped but didn't. I turned and went back to the kitchen table. I sat smiling to myself. Kera was singing in her room which lightened the mood, even more so that I indulged in happy seductive thoughts of Ethan.

CHAPTER 4

Traveling fifty miles to the east of Ethan's ridge, there is a town tucked into a ridge of its own. From the air looking down, the flat level ground is small and looks like a thick green carpet not stretched properly. On the ground, however, the area is wide and miles apart. The grass seems to grow thicker there. In this town, a man named Ben lives on the outskirts. He has a three bedroom, modest home that he shares with fraternal twin sisters. The twins were out and about town and Ben was at home in the bathroom.

He stood in front of the mirror looking at his face. He took his fingertip and ran it over the scar that ran the entire length of his face. He touched the top, just at the hair line on the left and slowly traced it over his nose and down to the right, stopping at the ear lobe. He had regretted getting it. It scared the simple minded people around him. He was an outsider here. Being an avid hunter and fishermen, he couldn't help but get into some situations that got him hurt. Besides, the boar was the best he ever tasted and he had his head mounted on his bedroom wall. He thought it a nice reminder of how close he came to dieing that winter morning. Only if he hadn't ate that hogs' liver that day things would be different. Today the scar was thicker to him and was slightly harder. He leaned in to get a closer look. The light purple he saw on any other day was deeper. "Must just be the lighting in here," he thought to himself. He closed his eyes and drew a deep breath in thinking "what's done is done." He had bigger fish to fry. That woman for one, has a lot of nerve to come so close to their home, to their property.

He threw on his t-shirt and walked out of the bathroom and out of the house. He had little time to get to the willow. He told Abbi and Gabbi he would be there in five minutes. He didn't want to keep them waiting. It takes a lot to get Gabbi out of her pacing mood if she starts.

Once he had arrived, he saw Abbi first. Her beautiful bronze-like hair that smelled of lilacs, framing those honey colored eyes. Her light complexion and her small frame could only be made by God. Perfect. He quickly looked away. Gabbi, of course, was pulling leaves off of the long limbs of the willow tree and dissecting them, not even looking while she stared off into the woods.

"Hey. Sorry I'm late," he said approaching them.

"Yeah, Yeah." Gabbi said rolling her eyes.

"What is it Ben?" Abbi asked. "What's wrong?"

"I went for a walk last night," he said getting closer to the tree. "I was going towards Ethan's." He reached the willow and Gabbi still picked at the limbs glancing at him. "I would have told you last night . . ."

"Yeah. You told us last night to meet you here. Go on. Just get to the point," Gabbi said throwing down a handful of molested leaves.

"Gabbi!" Abbi snapped dropping her knapsack. "Calm down."

"Alright. To make it short for you, Gabbi, we have another one of 'them' close."

"What!?" Abbi spoke up. "You've got to be kidding me? I thought they had given up on-"

"I don't know why she's here but it doesn't matter. We need to catch her. She is close enough now that she is probably in this area between us and-"

Gabbi giggled. "Neat. its been awhile." She was now closing the circle with Ben and Abbi whispering.

"Abbi. We need to catch her before she reaches Ethan's place." He hated to think of the repercussions of what Ethan would do if he broke his word to him. "She is young. She won't be that hard to kill. We all know the drill. Abbi be careful. Bring her right to me." He winked and took Gabbi by the arm. She glanced back at Abbi, who was now cracking her neck.

The tall, old willow trees outlined the woods and they swayed back and forth in the slight breeze. Ben could feel the warmth beginning in his chest. The radiating oven door opening. He breathed deep and his body broke out in a run letting go of Gabbi's hot hand. He had no control over what he would become. Just the final thought he held on to for dear life to steer his other half in the right direction. The beast within him would take it from there. He thought of the scent the woman left all over the woods near Ethan's ridge. His eyes closed. That was all he would remember until he got flashes later. They were all out in the forest stalking, hunting, panting.

* * *

A pair of honey colored eyes concentrated forward out in the distance. Every muscle wound tight with excitement, but disciplined. Crouched low to the ground with absolutely no movement, waiting for the perfect timing. Black tears streamed down the face to the mouth. Pupils dilated wide, then smaller, then wider as movement ahead caught their attention. The end of the tail now was the only thing twitching. Claws sunk into the dirt for traction. Two rounded shoulder blades protruded out above the spine. "It" was located between two pecan trees, poised.

The air was thick and still, no breeze. Its heart was racing full of anticipation. It began to move. When the front paw lifted, the back paw took its ground. It crept forward. The head was parallel to the ground and it never came higher or lower while it advanced. It slyly crept its way three or four yards.

Then it sprung, like a rubber band, from its camouflage. The back was so flexible that the paws met under it only to be bounced back apart in long strides. Zero to forty with no problem. The tail acted like a huge rudder as it turned. The object was quick but, never underestimate a determined cheetah. If the terrain wasn't wooded, full of big rocks and creeks, it could stretch its legs better and get up to sixty or seventy miles per hour easily.

The object ahead was a woman. That's what she appeared to be anyway. Tall with long blonde hair that whipped and snapped in the air. With as fast as she was running, impossible for a human, her hair ends were breaking off. The cheetah was gaining on her. As soon as the big cat got close enough, it slapped its paw on her ankle. The claws tore and ripped her Achilles tendon, severing it.

The woman tripped and fell to the ground with a thud. A low hissing poured out of the woman's clenched teeth.

Their eyes locked. The cheetah stood panting looking into the woman's gaze. They both paused. Fallen branches and twigs snapped under weight next to the cat in the trees. A brown blur came from the darkness, launching, landing on the woman's chest. Its lips pulled back over its long fangs, a snarl was followed by a thunderous roar. It had her pinned to the earth.

She made her hands like talons trying to dig into its neck. She arched her back, in a failed attempt to buck the lion off of her. All she dug into was its thick dark brown mane. Her abnormal strength couldn't save her. A cackling called from the other side of the trees. The woman's head jerked, facing the noise. A whooping sound came calling out next. It stepped into the ray of sun that penetrated through the trees to the ground next to the woman. It was a hyena. The hyena sprinted to the woman and placed her head in its mouth and crushed it. The cheetah stepped up and slashed the woman's veins in precise areas. Blood poured out creating a moat around her.

The lion nodded once to the hyena. It backed up into the darkness of the trees again. The lion stepped off the chest of the dead woman. He looked over at the cheetah. The spotted cat tilted its head from side to side. A cracking came from its neck. The cheetah playfully trotted and took its tongue and licked the scar that ran diagonal over the lion's face.

They played in celebration as they walked back to the area the chase started. The woman's lifeless body lie on the ground. This one definitely won't be getting back up. She had been drained.

∽◦∾

CHAPTER 5

I had been invited to a cook out at Ethan's house. I started by laying out clothes for Kera on her bed. She was wearing a cute outfit that had white and red flowers on a sleeveless shirt. The bottom was a red skirt with built in shorts. I sulked to my room dreading the chore of finding something for myself to wear. I began to sift through the stacks on my closet floor. I had thrown a lot of the clothes on my bed, but some didn't make it there. I stood frowning looking at the mess. It looked like my closet threw up.

"Okay. Concentrate." I took steady in and out breaths. "Now, do I want to 'wow' them or just blend in? Dressy or casual?" The water in the bathroom stopped running. "Your clothes are on your bed. Don't forget to brush your hair and teeth!" Kera yelled back something that I couldn't understand.

"No need to show off," I thought going back to my dilemma. So I decided to go with my favorite clothes. A crimson red tank top with see through black lace over lapping the red. The lace had a rose pattern on it. The skirt that I always wore with it was a long black one that came down to my ankles. It had similar roses grouped at the bottom to one side. The skirt had lace on it too. They made a perfect piece. Casual and pretty, just the look to fit in.

I met Kera in the bathroom finishing up. I took a quick shower, dried my hair a little, and put my makeup on. Light eye shadow, black eyeliner that made my blue eyes stand out more, mascara, and clear lip gloss. Lipstick always made my lips peel so I never wore it. Also, I get a kick out of men when they stare at my lips when I talk with gloss on. I went to the bedroom and dropped the towel from around me. A source of power crept into my person as the clothes slipped over my body snugly.

Not much after we finished up I heard someone knocking at the door. It was Zachary coming to escort us up the ridge.

"Is it time?" I asked.

"My dad said to come getcha."

"Let me get Kera and we'll head out, okay?" I smiled at him and looked up at the ceiling, hollering her name. She came storming down the steps. When she got to the door her eyes widened.

"Can I ride with Zachary?" She was eyeballing his four wheeler.

"No. I better talk to Ethan about that one, baby girl." I wasn't sure with Zachary being so young if he could handle someone else riding with him. I got in my truck with a little attitude from Kera. I gave her 'the look' and that was that.

We began to follow Zachary up the curvy, gray shale road up the mountain ridge. It's funny, we have been here for about two or three weeks and I have never been up here. I really didn't want to come to his house because that would be just too personal. Having him take control over my phone and the bill was already weighing on me. I really don't want to know how well off he was by seeing his living situation.

His house was two miles further than mine from the highway. Zachary slowed down as we approached the house. Ethan's house took my breath away. I had seen big houses before, but this one came from a mind of a genius.

It was a red pine log home with bolstered stone on the lower half. Wooden shingles covered the roof. Dark gray flat rocks, scattered, led the way from your vehicle to the mini-bridge before the front door.

Two log beams supported the king-post sized porch. A pair of old lantern lights hung in front of the beams. Multicolored pebbles flowed under the small bridge and pooled the length of the house on both sides. Enormous white rocks were like islands, placed with no sort of pattern. Two long, tall windows with the front door in the middle, had a cross shaped window above it. It let light in on the loft. Two large windows were on the sides of the front entry. They had no dividing panes.

The chink was a light gray, barely noticeable. Everything was wood and stone. The landscape was green and pink. Small Crepe Myrtle trees pruned into a large bush size bore vibrant pink flowers.

I was excited to see the inside of his house. The splendor outside was breath taking. What could the inside behold? Zachary parked his four wheeler, came over, and opened Kera's door. Ethan came to the front door.

"Hi. You didn't get lost!" His face was glowing along with his smile.

"I had a good guide." I winked at Zachary. We all walked to the entry and went inside.

"I still have a few things to finish up outside. I have to flip the steaks. Follow me and we'll go out back." Ethan's eyes were yellow-green again. He placed his hand on my low back guiding me into the house. Great. Don't touch me. Doesn't he know how hard it is to not grab him up and eat him. Focus.

The entry way was sunk down and the great room was enormous. My attention though, was drawn to the cherry log staircase. It tapered up to the loft from the great room. The bottom of the staircase was wider with railings and spindles that showed off natures perfect little imperfections. Five sky lights on the ceiling let the sun pour into the home, three were located in the loft, two others on each side of the highest beam.

As we walked up the little stairs from the sunken foyer, the two sided, wood burning, field stone fireplace with mantel was the focal point in the great room. The couch, loveseat, and recliner made a semicircle facing it.

"Here's the living room and Zachary's room is up there," Ethan pointed to the loft, "and there's the bathroom, first door on your left. Let's go out back and you can meet Shane and Josh. They are already here."

We walked through the great room, under the stairs, and into the dining room. The floors were red pine as well, all throughout the home. The dining room was lit up by the same widows that I saw at the front of the house coming in, no panes. All the windows were just one big piece of glass to peer out of and see all the green trees and colored flowers. A walnut table and hickory chairs were in the middle of the room. The house was so open. The rooms just flowed into each other.

To get into the kitchen you had to step up two steps. I thought that was neat. The kitchen had an island in the center of the room. The top of it made a 'D' shape. Hand made, tall stools sat around the rounded side of the island. On the flat side was a sink placed for easy preparation for meals, I assumed. The finishing touch to the kitchen was the black granite counter tops.

A stainless steel refrigerator shined, due to all the light the windows provided. Walking through the kitchen, Ethan opened the double doors to the outside. They too, were just long tall pieces of glass on hinges.

The backyard had a large jungle gym made of oak. Monkey bars, slide, rings, tire swing, everything. I was beginning to think Ethan has a fascination with wood.

The play set was to the left and there was an outside kitchen to the right. In the middle was a big rock fountain. Water squirted out the top, then flowed dripping down different levels of rocks and pooled at the bottom. There were beautiful Koi swimming about. White and gold fish with long tails that twirled and pirouetted elegantly in the water.

The kitchen area had a cedar overhead. The modest charcoal grill had lots of counter space on both sides. A sink with a small refrigerator underneath sat next to the grill. There was a table that sat six comfortably, that a woman and man sat at. Ethan took us to the table.

"Shane, Josh, this is Ivy and Kera. They are the family I told you about. They moved into my other house."

The woman had blonde hair styled in a pin up girl fashion. Bangs curled under, the long hair in the back pulled and tucked under with a blue ribbon tied in a bow. She had bright blue eyes, red lipstick on, a white button up blouse tied at the waist, and Capri blue jeans on. Her skin appeared to be made of porcelain. She stood up out of her seat graciously. She pulled her lips back showing off her white teeth on top, smiling. "Hello." Her voice swept the air. "I'm Shane, of course, and this is Josh, my husband. Please forgive his eyes, he is blind."

"Nice to meet you." I answered. Why do people say those things. What if it wasn't 'nice to meet them'? My eyes jumped to Josh. His eyes were closed. I wonder why he doesn't wear glasses like Ray Charles or other blind people did.

"What a delicious creature, Ethan." Shane whispered leaning behind Josh to Ethan's ear. I heard that. What was that for? What kind of people does Ethan hang out with?

"Hello. Are you ladies settling in alright?" Josh spoke, interrupting my thoughts. He was wearing all black. Black button down silk shirt with a casual pair of slacks. The silk shirt had a high triangular collar.

"Yes. You live around here?"

Shane answered for Josh. "We live the next town over to the west. You came from Paris, right?"

"Yes. I didn't live there long. I have been told I have gypsy blood in me." I smirked.

"Yeah, I could tell." She laughed and looked at Josh. Must be an inside joke. "We lived in Paris too, for awhile," she continued, "but the country suits our life style better." She sat back down in her seat. Kera started to run over to the jungle gym, dropping my hand to play with Zachary.

"What a beautiful girl you have there." Shane said. "Where's her daddy?"

"Hey, hey, play nice. Not too many questions at once." Ethan said saving me.

"It's alright Ethan. He's long gone by now. He left me before Kera was born. Anything else on your mind?" I took a seat right next to her. Nosy people always get put in their place when you tell them the real ugly truth.

"Ever heard of curiosity killed the cat? That's a flaw I have. I didn't mean to be rude." Shane paused then looked over at Ethan. "Well, your other guests are here. Fun, fun." Shane sounded strained.

"Well, I'll be right back." Ethan said to us with a glare at Shane. Shane just smiled like a child that just got the last word.

"So, you like it here?" Shane turned to me.

"Yes. It's so beautiful here. Ethan's house is, how do I put this? Wow!" I watched the kids playing and saw Josh out of the corner of my eye. He was leaning closer to me in his chair. I heard tires on the road approaching.

"Oh yes it is. He has a beautiful gift and we buy lots of things from him. I think the best work has got to be this house. He built it from dirt. He's absolutely fantastic, don't you think?" Josh asked. His voice brushed the thin hairs in my ear like moths wings fluttering in the air. It made my head spin like I wasn't getting enough oxygen.

Shane reached over my lap and found his knee. "Babe." Her voice barely audible. I straightened my face to a stone.

Ethan pulled open the double doors and brought out the others that had arrived to join us. I stood up to engage them. I was feeling a little on edge with my head spinning and all.

"Ivy, this is Ben, Abbi, and Gabbi." He pointed to each person as he named them. Ben had a scar over his face, it was light but nasty looking. He wore a warm smile with his gray t-shirt and shorts. Abbi was ridged while she stood a little behind Ben's shoulder. She was wearing a long, black, spaghetti strapped dress. Gabbi stood to the other side behind Ben, eyes locked on Shane. She was wearing jeans and a t-shirt with a yellow smiley face with a bullet hole in the forehead with some blood dripping out of it. I loved it.

"Hello. Nice to meet you." I was slowly losing the vertigo. I shook Ben's hand. He had a tight grip. Gabbi immediately went over to the children. Zachary jumped off the swing and wrapped his arms and legs around her.

"Wanna run?" Zachary almost lost his voice.

"Sure."

"No cheating this time." Zachary pointed his finger up at her. They both laughed.

"Does your new friend wanna run too?"

"Wanna run? We'll go to your house and back." Zachary said to Kera.

"Momma?" Kera looked at me with puppy dog eyes.

"Sure. Just check in when you come back." I was happy to see her having fun. I felt safe enough with Ethan's judgment letting Zachary alone with Gabbi.

"Love you." Kera wrapped her arms around my waist and squeezed. Then all three were off.

Abbi whispered something in Ethan's ear that made him straighten up and clench his hands into fists. Abbi broke away from Ethan's ear and proceeded with her eyes on the ground then over to the grill.

"Excuse me. Ben wants to talk to me for a sec." Ethan said.

"Before you go, will you show me where the bathroom is again?" I asked Ethan getting closer to him. His eyes were yellow. That same striking yellow I saw before when he was looking into the trees watching the kids play hide and seek.

"Sure. Ben, you coming?" Ethan opened the door. He shot a look at Shane and Josh. Ben followed behind me. Ethan took me to the bathroom and went into the room across the hall.

I stood in the doorway to the bathroom while Ethan shut his door behind him. I did the same. The bathroom was made up in dark blue and wood. A large vanity looked like a wooden dresser with a sink built on top. The sink was an old metal bucket. The faucet was old too. A rustic look. Dark blue towels hung on hooks matching the blue rug I stood on. Before I could get much of an eye full, I heard raised voices from another room. It was Ethan and Ben.

"I'm sorry! I didn't mean-" Ben's voice was saying.

"I don't care. You know how I feel. I made no qualms about what I want."

"I still came tonight to try to talk to you. We were wrong to-" Ben tried explaining.

Ethan's voice got louder. "I really don't care what you were trying to do! My son sleeps right here. Y'all messed up."

"Do you want to know? Or do you want to continue screaming at each other? You know I have to have a good reason for doing what I did." Ben spoke softer but still stern.

"What?" Ethan snapped.

"She was looking for 'her'. We caught her following . . ." Ben's voice started lowering to a whisper. I could no longer hear. I reached over and flushed the commode. I looked in the oval mirror and scrunched my curls and wiped my fingers under my eyes. I slipped out of the bathroom and walked fast through the house. I almost ran right into Abbi in the kitchen.

I jumped. "Oh, wow, you scared me."

"Sorry." Her voice was monotone.

I just looked at her puzzled. What was going on here? Abbi was looking out the kitchen doors at Shane. Shane just kept grinning at her. I walked out the doors and sat at the table. Shane got out of her chair and moved beside me.

"You alright?"

"Yeah, I'm getting a headache." I saw Abbi in the kitchen, eyes still glaring at Shane. "What's with Abbi?"

"She's just upset that we're Ethan's favorite . . . clients," Shane smirked.

My head really was spinning. "Has my daughter came back yet?" I felt the fight or flight response coming on. Time to go.

"No. Gabbi has the kids running. It will be awhile."

Ben, Abbi, and Ethan were in the kitchen talking now. I couldn't tell what they were saying but every so often Abbi would glance over at me. What did I do? After the conversation was over, Ben and Abbi went the other way through the house. Ethan came out the kitchen doors and he was visibly shaken, pasting a fake smile on.

"What's wrong?" I asked without thinking. It really wasn't my business.

"We'll talk later." Ethan said. "Are the kids back yet?"

"Not yet, but I'm sure they will be showing up soon." Shane answered.

Ben's tires crunched the rocks in the driveway heading down the mountain. Ethan went over to his grill and pulled some steaks off and laid down some hotdogs. Josh stood up and walked over to Ethan slowly. I watched him, puzzled. For a blind man, he walked with extreme confidence.

I stood up and went over to the fountain. I let the running water wash thoughts from my head and I focused on the fish swimming. It was peaceful. After my mind was clearer, the world around me started to come into focus, like a light fog was lifting. I hadn't even noticed that the kids had returned. They were sitting under the slide talking intensely.

Ethan had a pile of food on a plate at the table. He called the kids to eat. Like a magnet, we all hovered over the food, filling our plates before taking our seats. Shane and Josh had very rare steaks with blood on their plates. I like my steaks rare, but not that rare! They had Ethan just run the cow by the flames to add warmth. Zachary and Kera dug in and they were quiet for a little bit. The atmosphere shifted to a peaceful family time, not full of thick air and tension. I relaxed and was able to try to pick apart the couple in front of me. Shane moved with a flawless range of motion. Like the wind moves and changes direction, she made no abrupt movements. Josh was eating his steak in the same fashion, effortlessly cutting. If you have ever ate a rare steak, you know it takes some good cutting strokes to slice through it. They were making it look like cutting through butter. Ethan was sitting next to me, eating and talking to me.

"Jack told me some of the things that were happening in Paris. Has anything happened here so far?" His eyes were on his steak.

I was concerned that Jack had told him about that. I really wasn't shocked because I knew they were good friends. I looked over at Shane and Josh. They had stopped eating and were listening.

"No. I'm just trying to get a grip on how things work around here. Adjusting on my part."

"You will let me know, right?" His eyes climbed up my face stopping at my eyes. He was serious.

"Yes. I will." I really meant it. The same feelings I had about Jack, in the aspect of being able to tell him anything, I had about Ethan. Which was strange. Ethan is still a stranger to me. That fact known, I still felt some sort of trust there.

"Thank you." He continued to eat.

The rest of the meal was your everyday conversations, the weather, upcoming events, new furniture Ethan was building, Zachary's newest accomplishments, and then it wound down. Shane and Josh were getting ready to leave. Shane shook my hand and so did Josh. They both had porcelain white, velvet skin. Soft and cool. They said they were happy to meet me and they hoped to see me soon.

I helped Ethan clean up and do dishes while the kids played in Zachary's room upstairs. When we were finished, Ethan called me out back. It had begun to darken outside and mist was forming in the tree tops. The smell of fresh rain swept the back yard.

"I want you to know if anything is bothering you, at any time, you can come up to my house at any hour to talk. I can't go into details about the conversation I had with-. I'm sorry. So much has gone wrong tonight. I wanted you to have a nice time." Ethan spoke in a whisper close to me. Something was definitely wrong. I needed time to sort it all out.

"I did have a nice time." His haunting yellow eyes looked through me. Say something, anything. "Thank you for supper. It looks like it's about to rain. We better get going," I said. I needed alone time to think.

"You're welcome. Thank you for helping me clean up." Ethan took my hand in his and kissed it. Warm sensations jetted up my arm and my heart stumbled. I licked my lips and pulled my hand away gently. I was scared at how it was making me feel. Betrayed by your own body Ivy. Damn it. I restrained myself and smiled. I gathered Kera up and got in the truck. I turned the radio up so the thoughts would evaporate.

We headed down the road and reached home. My living room light was on. I know I didn't have it on when we left, it was still daylight out. Welcome to the twilight zone Ivy. I must be losing it. Feeling stuff for Ethan, going to his house, those weird friends of his, and now, not remembering the light? I went inside and did a scan. It smelled like vanilla all through out the house, upstairs and down. Kera thought it smelled like fresh baked cookies. "No more thinking until Kera's asleep!" I went to my room and undressed and got pajamas on. That made me feel slightly better. Kera was waiting for me on her bed.

"Momma, can a raccoon swim?"

"Well, I think so." I pulled the covers over her legs and tucked it under her arms.

"Ummm, I don't think they can 'cause Gabbi never came back up." She began intertwining her sheet in her fingers.

"What?"

"Gabbi went in the water and never came back up," she repeated.

"Okay baby. What does a raccoon have to do with Gabbi?"

"We were running and she cheated. Raccoons run really funny Momma, you should . . ." Kera closed her eyes and was falling asleep. I didn't wake her. I chalked it up to babbling. I kissed her little forehead and walked outside on the porch.

What a day. I held a breath in and slowly let it slip out of my lips. Now to sort everything out. The first thing I was sure of was Ben, Abbi, and Gabbi didn't like Shane and Josh. That was clear, the body language was loud. Secondly, Shane and Josh were different, very graceful and elegant. Shane's interests on where I came from and about me and Kera were slightly alarming. Third, Ben and Ethan had a disagreement about Ben doing something that Ethan didn't approve of. Ben did it anyway. Who was Ben talking about when he said 'she was looking for her?' Whom ever it was, Ben had caught her. I just wished I could have heard the whole talk.

Ethan asking me if anything weird was happening here, screamed at me from my conscious. Was there really something after me? Any hour, he said. Ben saying 'her.' It was all clicking. Maybe I'm not so crazy. Jack's, 'the situation is bad', rang in my ears. What is really going on? Everyone is involved. Ben, Jack, and Ethan. Why doesn't anyone tell me? I'm the one that needs to know! Kera needs to be taken care of and if something is stalking me, where does that leave her?

I hopped in the truck and slammed the door. This time it made me feel better to slam it. No time to hold back. Lairs, all of them. I sped up the road to Ethan's. I wanted answers and I knew he would talk if I could just push him to.

I slowed down as I approached his house and saw him. He was leaning on the rail of the small bridge in front of his home, like he was waiting on me. I jumped out of the truck and power walked up to him until my face was inches away from his.

"What is going on? I'm not crazy am I? Something was in Paris? You and Jack know exactly what's going on." I found myself standing on my toes trying to see eye to eye with him, but he was taller. The monster was coming out of its cage and no rational thought was breathable. Rage made my pulse strong and rapid. My ears felt like fiery flames about to explode.

Ethan placed his hands on the sides of my face. I thought of pulling away, but I paused for a split second. He put his lips to mine and pressed them together. I threw my hands on his shoulders. Not hard, just as a reflex. His eyes were closed, his lips were silky, soft, and warm. I shuttered as the reality of what was happening hit me. I kissed him back. All the rage melted down my legs and disappeared in the ground where I stood. He wrapped his arms around my waist and squeezed his hot body to mine. Our tongues touched and danced as if they knew each other. A tango that wasn't rehearsed, just known. We kissed for a minute and he eased his grip on me, but not letting me go all together.

"Are you thinking better now?" Ethan whispered to my face, his eyes were a vibrant yellow.

I was out of breath, but found some to answer with. "Surprisingly, yes." What did I want to say to him? I slowly got off of my toes and back to standing flat footed. Oh yeah. Now I remembered. "What is going on? The truth. Just spit it out. Please, I hate being in the dark. I need to see my enemy in what ever form it's in. Who is it?" I wasn't mad any longer, I even said please.

"The word 'form' in your sentence is more accurate then who." Ethan completely releasing my body but still held my hands.

"Okay. Run that by me again. I keep getting lost in conversations tonight like I'm speaking a different language. First with Kera and now with you."

"A man wants to harm you. So, Jack thought it would be better to relocate you and maybe he would lose interest," Ethan said shrugging.

"Who is it, and what did I do to him?" Crap, the past is catching up with me. Which one of the many, many people I've hurt was looking for me. I probably deserve it.

"This may sound strange but, hear me out. The man is really not a man, Ivy. He's a vampire." He stopped talking.

Did I hear him right? A vampire? Those aren't real. I don't believe in fairy tales or fairy tale monsters. This was the real world, were good people are taken advantage of, and poor people, down on their luck, get kicked when they're down.

"He's been following you for quite awhile. He wouldn't come close enough-Thank God Jack was around-" He continued.

"I can't believe you're telling me vampires exist."

"Vampires are real. The things in your home moving around, that was him. Your truck being moved, him too. The cold spells when your alone are not coincidences either. I'm not quite sure why he's toying with you though. You are interesting to him or he would have killed you by now. I'm not quite sure who it is yet. I have Ben and the sisters on that one." Ethan's words were pouring over me and drowning me. I was not processing any of it at this point.

"So, what do I do? How do I protect myself and Kera from a Vampire?"

"You don't. You get me and I'll handle it." His voice shot out at me. "He won't come near here. Everyone knows, vampire or not, that I live here."

"You? What do you have that could make a vampire afraid? Silver bullets? A cross?" I laughed but everything in me wanted to run.

"Ivy, one thing at a time. You need to be at home with your daughter. My dogs are house sitting for the night already. They are in the tree line watching. If anything goes wrong, they will alert me and I'll be there. Be careful and get some sleep. There's a lot to talk about tomorrow. I'll be there early. I'm sorry you got dragged into my world." Ethan strolled down the bridge and put me in my truck. He never let go of my hand. I sat in the seat, frozen on the inside. All I wanted to do was just wake up. This dream sucked. All but his kiss.

CHAPTER 6

I was in my driveway when I noticed I had drove home and had made it in one piece. My thoughts playing with the idea of vampires. I always thought that it was a neat idea, vampires, to never age and be invincible. Was I in some weird parallel universe, where everyone is insane? Vampires, now really! I really don't think Ethan was a crack pot, but one does not just accept this and swallow it lightly. If they do exist, I want no parts of it.

My life was based on reality. I never did acid because I knew it would alter it. The truck I'm sitting in is supposed to be sturdy, not melt before my eyes. This new discovery will, and is, adjusting my reality. Adjusting is an under-statement. How do you really adjust reality to accommodate monsters?

I knew there would be some ultimate price for me to find and feel love. This is it. I really am poison. Destroying all around me, never letting me love or find love, if I'm capable of it. Now I'll never know.

I scanned the tree line and saw nothing. That's when I realized it had started to rain. As a matter of fact, it was pouring thick, long sheets of water. The rain drops were big, bigger than I ever saw. It must be a country thing. I got out of my truck and ran to the house.

After I hit my porch, I saw that my front door was slightly ajar. I was so mad when I left earlier that I didn't close it I guess. That familiar vanilla smell was oozing out the crack in the door. I pushed the door open with one finger and there he was. Standing in my living room, still as a statue. He was about 5'8". Long black hair pulled back in a pony tail. Green piercing eyes staring me down. He had on a trench coat that was dripping water in a puddle on my floor. A white t-shirt peeking out from under the coat with a pair of black jeans on. His hands were balls of fists at his side. He was in my home! So much for the dogs warning Ethan. Oh my God, My daughter!

"Who are you? Why are you in my house?" I spat through my lips trying to keep my voice down for Kera's sake. "Where is my daughter?!"

"You have been an elusive minx, my pet. I'm not interested in her. She sleeps upstairs soundly. Don't worry." He slithered out the words as he started to walk towards me. I tensed up all the muscles I could and took a step in his direction. I was terrified. He stopped in his tracks. His eyes widened. "Do you know why I'm here and what my intentions are?" He grinned at me and my skin felt frigid, like I was being covered with a cold blanket.

"No, and I don't care. You're going to get out of here and leave me alone before you see the kind of monster I can be!" I took another bluffing step and clenched my hands into fists too. I was trying to make my eyes like daggers to wound him. He threw his head back and let out a loud challenging laugh.

"So you do know what I am. How sweet." He was smirking at me while he talked, and in an instant he was sitting on my couch. I didn't even see him move. He was getting it all wet. "You killed my messenger and made me come all the way out here to mosquito-ville and leave my house." He playfully touched his finger tips to one another, rolling them over and over. "This is unacceptable." The rage immediately warmed my joints and extremities. Unacceptable? Kill his messenger? What?

"I didn't kill anyone and I didn't make you go anywhere. What do you want so that you can get out of my house and stop making everything wet!" This was irritating me, this cat and mouse game. Tip toeing around the real reason why he was here. I wanted to get rid of him, so what did I have to do?

I never saw him move. His icy hand was on the back of my neck. His breath was intoxicating, full of that vanilla aroma. His other hand was on the front of my throat. He wasn't squeezing it, just holding it firmly. My body quit moving and fighting. His eyes fixed on mine. He pushed his cold wet body against me. I jumped.

"Now. That's better. No more fighting. No more running away. Would it help if I did this?" His hands become hot almost burning around my neck. His body radiated warmth pushing into me. His clench got tighter. I could no longer breathe. "My name is Azrael and I will have you stand at my side as a beautiful dark angel." His eyes flashed to mine, curling up his lips in a grin. "You have a monster inside you just begging to come out. You keep it locked up, don't you? Let it out." He whispered in my ear, lightly licking my lobe. My head started to spin. Black spots appeared in my sight, sporadic at first. My vision started to become a long tunnel. His grip loosened letting go of the back of my neck, but left his other hand in front. "Don't go to sleep just yet minx." He ran his nose down mine, down my lips, over my chin line, in my ear, and down my neck, taking long inhales of my scent. I found I could talk again.

"No!" It was all I could get out before he tightened his hand. My body was not moving. It was doing nothing except letting this man put his hands on me and sniff me like a dog! I wasn't weak. I can fight this man off like I did so many others! Rage came to the forefront of my thoughts. I was stronger with it.

I made my right arm move and I jerked, hitting his head that was now at my stomach. He caught my wrist on the back swing. His green eyes looked up at me from my navel. He must have pulled my shirt up to expose it. He slid his mouth across my skin and cut me slightly with his teeth. I was feeling nothing because of my anger. Blood came sliding out of the small cut that he licked.

He closed his eyes rolling his tongue over his front teeth. "Wow, you really are monstrous if you want to be, aren't you?" His eyes shot open. "Do you really think that Ethan can help you?" He lifted me up off the floor by my throat that he still had in his hand, and slammed me on the couch. A gust of air escaped my lungs and I struggled to get another breath, pulling my hands to my throat. He let go of my neck and wrist. He grabbed the bottom of my skirt and with one quick movement, ripped it up the center showing off my panties. He placed his hand on the back of my knee and sank his teeth high into my inner thigh between my legs. I screamed as he wrapped his other hand around my hip on the left side as he sucked the blood that seeped out of the bite.

I took my hands off of my neck and grabbed two hand fulls of hair. I pulled with all the strength my arms would give me. It didn't phase him. He drew harder with his suction. I began to weaken and become cold again. He released me to move his face to mine. I couldn't move. I felt the icy coldness creeping through my body and thought, 'This is what it must feel like to die.'

He smiled and my blood trickled out of the corner of his mouth hitting me on my cheek. "You have lived a fascinating life I see. You will be perfect. Unfortunately for you, this is the painful part." He vanished out of sight. I could feel his fingers petting my leg where he had bit me. The circles he was drawing undoubtedly were streams of blood. He was letting out gasps of air along with low soft moans. Then I felt the heat of his mouth covering the wound. I let out a blood curdling scream when he sunk his teeth into me once more. This bite was warm and got warmer as it spread up inside my body, dispersing. Warmth turned to extreme heat. He was on his knees by my head watching me. He was breathing heavily and shivering.

I heard a howl outside from the open front door. A growl infested the house all around me. Azrael whipped his head to the door, paused for a minute and returned his attention on me. "My beautiful minx." He swept his fingers through my hair. "The damage is done to you, there is no going back now." His tongue lapped up the blood droplet off of my cheek. He then slowly stood up and stepped out of my sight.

I didn't care, he was gone. I was on fire all over my body. A painful cramping in all of my muscles. The big muscles were the worst. My fingers curled up into claws. My jaw felt like it was wired closed. My feet pointed and my knees locked. I was in hell. A kiln roasting me from the inside out. My skin felt as though it was blistering and boiling off. I tried to lift my head but couldn't. I tried to swallow or scream out and the same thing, I couldn't make my body move! I was becoming stiff. I tried to close my eyes and will this oven heat away. I couldn't even do that now. My heart sputtered irregularly. A loud roaring came from outside. Thunderous booms rang in my ears. The house shook as if there was an earthquake. The banging and shaking ebbed out of my hearing and with my eyes pinned open wide I could vaguely see Ethan. He was looking me up and down. Tears formed on the bottom of his eyelids. He knelt down next to me in the same place Azrael had just been. The tears overflowed down his face, to his chin, and dripped to the floor. Ringing blared out in my ears. Darkness slipped into my eyes in little dancing dots. The heat intensified, but I didn't care. I was welcoming the dark. "Is this what it felt like to die?" I repeated in my mind, that was now the last place my voice would ever be heard. I knew that just as well as I knew I would never draw another breath. A thin black sheet covered my eyes. My mind and body faded away.

CHAPTER 7

Ben left Ethan's house in a hurry with Abbi close behind. He drove his teal Mustang down the curvy road towards the highway. He drove slower than he wanted to because he knew Gabbi was somewhere playing with the children. Hopefully he would run into them on the way.

"Crap!" Ben thought. I knew this would happen. "I have to make this right. I have to." He scanned around looking for anything moving. He pushed the window button and lowered it. He stuck his head half way out of the car and smelled the air. Abbi was silent in the passenger seat looking out the windshield with wide eyes. He knew she would be concerned about her sister. As he searched for Gabbi, he couldn't help but to catch whiffs of Abbi. She was intoxicating to him. He glanced over at her. She was fiddling with the bottom hem of her dress breathing quickly. Her collar bones delicate and small. Her neck was thin and soft. He could tell from here. He wanted to bury his nose in the gape of her neck and inhale lung fulls of her scent. She looked in his direction and he quickly smiled, halfheartedly smiled, and looked away.

"Now was not the time," he grunted to himself. Where in the world was Gabbi? They were almost to Ivy's house and not a sign of her. Then the trees moved out Abbi's window and he stopped the car. Gabbi emerged out of the thick trees and she was dripping wet. Her red hair was matted down to her head and she was covering herself. What in the world?

"Gabbi! What happened?" Abbi hollered. Gabbi sprinted for the back door and got in. "What is going on?"

"Zack thinks he can out run me but I showed him. If this keeps up I won't be able to-"

"What were you thinking? Have you lost your mind?" Abbi's voice was screeching. "Did Kera see you shift?"

There was no response from Gabbi. Ben knew that Abbi would continue yelling at her if he didn't do something. He placed his hand on Abbi's knee. He looked over at her and gave her a soft glance. She was angry and had every right to be, but her temper could get out of control. He had to replace dishes all the time because of it. He held her knee for another moment and rubbed it gently. Her warm soft skin tingled the palm of his hand. He enjoyed the moment and released his touch. He understood the dilemma of why it would never work, but try telling that to his heart. He had to get those feelings back into the darkness of his mind. He looked in the rear view mirror and waited for Gabbi to finish drying off with a towel. He had stocked the trunk of the car with a few sets of clothes and towels just for times like these. Gabbi always shifted in the most inconvenient places. She very well couldn't run around naked.

After she was dressed, he looked in the mirror again. "What were you thinking?" he asked Gabbi, who was hand drying the rest of her hair.

Gabbi rolled her eyes. "Zack was racing with me and he started to pull ahead of me-" She folded her arms and sighed. "I don't know."

"What about Kera? Did she see you?"

"She won't say anything. Don't worry about it. Man. You guys are just overreacting as usual!"

"Are you serious?!?" Abbi flipped in her seat glaring at her.

"Yeah. You and him always make it seam like we need to hide the fact that we're different from everyone we meet. Kera's cool. She won't say anything." Gabbi stared out the window.

"You have got to be kidding me." Abbi faced forward in her seat.

"Now hold on a minute Abbi." Ben placed his hand on her shoulder. "Gabbi? How do you think we have stayed safe all these years?" He glanced at her in the rear view mirror.

"I know, I know," she said. "I'm wrong. Of course!"

"This is not about who's right and who's wrong, Gabbi. This is about how things have always been done. It's tried and true. We don't shift in front of strangers. We don't expose ourselves to unknown elements. Ivy and Kera are just that. I'm not saying they'll do something drastic but, well, we just need to be careful." Ben kept driving down the highway. He wondered how he was to ask Gabbi a favor after he just grilled her and treated her like a child, as she would put it. She would have to read the woman they killed. He knew she had the gift but would it work? The woman was dead, sure, but Gabbi never tried it on someone that was very dead. Would it work on a vampire even? She had success on Ethan's wife, but that was different. She was a living human being and then died.

This woman in the forest was the undead, a vampire, killed, and a full day had passed. If he knew Gabbi, and he did, she was not going to like this. He had no choice though. He thought of Ethan. He was fond of him and their friendship. If he was Ethan, he would be upset too. He should have called Ethan first and told him about the woman. Something. Anything. He just needed to fix it. "Gabbi." He spoke softly trying to lighten the mood. "While you were out with the kids, Ethan and I had a talk. An argument really. He knows about the woman."

"Really?" She didn't look up from her window. "How—Never mind. Is he mad?"

"Yes. He feels betrayed. I would be too if I were him. The way I see it, there's only one thing to do. We need to see where she came from and if anymore are coming."

"Oh?" Gabbi locked eyes on his in the mirror.

"He mentioned Jack and other people that I don't know. This has got to have something to do with Ivy. Ethan didn't go into details, just expressed his unhappiness with us killing her on his property. So, I told him we would clean it up." He slowed down to make the turn off of the highway towards their house. Abbi was unusually quiet in the seat next to him. About two miles down the dirt road, Gabbi cleared her throat.

"So . . . what does that mean?" she asked.

"I need you to read her."

"What? No way!" Gabbi curled her lip up. "Yuck."

"Think about it. This woman came here for some reason following Ivy. Ivy and Kera now live on Ethan's ridge. If things get heated up there, if more come, how long do you think Ethan's going to stand by and watch? He's going to get involved." Ben looked at Abbi for comfort, support, something, but she was just sitting there not moving or helping. What could he say to convince Gabbi to read her? "Gabbi, Zachary's up there. Do you want something to happen to him?"

"Of course not. Don't be stupid!" Gabbi snapped.

"I told Ethan we would see what the woman was doing here and give him a call. It's the least we can do."

"Well, seems like I don't have a choice do I?"

He pulled the car into the carport at the house and turned the engine off. He sat still for a moment and then opened his door. He got out and walked to one of the shelves on the walls and grabbed a bottle of lighter fluid. He continued through the door that led to the backyard. He stopped and looked around for his gas can. The pond was unusually still. The frogs were grumbling their normal sounds and the sky was filling up with thick, dark clouds. Rain clouds. A breeze swept lightly through the woods to their yard about five degrees cooler. It was probably raining at Ethan's, or about to. His grill lid was open from a cook out a few days earlier. He walked over and shut it. Abbi's face came to his thoughts from the back of his mind. He was focused on the task at hand, but the bathing suit she wore the day of the cook out took his breath away. She really was a beautiful woman. A lady. She was really too beautiful to spend the rest of her life alone. She didn't date anyone around town and hadn't for a long time. He knew all to well what happened the last time someone was in her life.

"Are you ready?" Abbi asked. She came over to his side and put a hand on his shoulder.

Stumbling out of his thoughts, he cleared his throat. "Yeah. Just looking for my . . ." He walked to the patio table and picked up his can pushed up against the house, ". . . gas can." He flashed a half smile at her. "Let's go.

The rain will be here soon and I want to get this over with."

He broke out in a run towards the faint smell of death deep in the woods. Abbi followed with Gabbi right behind her. Flashes of the hunt forced their way to his thoughts. The cracking of bones, the cackling of a hyena, the cheetah's dark spots and black tears, and the bitter taste of vampire blood. The memories came with a price. Knife-stabbing pain with each recollection in his brain. It took some getting used to. The first time it happened, he lost consciousness. Passing in and out for a few hours remembering the distant things his other half did. He could never get the whole thing or the memory in chronological order. A jigsaw puzzle of the beasts' happenings.

He was getting closer. The smell overwhelmed his nose and his gag reflex began to kick in. The pungent odor of decaying flesh and old coagulated blood tantalized the fresh air, destroying it. Abbi threw her hand over her nose and mouth. "Oh my."

"And you want me to read her? Are you nuts?" Gabbi whispered through her fingers. Gabbi squatted there in the grass looking over the deformed woman. She looked nothing like the person they had hunted down just yesterday. Long deep lacerations dug into her wrists, neck, top of her foot, inside her thigh, and behind her knee. One of her legs was two feet away, probably from animals. Her face was caved in from the eyebrows down to the mouth. The skin was stretched over her bottom row of teeth and only one eye was visible. It was popped and jammed into her brain. Her shoulders were flat on the ground. Her hips were facing backwards, and her leg, the one still attached, was mangled. Thick clumps of blood gathered blades of grass together and fanned out around her body in an outward circle.

"Gabbi?" he said. "Do you think it's possible?" He took a step forward, closer to the mangled mess and placed the gas can and lighter fluid on the ground.

Gabbi rocked to her hands on the balls of her feet. She cocked her head to one side. "I can try." Gabbi sighed and crawled up to the morphed head. She tilted her head to the side so she was looking straight at the face. She took a deep breath in and let it out. Gabbi took her forehead and placed it on the dead woman's forehead. She put her hands on the woman's hair line just above where her cheek bones were supposed to be. The ground started to shake. The leaves on the trees in the immediate area began to quiver violently. Gabbi began to blur and shiver. She gulped for air. She kept trying to inhale but her body was turning a slight blue color after a minute. She still gulped, but harder now.

"Gabbi!" Abbi screamed. She went to run to her. Ben threw his arms around her waist. He didn't want Abbi hurt.

"Shh. If she's in trouble you know she'll let go. You could hurt her or yourself. Just give her a second." He spoke in the crook of her neck. He wanted her to clam down. He held her tight but still watched Gabbi for signs of not being able to let go. That had never happened before, but there is a first time for everything. Abbi started to relax in his arms. Holding her so close hurt him more than the broken heart he learned to tape up everyday. Her warmth was seeping into his body. Her soft skin rubbing on his. Her heartbeat thumping in his ears, her hips pressed to him. He hoped that this woman, dead before them, would be alone or was a freak thing with her coming here. He couldn't lose Abbi. He couldn't live without her and wasn't going to.

It was about ten minutes of Gabbi gasping and shaking before the blur came into focus and she threw her head back taking a long deep inhale of air. She sat on her knees in the grass. Abbi broke his loose grip on her and she ran to her sister's side. "Gabbi!"

Gabbi put her arms around Abbi's neck and held on tight. "We got some big problems Ben," she said after she got a good peach base to her face.

"What is it? Who is she?" Abbi placed both hands on her sister's cheeks.

Gabbi looked at Ben sliding Abbi's hands away. "This woman was in the dark Ben. No memories of before being turned, being a vampire, nothing. It's like she was brainwashed."

"How can that be? Have you ever seen that before?" he asked.

"Yeah like I go around reading dead mosquitoes." Well her humor was back. "Her thoughts were like a thick fog. There was only one name that was floating around in there." She swallowed hard. "It kept repeating and repeating like a chant. Azrael," Abbi gasped.

"Did you get anything else? Anything at all?" He knew exactly who he was, but there had to be something else.

"I'm betting on her being his puppet from the feel of her mind. He wanted her to remember nothing else like, as if she was caught, she would be no use to the person asking her questions."

He picked up his can and fluid, "Torch it Gabbi. We need to tell Ethan and tell him now. He needs to know

Azrael has sent this woman here. He needs to be warned. If I know Azrael, this is only the beginning of trouble."

Gabbi took the gas and poured it all over the body and around it. Ben had turned towards the path to the house. He didn't even wait to see the woman set on fire. He walked at a fast pace and tried to clear his mind. Nightmares were inspired by Azrael. If he thought too much about why she was sent here, or what he wanted with Ivy, he would drive himself insane. His mind just didn't think on Azrael's level. He was pure evil. It was going to be a very long night after they got back to Ethan's.

It was very dark now and the clouds above began to cry thick sheets of rain. Abbi and Gabbi had caught up with him several feet away from the house.

* * *

"Great." Ben thought to himself, Josh and Shane are still here. Just the complication he didn't need. Their red Jeep was tucked in on the side of Ethan's house. He put the car in park and turned it off. He twisted in his seat and faced Abbi sitting next to him. "Josh and Shane are here so we need to be careful." He pointed to the Jeep that was almost invisible from the driveway. "Gabbi stay close to me and don't talk. Your attitude won't help us here. We know how you feel about vampires and so do they. Please remember that when we are inside." He really wasn't ready for Josh's crap right now. Josh and him don't have a good rapport. He didn't like his smell. Not the vampire smell, not that the reeking death vampires oozed didn't burn his nose to the brain, but he just smelled off. Josh wasn't right. He was sneaky, sly, and a lair. Something screamed at him from deep inside, perhaps his other side, to be weary of Josh.

They all got out of the car and Ben walked in front. If something was going to happen, he wanted it to happen to him and spare the ladies. He could put up a good fight while they escaped. It was dark outside and the rain had slowed to a mist on the drive here. He could smell Shane's scent along with Ivy's. Ivy's scent was different, changed somehow. He couldn't put his finger on it. He stood on the porch before the front door, held his hand up to knock, and the door opened.

Josh stood in front of them with his eyes closed. "Welcome." He took a step back and extended his arm with a sweeping motion into the foyer, bowing. His smile was contentious as he stood back up. Ben didn't like the looks of this. Thunder rang out around them. The rain picked up and thick drops plopped on the ground behind them. He walked in and while keeping his eyes on Josh, he put his hand out for the twins. Abbi took it first. He escorted her past Josh. Gabbi didn't take his hand but she made a wide circle around Josh, snorting at him while she passed. He protectively guided them like precious cargo past the vampire. They were not on the menu and he would be damned if Josh was going to hurt them.

Ethan was coming down the stairs from the loft and his shoulders were slumped. He came down the stairs slow and sighed as he stood on the bottom step. "Let's talk outside. Kera just fell asleep." He led the way through the kitchen and out the back door. Ben kept his head down with his peripheral on Josh, who was close on his heels. The rain had changed in the little time it took to walk through Ethan's house. The rain drops were getting bigger, or was it his imagination? Thunder rolled overhead. Ethan stopped at the fountain and was looking down at the fish. He took several long breaths in and then faced him. Ben had the ladies on each side standing slightly behind him. "Here we go," he thought.

"Did you do it?" Ethan asked.

Ben noticed Josh creeping to Ethan's side with a grin on his face. Why is this any of Josh's business? What's up Josh's sleeve? "Yes. We went back to the woman. She was brainwashed Ethan. Gabbi was able to extract a name from her."

"Interesting," Josh murmured.

"You shut up and stay out of this batty!" Gabbi yelled.

Ben jerked his head to her. "Gabbi!" he said through his teeth. She immediately slammed her mouth closed and looked down. "Sorry Josh. This is hard for her. You know what happened, why she's this way." He glanced at Josh's face. His eyes were slit and he was no longer grinning. "Ethan," he continued as he pushed water off his brow, "this woman was someone's puppet."

"Do you know whose?" Ethan asked.

Ben found Ethan's eyes in the dark thick rain. "Azrael's." He paused waiting for a response. There wasn't one. He just stood there looking tired and beat. He knew! "What's going on here Ethan?" He raised his voice.

Ethan spoke in almost monotone. "He came here."

"To your home? Why?" Lightning struck in the woods behind Ethan and Josh. Every moment that passed, he felt like he was being watched and not from someone in the group.

"No, the other house." Ethan stopped. Josh placed a hand on Ethan's shoulder.

"Is everyone alright?" Ben asked. All seemed well in the house, quiet and still. Outside was getting louder and anxiety was creeping into his mind. This vampire was so close to their home. What was going to happen to him and the twins? Was he gone for good? So many things to worry about now. Azrael has been too close to him and the ladies, being what they are, he could have caught a whiff of them. Never ends well for them.

Josh interrupted. "No need for concern. Ivy and Kera are just fine."

"Really?" Gabbi chuckled and threw her arms on her hips.

"Really." Josh smiled at her. "Ivy is in the basement with my wife and Kera is sleeping like a baby in the loft."

A gust of wind blew cold, stinging rain in Ben's face. It stung like a scorpion's strike on his eyelids and lips. He put his hands over his face pushing, soothing his battered skin. A tree branch fell close by. The rain came down faster, slapping the leaves and ground around them. "Ethan? What happened with Azrael?" He just wanted to get out of here and get to their house so he could get a grip on things.

Ethan's eyes searched the darkness around the backyard as to look for the words wrote on the grass or play gym. "He attacked Ivy."

"What?" Abbi spoke up. "Why?"

"I'm not really sure. He bit her Ben. I got there too late. Shane is in there right now trying to get her through this." His voice drifted off, muffled by the pouring rain.

"What about Azrael?" Fear struck him in the gut and ran rampant throughout his extremities. He swallowed hard waiting for a response.

"I got there right after he bit her. He came outside, we exchanged some blows and he ran away."

"You let him get away?!" Gabbi yelled. She threw her wet hair back out of her face.

"What was I suppose to do? Tell me. Let him kill her?" Ethan yelled at Gabbi.

"Not get away!"

Ben stepped in, "Ethan? Why would you get involved with that? I understand it being your home and property and all, but, he could have killed you. Why risk making Zachary fatherless." Lightning was growing around them. Streaks here and there and blasts of light illuminating the backyard. Dark shadows danced between the tree trunks as though someone was ducking and hiding.

"You know very well why I had to step in. You remember my wife don't you? You think I'm going to allow another woman I love to get killed here?" Ethan's voice was strained and cracking. His arms were folded over his chest now, his biceps were flexing, his jaw locked, and he was grinding his teeth.

"Your demons have nothing to do with this. We all know what happened to her but this is different with Ivy. You didn't marry her. Azrael will come back! You know this. Even if you don't want to own up to that fact, where does that put me and my family? You should have thought of that." Ben was on the edge of losing it. The storm was only getting worse in the backyard along with the storm within him beginning to twitch. He needed to get the twins in his car and out of here. Watching eyes and panic were tugging at his guts.

"What do you know of my demons Ben?" Ethan threw his arms down to his sides. He just stood there a moment and the anger fled his face. "Oh never mind. I did the right thing."

"Is she changing?" He knew he was being blunt about it but he didn't care. He wanted out of here. The thunder and lightning were getting in sync. His nerves were becoming frazzled.

"Yes" Josh interjected. "But don't worry. My wife will teach her everything she needs to learn. Ivy is in good, capable hands."

"Are you for real?" Gabbi asked. "Good hands? Teach her well? Make sure she knows the truth. That's all I want." She began to advance past Ben's side. "Tell her about your dark side and messed up escapades!"

He had to grab her elbow so she wouldn't get too close to Josh. "Gabbi, please. Ethan? Is she staying here after she's done changing or are Josh and Shane going to take her away?"

"Absolutely she is staying here." Josh said.

"Ethan?" Ben repeated. He wanted his friend to tell him not this lowlife.

"Yes. She will stay with me. I did this," he whispered.

"Well, that's that then. Ethan, you understand my concerns. We can't be having all these vampires around with how they feel about our blood. Just keep her out of our land." He glanced at Josh, "Make sure you teach her right. We will defend ourselves if anyone gets too close. I wouldn't want any more blood on Ethan's hands." He knew Ethan really took everything so personally when it came to violence. The chaos of the weather appeared to put a close to the argument by becoming too loud for anyone to hear over. Ben decided to start backing up and putting his hands out to his sides and guiding the ladies backwards. Josh appeared in front of Ben's nose.

Josh whispered with venom in his voice, "Thanks for stopping by. I'm sure you know the way out. Unless,

unless you need some help?" Josh's eyes began to open. A knife of fear struck Ben's gut.

"No. We're good. We know the way. Later?" he asked. Josh could hurt all of them there. Getting out right now in one piece was the plan. Just for now, then later they could continue the dance.

"Later." Josh smiled closing his eyes. He returned back at Ethan's side a moment later.

Ben didn't waste any time. He shuffled the twins to the car and got out of there. What the—what was he to do now? Falling out of favor with Ethan and now that viper is slithering in his ear, what was he to do? They rode in the car in silence. He just wanted the familiar sight of home. Where everything was calm, safe, and uncomplicated. Tonight had gone terribly wrong.

CHAPTER 8

My eyes were open when I realized I was awake, awake and alive . . . sort of. I still couldn't move them. Actually, I couldn't move anything. I could feel there was a bed under me and a pillow under my head. I could hear some noises of birds outside through an opened window. My body was cold and like stone. The rest of the warmth that I had had was fleeing out from under me where the sheets had held its escape. I could hear footsteps approaching were I lie.

A door opened, the air in the entire room went sucking out. A familiar voice filled the air. "It's me . . . You better get over here." It was Ethan. "He got her . . . He got Ivy!" Ethan's voice was strained. "Azrael!" There was a short pause. "I almost killed him . . . He ran away!" He was pacing and I could hear his shoes tapping on the floor. "No she's here with us. She's fine . . . Not good." Ethan came into my sight and I saw a small phone to his ear. He caressed my face, brushing his finger tips down one side then the other. "She's cold . . . and . . . she looks dead." He knelt down next to me on the floor and started to cry.

"I'm not dead!" I wanted to scream. "I'm right here!" Why couldn't I talk? Interruption of a memory played in my mind of being at school. The plump history teacher, always trying to find new ways to get her class interested, drew up on the blackboard a sketch of a tombstone with a line representing the ground. Deep below a stick figure of a person with a sting tied to a foot. The string lead to the top of the tombstone with a bell attached. She told us of how people were buried alive and it was a frequent mistake. Doctors at the time were just babies themselves to the human body and science. So all night long for a couple of days someone would sit and wait for the bell to ring out. That's were the expression 'graveyard shift' came from.

Ethan sniffed and cleared his throat. "I'm here . . . Why? . . . okay, just hurry." He hung up the phone. His eyes climbed up and down my body. "I am so sorry."

Why was I like this? What is going on? My skin so cold I couldn't help but think I was numb somehow. Ethan's touch was so warm when he placed his hand softly on my cheek. He laid his head on my chest. When he touched me, I felt a thud in my ears. Ethan jumped.

Was that my heart? It sounded like it. Why did my heart do that? Wasn't it beating before? I concentrated on listening in on it. There was only silence. Ethan stood over me staring. He watched my fingers, legs, face, and eyes for a long time. I wanted to scream at him. "I'm not a bug, quit staring at me!" That drives me nuts! He put his fingers on the side of my throat and waited. I can't talk and can't move. How do I tell him I'm here? I dismissed trying and decided to ignore him. Even in this state of mind I am impatient. I tried to listen in on my heart again when I heard a wonderful sound. I heard my daughter's voice. She was giggling. From the sound of it she was playing on the jungle gym outside. I could hear the chains creaking. If my body was working, I know tears would have came pouring down my face because her laugh was purely angelic to my ears. But my body wasn't working, so nothing happened.

Another sound came crashing into my ears. It was the sound of tires on shale. Someone's coming up the road. It grew louder and louder. By the time they stopped, the sound was piercing my ears. Two doors shut. I heard a few footsteps on the wooden bridge. Ethan was gone from my side. I could hear people talking but I wasn't paying attention. My focus kept slinking off to listening to my daughter.

Louder than before, a woman's voice tumbled in my ears. "I brought some space heaters. Are the windows closed in the room?"

"Yes. She's in the basement. I wasn't sure if she would attack us. I had no idea what to do or expect. I don't know what happened but her chest thumped." They were coming closer. The door knob twisted and the air escaped the room again.

"Don't worry Ethan, I'll take good care of her." I recognized her voice, it was Shane. "Put one there and one there. If we warm up her body, it will get function again."

"So . . . She's going to be alright? I really don't want to lose her." Ethan came into view. "I think I'm falling in love with her." He wiped his cheeks free of moisture.

"I know Ethan. She'll be fine. Now, leave us alone and I'll bring her up when we're ready. Josh, help Ethan with the kids."

In the room was a constant low humming. It was similar to the sound a refrigerator makes. Slowly the noise quieted as the guys left the room and Shane lowered her head until it was directly over my face.

"Hi, sweetie. You're doing fine. Just hang in there. This is the worst part. You are in the rigor mortis stage. It won't be long now until you are through this process and you will be a vampire. The heat will help that along. We're going to take good care of you. I have wonderful things to show you when you're more yourself."

What did she just say? Vampire . . . Okay, I have done lost it. I can't . . . I'm going off the deep end . . . Everyone around me is certifiable! This can't be . . . God help me I am going insane . . . Get a grip Ivy! Calm your . . . What is going on? This is not happening. I would be hyperventilating right now if my lungs were working.

Shane fidgeted with the heater next to the bed, interrupting the madness consuming me and continued to talk. "So, let me see. Azrael was the vampire that did this to you. I wasn't sure if Ethan told you. Disgusting thing, Azrael is. He's gone and if he knows what's good for 'em, he'll stay that way! He bespelled Kera and put her in a deep sleep, but when he ran away, it broke his grip on her. She knows nothing and hasn't seen you, even when Ethan brought you up here." She smiled, shut her eyes, and inhaled deeply through her nose. "Nice. It's just about time." She placed her hands on different parts of my body, lightly pinching. She kept on talking, "It's wonderful about Ethan, huh? He hasn't taken a second look at a woman since Evelyn. That was his wife." Shane moved my head from side to side looking at my neck running her fingers over my skin. She moved to my arms and searched them. The puzzled look was quite amusing on her face. What in the world was she looking for? "She died five years ago." She stopped talking and tilted her head. "Where did he . . . Never mind. We can talk later when you can input your part of the conversation." She sat down on the end of the bed and sighed. She was still looking at me like I was about to do a trick or something. My mind was more at ease knowing Kera was safe. I tried to empty my mind of all the thoughts racing around. I just stared off into space.

I lie there looking at the ceiling and I could start to see the wood more intensely. The swirls that were throughout it, the knots and the lines, were magnifying. My sight was intensifying. It felt like my eyes had been asleep my whole life and they were waking up for the first time. They were shaking the sleep off of them.

I could feel that tingling feeling you get when the blood is going back into a sleeping foot or hand. The sensation was beginning at my finger tips and toes. My body felt like it was thawing. Shane seemed to be glowing while she watched. I was able to move my fingers, then my wrists. Then my feet were able to rotate and finally my eyes were capable of moving. I glanced over at Shane. I took a breath in, but it didn't feel the same nor did it have the same effect on me. I didn't feel better taking it. How strange. I licked my lips and the skin felt odd. They were not my lips. My teeth were different as well, pointier, sharper. I must have been making a funny face because Shane was rolling with laughter.

"You'll get used to all the different tastes and smells. You're almost completely done." Shane brushed her hand under my chin.

I blinked once. It was awesome to move again. I got full range of motion back within a few minutes and had scooted over to the end of the bed by Shane. I was studying every detail I could. I really liked looking at the bed spread. It was blue, white, and thick. The stitching was impressive with my now eagle vision. Every thread popped out at my eyes. They had a swirl about them, like a wave rolling in. I placed my hand over the stitching and ran my fingertips over it. I could feel the individual threads. They were elevated somewhat, like braille.

Shane was laughing again at me. "The fabrics can wait. Let's try something you will need to learn to get out of this room. Like, for starters, try walking." Shane flowed over to stand a couple of feet away from the bed.

I felt like a toddler. 'Momma wants me to walk to her.' This is silly, I know how to walk. I stood up, walked to Shane and stood next to her. See, I know how to walk.

"Okay, let's try that again. You'll freak everyone out if you do that. Remember, you're a vampire now. There are a lot of things you're gonna have to learn all over again. When you walk, slow your thoughts down to think of every action you make. This will help you to not appear in one place, then another like you just did. Try again. Walk to the bed."

The word vampire stuck in my mind. I didn't want to move. Was I ready for this chapter in my life? I caught a movement out of the bottom of my eye. It was my hands. I lifted them up to look at them closer. My skin was whiter, different as I ran my thumbs over investigating the other four finger tips.

I flipped my hands over and looked at the back of them. Beautiful white complexion with no scars. I had one from a knife wound that was on the back of my right hand. An ex-boyfriend had given it to me. A reminder of what would happen to me if I ever left him. He paid for what he did to me though. I dismissed the thought of him immediately. That's the past and now the scar was gone just like him. When I lifted them, they revealed another strange sight. I was seeing traces of them. I moved them back and forth and I could see a delay in their movement. How wonderful.

"You'll get use to that too. Your vampire mind will be able to sort out all these new things. The tracers will fade slightly after awhile. Focus. Try walking first." Shane looked like a kid in a candy store. Giddy and excited at my discoveries. I took another pointless breath and concentrated on placing one foot in front of the other walking to the bed.

Clapping chimed out in the room. My hearing was acute and the sound hurt my ears. "Very good. Now do it again." I turned around slowly and step by step I walked to Shane. "I know it feels like you were doing everything in slow motion, but, you are moving faster than you think. That walk will work until you get use to your speed. Everything will grab your attention now. A butterfly flapping its wings, a bird soaring in the air, even dirt lingering on the road after a car has stirred it up, will intrigue your sight. Focusing will be very hard, but you'll be able to do it in no time. I have brought you something."

She pulled a flat black object out from a duffel bag that she had stowed under the bed. "This is going to shock you. I must say that you are gorgeous in your vampire skin." When she handed it to me I realized immediately what it was, a mirror. I tilted it to see my face and dropped my jaw. My curls were shinier, reflecting the light off of every strand of hair. The black color of my hair had deep rainbows in them. Rainbows of blacks, shades of midnight from light black to pitch black and everything in between. Shining brightly, not dingy or dull. It was marvelous. My aqua blue eyes were no longer that color. They were a pale blue, almost an icy color. The structure of them had changed as well. They were like a cats' eyes only the pupil was the same round shape. Glassy, thicker, deeper. The scars I had on my face were gone. The break I'd suffered to my nose was fixed. All these subtle things no one would notice but me.

My lips were a deeper red now, like I had robbed Mother Nature's palette she used for her roses in gardens. They were silky like rose petals too. My eyelashes were thicker and fuller. I was mesmerized by my porcelain skin that framed all the new beautiful colors.

My sight was defined. Everywhere I looked I saw a rainbow spectrum. Each color had its very own sparkling dazzle and every color swirled at me. Waving like the ocean current moving the colors around. I looked up at Shane and a tear escaped her eye.

"What?" I asked. My own voice was new to me. Everything was clear as a bell. Each sound rang in my ears intensely.

"Nothing, I'm just weeping at your beauty. Now I know why my maker wept at me." She wiped the tear away and lost all expression in her face. She stepped towards me. "Are you thirsty? If you are we cannot go upstairs."

"I don't know." I wasn't sure. I didn't feel hungry. I didn't feel anything. I was searching my body from the inside looking for any sort of feelings. Then I found one, a red hot poker stabbing me in the gut. I folded over in half. A burning wild fire spread through my abdomen ripping and tearing me from the inside.

"I'll take that as a yes." Shane nodded and returned to the black bag retrieving a green metal thermos. "Here. Drink this."

I was in agony. I dropped to my knees gripping my stomach. I could barely lift my arm to take it. I twisted the lid off with no difficulty, but it was surprising with the amount of pain I was in. The top spun off and spiraled to the floor. I put the thermos to my lips.

"Brace yourself." She was kneeling beside me while I started to drink the red stained drink. My ears rang out with an enormous symphony of chimes. Louder than any noise I had ever heard in my life. My hands clenched around the metal thermos. I shut my eyes tight. The taste swirled on my tongue and drained down my throat. A scrap book of pictures flashed before my eyes. A scene from a beach with people smiling. A boat with someone holding up a fish. A baby being born. A hospital bed with an old man hooked up to tubes. A blue sports car parked at a curb. A child riding a bike with a man holding on to the back of it. Flashes of photos projected into my mind. The pain in my stomach began to subside. I held the drink up in the air until there was nothing left. I opened my eyes and saw I had crushed the outside of the thermos.

"Do you feel better?"

The drink was refreshing. Revitalizing. "What was that?"

"A secret stash of mine. The photos you saw were memories from the person it came from. Every time you drink human blood you will get those flashes. Animals are different. It's not that intense. You'll see a forest setting. That's about it. You won't have that clenching feeling either. Ivy, everything will slowly fade to a constant and you will do just fine." She put the dented thermos back in her bag along with mirror.

Vampire. Human blood. I just drank someone's blood. Funny really, I didn't feel nauseous by the thought that human blood was now sitting in my stomach. I was powerful. I could feel the strength beginning to grow in my body. This world was nothing I could ever have imagined. Every sense a human has, mine was ten times more acute now. I stood up reminding myself to do it slowly.

"How do you feel?"

"I feel great. Any other instructions before I can go outside?" I really wanted to see my daughter. I wanted to see Ethan too. I wonder what the outside world would look like through my eyes. My vampire eyes. The word was getting easier to hear in my head. After all, that is what I am now.

CHAPTER 9

"Let's just sit for the moment. I have a couple things to fill you in on about your new body before we can go upstairs." Shane was smiling and holding perfect posture. She sat on the end of the bed patting the thick blue and white comforter.

I made sure to think of all the motions it took to walk in my mind and flowed over to her. I sat right next to her with one foot on the floor and the other pulled up on the bed under me. It was then I noticed I was wearing different clothes. I was wearing a pair of jeans. I remembered then that Azrael tore my skirt and Ethan must have changed me. I just dismissed it. It would make me blush.

"Now. Your body is under your control. Before, your mind was at the controls. You didn't have to remind yourself to breath when you were sleeping, make your eyes blink, things like that. Now you make these things happen or not. Take breathing for example. It doesn't do anything for you anymore. But, when you were human, it made all the difference in the world. First, what do you think you know about vampires?" Shane folded her hands in her lap.

"Umm, just what I have seen on TV and read in books." I tried to pull the memories forward but was drawing a blank.

"Start with what hurts them."

"Okay. They can't go in the sun. It kills them. They can't touch crosses, it burns them. They have to sleep in coffins."

Shane shuttered and made an 'ew' sound. "Alright. Sunlight is hard for us to be in because you already know that our eyesight is perspicacious. The sun magnifies and brightens what we can already see. It burns our eyes. When you were human, you wouldn't look directly into the sun because after you did, you would be seeing a circle for a few minutes. As far as crosses go, they are a preference just like being an atheist. Your belief in God, or the lack of, is your faith and your decision." Shane sat straight as possible and said, "I most certainly do not sleep in a coffin. I did have a water bed for awhile and the water sloshing around under me was too noisy and I got rid of it." She chuckled again. "What else do you think you know?"

"They have to drink blood to live. Umm, they are strong. Some can read minds, fly, depending on who made them up." I was trying to pull up the facts I thought I knew but they were eluding me. My attention kept wandering to sounds around me. I could hear the hum of the refrigerator upstairs, the hot water heater coming on, and Ethan has a mouse in Zachary's room.

"Hello. Focus. Remember." Shane waved her hand in front of my face. The air from her hand caressed my skin.

"Okay, this is nifty. Feel my hand." She held it out. "Is it cold?"

I took her hand in mine. It felt like the same temperature to me. "No." I said but was quickly corrected as it began to warm up.

She sat smirking at me as I held her hand. "Your body can be warm just like when you were human just by making your blood move through your veins. The faster you make it move the hotter your skin will be. You try. Focus in on your hand. Make it warm. It's just like thinking about moving your foot. Focus in and do it."

I concentrated on my hand. I could feel every tendon, every muscle, and every vein from the inside. I pushed my blood through them. I tried to make it move faster. I focused harder and stared off trying and then something happened I couldn't explain. A loud thud came from my chest just like when Ethan was crying on my chest when I couldn't move. I jumped up off the bed.

"It's alright." Shane held her hand up. "Calm down. You just went from vampires 101 to chapter 6. Your picking up on things at a higher rate then I thought you would. That, my friend, was your heart beating. Well, beat. You can make your heart beat whenever you want. Just like warming your body. Neat huh? It helps if you get a good job and have to go get a physical." She folded her hands back on her lap. "Try again. This time forget about the hand and do the heart." Shane was fidgeting with her fingers again. I settled myself back on the bed and tried again. This time zeroing in wasn't hard. My heart beat to my command. It was irregular at first but I got it into a good rhythm in no time. I looked up at Shane, I could feel the warmth spreading throughout my body. This was awesome.

"Your body heat will throw people off to the fact that your different. You can control your healing as well. If you're cut or damaged, you can fix yourself. Everything you can do is to make you a better predator. Consider your prey. Animals that are aware of noises and smells. Also, humans think different people need to be avoided. You need to get close to both. You can drink animals blood but you can't live on it. Human blood is stronger. Therefore you get stronger when you drink it. Look in the mirror again." She retrieved the mirror from her bag and handed it to me. "Look at your eyes now." I looked in the mirror. My eyes were more of the aqua color I was so accustom to see staring back at me.

"That's what happens when you drink human blood. The more you drink the darker your eyes will become. The less you drink the lighter and less powerful you will be. With the whole mind reading stuff, each person is different. The poison will change your body but not your soul. Any talents you had as a human explodes into a gift. You'll know what yours is when you notice it." She laughed. "Now, run your tongue over the roof of your mouth."

I put my tongue to the palette of my mouth and found it was harder like something was under it.

"Those are your venom sacs. If you bite someone, you won't turn them unless you force your poison out. It seeps out of the top of your mouth and gets into their blood. Then their body does the final act by circulating the poison around inside them."

My thoughts veered off from her talking. I wonder why she was helping me. I quickly knew why I was so fascinating to her. Something echoed in my mind. She had a hole in her heart from losing a child. Why did I know that? Where did it come from? "Have you ever had children Shane?" She stopped talking to me and just sat there. "I'm just curious." She sat there staring off. "Shane, tell me about it."

"Yes." Shane's eyes found the floor and she caressed her one hand with the other while she held her hands clasped. "I lost my daughter when she was very young. I have tried to tell myself that giving in and making a vampire child is not the answer." Shane threw her hand over her mouth and her eyes widened. "What did you just do to me?"

"What do you mean?"

Shane stood up slowly, eyes wide, and backed away from me. "You bespelled me! I have never in my vampire life ever seen a vampire bespell another!"

"Okay slow down. What is bespelling?"

"Bespelling is when a vampire tells a human something and they have to do it. I was not able to stop the words coming out of my mouth. We, Josh and I, don't speak of this. No one else knows about it but us." Her eyes began to gloss over and filled the bottom rim. She wiped them with her hands before they could flow down.

"I have no idea how I did that. I'm sorry about your little one Shane." I don't want her in pain, especially with her helping me get a grip on my new life. I waited what felt like forever trying to let the feeling of heaviness evaporate out of this small space. Shane slowly came back around to the here and now as she shook the memories that I have no doubt plague her. "I will try to never do that again. I guess that will be a chore for me if it came so easily."

"It's a form of manipulation. Only old vampires have perfected that art. You have a powerful gift. No need to be too hard on yourself." She walked back to the bed where I sat. "Don't worry, I'm fine." She hugged me tightly. I am not really a touchy-feely person, so I reminded myself she needed this after I just violated her. I hugged back.

When she let go of me I wanted to move around, get out of this room. "You think we could go upstairs now, to see my daughter?" I was excited to see her. I wanted to see what my eyes would reveal of the world outside. Ethan was another reason I wanted to go. I wanted to thank him and apologize for the way he found me.

"Yeah, the air is cleared up there now. We could go if you want."

"The air?" I asked.

"We had some company over that Ethan and Josh had to tend to. Ben and the twins. They had an altercation with someone yesterday. They went to clean the mess up. They had some information to relay to Ethan. Let's go up and I'll let him tell you. He's going to be shocked by how beautiful you have become!" Shane grabbed her enormous bag that she called her purse, and headed to the door. Quickly she turned around and giggled. "Not that you weren't before." She opened the door to the room and a wonderful smell teased my nose.

"What is that?" I took a long breath inhaling the aroma. It was like being in a Hershey's factory. A sweet, edible smell that made my stomach gurgle.

"That's Ben and the twin's scent. I was hoping last nights storm would have dissipated the smell some but you have so many promising gifts." She just looked at me. "Let's go." She began up the stairs.

Wow, they smelled so good. I'm not sure what was wrong with me when I was human. I'm positive I would have been able to smell that as strong as it was, and remember it too.

Shane and I stopped at the kitchen island and she placed her bag down. She began digging through it. "Ah ha!" She pulled out two pairs of sunglasses. The night had passed and the morning had come while I was downstairs.

"Here. I'm so glad the big bug shades came back in fashion. I loved them the first go 'round. They are much better for 'us' than the small frames that they were wearing. The sun shined in through the top and sides. Really no point to 'em." Shane laughed and walked over to the double doors. Ethan and Josh were making their way across the yard from the fountain when they saw us. Ethan stopped and just looked at me. Josh smiled. I heard a low humming again while I put my sunglasses on and followed Shane outside. It was the same humming I had heard while I was frozen on the bed. Kera and Zachary were swinging on the swings.

"Morning Momma, you sleepy head!" Kera started dragging her feet on the ground slowing herself. The dirt lifting off of the ground glittered with rainbow colored browns. The swing chain was loud and the clanking was hurting my ears. Kera made it to me and wrapped her arms around my waist. "What's the matter Momma?" Her eyes looked up at me. "Are you sick? You're cold."

"No. I just sat too close to the air conditioner vent." I lied. "You having fun?" I asked while I thumped my heart into rhythm.

"Yup. Josh said that we might spend the night at their house! Can I, please?"

"We'll see. Maybe." I looked down. Her sapphire eyes were deeper, her hair brighter, and her skin soft and warm under my finger tips. A warmth drew in my stomach suddenly. My mouth watered and the urge to drink filled my mind. "You go play, baby girl. I want to talk to the grown ups for a minute. Love you." I kissed her forehead like I had done so many times before, but this time it was different. She was appealing to me. She smelled so good. What had I become? I clamped my jaws together so tight that I thought my teeth would shatter from the pressure. I shot my eyes to Shane. She understood because she was there in a heart beat, escorting Kera to Zachary. Shane was telling Kera that Ethan and I were going to make a big breakfast soon.

I tried to take a calming breath to remove the hunger and that didn't help at all. I started feeling something deep in my core. Deeper than hunger. I was scared. There was a lingering warning in the air. It was pulling at my gut, whispering for me to run and run fast. Walking, step by step, I made it over by Ethan. I wanted to throw my arms around him and never let go. I wanted to kiss him passionately again like we did in the rain. It was not until I got closer that the pain turned to agony. My body wanted to flee. It wanted to turn about face and run. I stood there confused. All I could think of doing was call out. "Shane? What's going on?" My voice was shaking. If anyone would know what was wrong with me, it was her.

She was at my side immediately. "It's Ethan." Her hand took mine. "It's okay. He's not going to hurt you. Let's go sit. We'll cover all the questions you have."

"Ethan? I don't understand. Hurt me? I need to go back in the house."

Shane started walking me to the table. "Come on." Ethan backed up and sat down at the table on the far end. I saw his tear filled eyes from were I had come to sit. They were yellow and full of pain. Josh sat on one side of me and Shane sat on the other.

"You are experiencing vampire fear. Actually any feeling you will feel is a vampire emotion now. They are very strong. Humans feel a fraction of it. Our road rage ends in death." Shane chuckled but I knew it was forced. No one laughed but Josh. "Alright, on a serious note, Ethan is a transbear. You may not have heard of them because they are becoming extinct. There's only a very few of them left here in the U.S. There are more overseas but that's for another time. Ethan has bear D.N.A. encoded in with his. He is more powerful than us. Our poison has no effect on him. Our bodies, being vampires, know that he can hurt and kill us, so our fear elevates." Shane stopped talking and I looked down the table at Ethan. Is that what it was all along? A big strong bear under his skin that made me feel safe. Shane's words played in my head from down in the basement. "You're at the controls now," she told me. Let's put it to the test. I stood up gracefully out of my chair and stepped towards Ethan. All of my insides were twisting and creating pain, grabbing my attention. I shoved them down, down deep inside my abdomen ignoring it. Step by step getting closer and closer to him. Pain trying to make me run coursed through my body. I shoved it harder, demanding it to stop. Shane let out a breath of air when I reached Ethan's side. He just looked up at me.

"Are you not going to talk to me any more?" I whispered to him because talking would have given away the shaking in my voice.

"I am so very sorry I didn't get there quick enough." A tear left the corner of his eye. I wiped it off with my finger gently. I used my thumb to swirl the tear on my fingertip. The sunlight danced on the outer edges of it sparkling and shinning. I slowly opened my mouth and tasted it. The tear was liquid salt. "You are stunning." Ethan whispered back.

"Thank you. I'm sorry you had to see me like that last night. What happened to your dogs?" I smirked and pulled out the chair next to him. Once I told my body that Ethan wasn't going to harm me and forced it to move over here, it subsided. Not all the way, but enough that I could sit and talk to him without having an escape route planned.

"They were distracted by the bad weather. Nomad was the one that alerted me." Ethan's eyes were drying up but, his voice was still uneven.

"Don't be upset anymore." I placed my hand on his on the table. His hand was hot to the touch.

"I'm upset about not being able to protect you but I'm crying because you are okay and here with me." He put his other hand on mine. Now my hands were encased in an oven. I warmed up mine to accommodate and it wasn't as bad. We sat in silence for a moment or two just looking at each other. I was looking into his eyes that were so much deeper and more colorful than yesterday. Yellow and green have so many different shades. "So, how you liken' your new body?" He grinned at me looking me up and down. "I do."

"There's a lot to sort out. All my senses are turned up. Oh, before I forget, how's Nomad?" Ethan placed his fingers in his mouth and whistled. I dang near jumped through the over hang of the patio.

Everyone was laughing at me. "Sorry." Ethan said. A bark was let out in the air responding to the whistle. It was Nomad and he came right to me. I pet the top of his head and thanked him for telling Ethan I was in trouble. His fur was smoother than when I had pet him yesterday at my house. My touch was defiantly different and I could feel every hair individually.

"Bear DNA huh. What does that mean exactly?" I asked after Nomad and I had a minute.

"It means I can morph into a bear," he said.

"Wow! What kind of bear?"

He leaned in smirking, "What kind of bear would you like?"

"You can do any bear?"

"Yup."

"Cool. You have to show me one day." I was turned on by his teasing.

Ethan smiled and returned my flirting. "I can't wait."

"Guys. We're still down here," Josh said as he and Shane came to join us.

Ethan cleared his throat and leaned back into his chair.

"How would you like to go hunting with me in a bit?" Shane offered. "Josh and Ethan have talked about it and they will watch the kids."

"That would be fine, I guess. Where do you have in mind?"

Shane giggled. "Around a more populated area."

Populated means more choices. That will work for me. Will I be eating a person? Would I be able to? I dismissed that one quicker than it came in. I'm a vampire, sure I'll be able to. Will they put up a good fight or will it be quick? Does the person I kill have a family, a child, or someone needing their return to take care of them? Will any family member catch on to the fact that their loved one is missing? "How do you get away with killing people and the cops not catching on?"

"You have no idea of how many people go missing each year and are never seen again. I personally prey on the wife beaters and child abusers every once in a while." Shane smiled over at Josh.

"What a concept. Being able to right some wrongs while being a vampire. That thought never crossed my mind." As I spoke Josh stood up. He smelled the air. About the same time I caught a whiff of it as well. That chocolate smell. My body reacted before I could think. I was in a fast sprint. Smelling the air as I went tracking the sweet aroma and gaining on it. I was running faster. It smelled like a deer too. How weird. I ran through trees, over streams, and somersaulted over huge rocks. I was flawless while I ran. The sun rays penetrated through the trees and then disappeared were it was blocked, kind of like a strobe light.

It was early morning and dew perched on the end of each blade of grass. Round droplets on everything. Reflecting the sun making them all look like millions of diamonds. My eyes focused in like the zoom on a camera. In and out trying to see where the animal had gone. Tree limbs moved and my eyes reacted to the tracers. I was not alone. I sensed another person other than the prey with me.

"Ivy! Stop!"

I slowed down and whipped my head in the direction of the yell. It was Shane. She was on my heels.

"Did you smell that?" I scanned the woods looking for it.

"Let's get back. There's so much more we need to talk about." Shane turned to leave.

I reluctantly turned and broke pursuit. I really wanted to see what it was. I couldn't keep my feelings bottled up and I growled to let it out. Shane stopped in front of me. She pivoted on the ball of her foot and smiled at me. "It'll be alright. Think of something else to distract your frustration."

I shut my eyes tight, then relaxed my face. "Easier said then done." I looked around me and was unfamiliar with the surroundings. Shane lead the way through the woods. The birds were calling out songs and chirps. I could locate them when they did. It was amazing. To be able to hear a bird and then find it. Blue jays, cardinals, swallows, all kinds of birds. They shone in the morning sunlight becoming brighter more vibrant in color. It was like a switch inside them that when flipped, lit them up. Rocks that were tiny pebbles in size, to bigger than me. Rocks of assorted colors, white, brown, maroon, gray, dingy yellow, speckled, striped, so many colors and shapes. Flowers of a wide variety as well. Black Eyed Susan's, butter cups, Indian paints, daisies, dandelions, and other weeds I can't name.

I must have been running incredibly fast to have gone so far. It took me and Shane half an hour jogging to get back. Ethan and Josh had the kids in the kitchen serving up breakfast. Muffins that I could smell when we were half way there. Josh applauded when we came in.

"Don't encourage her!" Shane snapped. "I was almost too late." She slapped him on the shoulder as she passed him.

"Hey kids? Wanna have a picnic out on the patio?" Ethan asked as he packed the muffins on a plate and headed to the doors.

"Yeah!" The kids answered in unison. They ran out the door and Ethan made them a spot outside to eat at. He already had an Indian blanket lying on the ground. He returned and shut the doors to the kitchen.

Ethan had no expression to his talk or walk. "Let's go into the living room and do this." Josh lead the way. We all sat in the big living room in front of the fireplace. Ethan sat next to me and Shane and Josh sat together. The kids were playing outside, I guess they were done eating. With my vampire ears it sounded as if they were right next to me. The air in the room thickened with an imaginary fog. This talk would no doubt change my life on top of all the rest I have learned in the past 24 hours. I found that very amusing.

CHAPTER 10

Pushing on the pond bottom, Gabbi's toes sunk into the thick sediment then became solid enough to propel her to the surface. Big lime-green lily pads stood in her way to the bank. She threw her arms about, splattering water all over her face while swatting them. "Stupid things!" she called out. "Get outta my way!" She stomped her bare feet on the pond floor and stumbled out of it. Mud covered her ankles. She shook her arms at her sides shaking the water off but kept hitting her fingertips on her thighs. "Ouch!" She clenched her teeth. She took several long strides to the back porch and grabbed her robe. It was hanging on a hook that Abbi insisted on installing for her. She had said, "I can't have you running around here naked so, here, use this." She mimicked her sister scrunching up her nose and frowning her mouth. The screen door to the back of the house slapped the back wall as she flung it open. "Hey!" she yelled entering the kitchen. "We need to go to Ethan's." She didn't skip a beat. She continued down the narrow hall and went to her room. Slamming the bedroom door, she walked over to her dresser. She opened the top drawer and grabbed a pair of underwear before shutting it. "That flea!" she grumbled, "Who does she think she is?" She pulled the bottom drawer out but, pulled too hard. The wooden thing dropped on her toes. "I have had it!" Gabbi screamed. Grabbing shorts and a shirt, she plopped on the bed and got dressed. She stomped down the hall to the living room where Ben and Abbi were. "Didn't ya hear me?" she stood over her sister sitting on the couch.

"Slow down Gabbi. What happened?" Ben asked. He sat on the edge of his chair in the corner.

Gabbi stood shocked at them not moving. Wasn't he the one who told her to spy on them? You would think they would get the picture that there was something totally wrong. She tried to dig a hole in the back of Abbi's head with her eyes. She hadn't even looked at her since she came into the house. She was wearing a silk robe and her hair was wet. "I did what you told me to do," she said glancing at Ben while she talked, "and that mosquito ran after me!" Abbi flipped her head around. Her mascara was running down her face.

"What? Whatcha shift to?" Abbi asked.

Gabbi went around to the front of the couch and plopped down next to her. "A deer." Abbi's face blanked. "Well, I couldn't very well have done the squirrel now could I? I can't hear as good. Anyway, I feel nuts like that. I wanted to try and remember as much as I could." She went to put her feet on the coffee table and couldn't because there was a towel and some other stuff on it. She took her hand to push the crap to the side, but Abbi quickly got up and grabbed all the things with one swipe to take them out of the room and down the hall. "What was that all about?" she asked Ben.

He shook his head. "Never mind. Focus. What did you see?"

She glared at him. Focus. Did he really say focus to her, again? "I am focusing! I'm not a child or you wouldn't have sent me to watch Ethan's would you?" He constantly treated her like a kid. Abbi came back into the room pulling her hair back.

"Calm down Gabbi. Who chased you?" She sat down next to Gabbi.

She tried to keep her anger in the forefront of her mind. Abbi and Ben had tones in their voices that contradicted her feelings. It always felt as if her feelings were not justified. "I guess it was Ivy. I dunno for sure." Anger was slipping away, great! "The way I see it, it don't matter who it was. They should know better!" She looked at Ben. He stood up out of the lazy boy and began to pace. "I did what you told me to," Gabbi huffed. Abbi sat staring off at the muted TV.

Ben went to his room and returned with a phone. He held it in his hand rubbing the 'talk' button with his thumb. "I told you to keep a good distance from them also. You said one of them chased you? Then Ethan for sure knows that you were there. I need to fix this. I don't-"

"You've got to be kiddin' me! They try to eat me and you want to fix it?" She stood up and grabbed his elbow. "Don't act like this. Defend our land. That's what you said. Well, seems to me we did nothing wrong."

He tugged his arm out of her hand. "No. You were on his land. That makes us wrong. Ethan has a lot on his plate and complicating it more is just insulting. I really wish you would have shifted to something better." Ben left the house and stood in front of the bay window. His voice carried, but not enough for her to get the whole conversation.

"Not exactly. Put yourself in my position . . . Out-numbered . . . I'm sorry. Yes."

Gabbi's mind ran off with fear. How could he take their side over mine? He did tell her to spy on them. Maybe not those words, but dang close to it. They were kissin' butt, Abbi and Ben. They didn't know what it was to fight. They always wanted her to be calm. How can they be calm with all 'that' going on over there? Mother wouldn't have stood by and done nothing, bein' all calm. Maybe Abbi didn't remember the fighter she was. The fight she put up. Gabbi shook her head. Thoughts of mother had to go away. Not now. Not here. Mother would only fuel her rage.

Ben returned in the house and slumped down in his chair. He was fiddling with a black hair tie, rolling it between his pointer and thumb.

"Well?" Abbi asked.

Gabbi asked louder from no response. "What happened?"

"We might want to move." Ben said.

Gabbi stood up. "I think not. How could you say something like that? I'm not going anywhere. Mother died-" Gabbi stared down Abbi. She didn't comment on moving, she was just to blame for her outburst as Ben was. "Screw this. I'm going over there and getting this taken care of 'Mother style'." Gabbi ran to the door.

"You will not." Abbi huffed. "You will calm down and wait until Ben and I think of what to do next."

"Calm. I really hate that word." Gabbi opened the front door and focused. The furnace door in her chest flew open. Ha ha, she thought. Every time I shift this close to the house Abbi has to clean up broken dishes and rehang pictures on the walls. Serves her right. She should be loyal to me, not Ben. I'm her sister. Thoughts ebbed out of her mind and the scrambling thoughts of another took over. She would run up trees, tight-rope on power lines, and play chicken with cars. Carefree and wild. Just what she needed right now.

CHAPTER 11

We all stirred in the living room at Ethan's house getting ready to have a very intense talk by the looks of it. I sat on his dark blue couch listening closely. Josh started the conversation.

"Ivy, you were changed by a very powerful vampire named Azrael. First of all, to understand him, you need to know his eating habits. That's the quickest way to get to know a vampire. Their trademarks, techniques, so on. He plays with his food, so to speak. Hunting, stalking, and taunting them. He does this for a couple of weeks. He enjoys it. He was hunting you in Paris. Jack threw him off his game plan and made Azrael think twice about touching you, I would assume. Jack is just like Ethan, a transbear. Azrael must have been real intrigued by your defenses against him and the fact that you had a teddy bear for protection. He challenged the boundaries by going into your house knowing what Jack could do to him. He just didn't care." Josh shook his head.

Ethan jumped in. "He has some very powerful friends too. They will not like the fact that I attacked him. They might come back here in bigger numbers when Azrael tells them. I give them awhile though. He already erased one woman's mind, turned her, and sent her to hunt you down. Ben and the twins took care of that and Azrael came alone when he came to take you or whatever he had planned for you. That gives me the idea that he told no one about what he was doing."

Shane cleared her throat and all eyes went to her. "It's really an unwritten rule of ours, vampires, that we don't torment our food. We just eat like anything else does." Josh sighed and she quickly added, in a not so nice tone, "Some of us have the cat tendencies though. I think that is terrible. Eat it and get it over with."

Josh stroked the back of Shane's hand and grinned. "Not everyone is as kind as you, Sweetheart. Ivy, a more pressing matter, Ben and the twins. They call themselves 'changelings'. Any vampire can tell they are different by that sweet smelling aroma they place in the air. They are very good eatin'." Josh smiled big and smacked his lips. I had to chuckle.

The phone rang and I jumped. This hearing of mine is so acute. Shane threw a smile at me. Ethan went over to the phone in the kitchen.

"Hello." He carried the phone into the room where we were. His stance changed immediately. He straightened his back and placed his feet shoulder width apart. "Are you spying on us? . . ." An eery feeling twanged my gut. Like when you know when something bad was about to happen. I smelled the air and didn't notice any change in the quality. Ethan continued, "What would you call it then? . . . I'm not in your position. I'm concerned for my family's well being as well! You want us to stay away from your town and then you pull this crap!" Ethan looked over at me. I felt my heart beating more rapidly then the timed rhythm I had set for it. My muscles tensed in my arms and core. Ethan spat into the receiver, "That's not my fault! You dissolved our friendship. Not me. From where I stand, you have been making stupid decisions lately." I was feeling a pull from anger to irritation inside me. I looked at Shane and she sat motionless as Ethan huffed into the phone and veins popped out of his forehead. "Why did you call then? . . . Get it over with. I have a lot of explaining to do to Ivy and you're interrupting, again . . . Is that all?" Ethan walked over to the mantel in front of all of us. He growled into the phone. "Then let me make myself perfectly clear, Ben, if you come onto my property, y'all are fair game. So be warned." Ethan pushed the 'end' button and slapped it down on the ledge. The sound of his teeth grinding made my mouth water and cringe. He returned to his seat next to me.

"Wow! Good for you Ethan," Josh said clapping his hands. His outburst startled me and waved a sense of joy in the air.

"What was that all about?" I inhaled the calming vibes from Josh and settled my thoughts. "I thought Ben and them were friends with you?"

Ethan breathed in and exhaled slowly. "We were until they made me choose." He placed his hand on mine.

"Choose?"

Shane interjected. "Let's go back to the conversation we were having and it will all make sense to you."

I diverted my eyes off Ethan's tension to Josh that cleared his throat.

Josh continued. "Anyway, Ben and the twins live to the east of us here. The reason they call themselves changelings, a fancy way of saying they are not what they seem, is they can change or shift into animals."

I was shocked. This rabbit hole keeps getting deeper. I feel strangely like Alice, only there's no furry white rabbit. I'm stalking dark shadows of the imagination. To shift into animals, incredible. "Wow." I let the word escape softly from my lips.

"Yes. It is pretty cool but they are nothing but a disease. They infect your blood." Josh turned up his nose and shuttered.

Shane patted his leg and added, "Not everyone can be infected and not everyone survives the change either. At least that's what we gather. Your soul has to be a strong willed one."

"No. Not everyone can." said Ethan. "You see, the vampires and changelings are both my friends so I know things about both. I have remained neutral in the fighting between them. They both respect what I'm capable of and we have no problems. But, Ben and the girls didn't like the fact I stepped in and fought Azrael. They think he will come back and bring more vampires. Then they found out about your changing. They feel out numbered and vulnerable. If only I had been quicker to stop all of this from happening. If I could have killed-" Ethan stopped and sighed. Sorrow filled his being.

"This in no way, is your fault." Shane raised her voice. "So don't feel like it is." She shifted her eyes to me. "Your changing was just another thing that just happened. They gave Ethan a choice between them and us. If Ben was any kind of a friend, he would have never done that."

So much has happened in such a short amount of time. I am a new vampire and Ethan just lost half his friends. His pain was seeping into my hand. I could feel it like hot or cold. "I'm sorry Ethan. Is there anything I can do?"

"Not really. Just don't antagonize Gabbi. She is a hot head and if this does explode, she is the weak link."

"I'd like to." Josh laughed. He quickly stopped when he glanced at all of our faces. I kept mine like stone. I liked his upbeat manner and hidden meanings. With all that was going on, feeling what they were feeling, and Ethan's very sharp pain infiltrating me, I didn't want to side with Josh and make everyone hate me.

"What else about them Ethan?" I wanted his pain to stop and so I thought if I changed the subject, I could do that.

His hand lightened some and the heat of his touch was coming back. "They need to submerge their bodies in water after they are ready to change back into human form. The shift, as they call it, heats up their bodies. It will cook their brain if they don't cool off."

"What do you think Ben's game plan will be?".

"He will run. He's not a fighter."

"Let him then. We won't have to fight and hurt any of them." I said.

"Are you sure you're a vampire?" Josh's face turned to me. His eyelids were slit. I saw no color, just the bottom of a round black orb surrounded by white.

"Yes. I'm sure. Did Shane tell you what I did to her?" I taunted. After a short pause in the room, I couldn't decide if that was a good thing to say or not. Josh had opened his eye lids more and there was my answer. Well, now I'm screwed. Just when I didn't want them to hate me, I blurt out something like that. I cleared my throat, and asked the first thing that popped in my mind. "How long have you been blind?"

Josh didn't move at first until Shane rubbed his hand. "I was in a car accident a long, long time ago."

"Tell her about it. I always love hearing your stories. Even though I have heard them for so many years, I love the way you tell them." Shane reclined back and placed her head on his shoulder.

"How could I refuse?" He pet her hair smiling. "When cars first hit the dirt road, the glass in the windows were made of real glass. They didn't have seat belts either. I was in the front seat with my father going to the grocery store. We lived somewhat out of town and my father would see how fast we could go. I was around seven or eight years old and it was the cat's meow let me tell you. Being that young, my father was a hero in my eyes and thought he could lift the house if need be," he chuckled. "This day was different because there was a car that stalled in the road ahead of us. He was crossing the road we were on. He was cranking the engine trying to get it started. Our car didn't stand a chance. I flew through the front window and the glass ripped into my eyes. Glass had gotten lodged in and around my eye sockets. One of my eyes was completely cut in half. The doctors back then couldn't do anything for me as far as the eyes were concerned. They wrapped my head and tended to the other things they could fix. Shattered ribs, broken legs and other things. I lost my father that day. Some hero he turned out to be. I was shot several yards down the road and in a ditch while my father molded to the steering wheel." A long pause of stagnant silence fumigated the room. Shane rubbed his hand so tenderly. "It was a very long time ago like I said. When I was turned into a vampire they healed up to look like this." Josh opened his eyes wide at me. They were the most fascinating eyes I had ever seen. White with a black center. The black even looked as though it had a swirl to it.

"So you're still blind? Even after the poison fixed them?" I asked.

"No. I have better vision than you do." Josh laughed. "I have sonar. Like a bat, no pun intended. I can see with them closed or open. I make a noise too low and faint for humans to hear."

"I've heard it." I was so intrigued with his unusual eyes, that out of the blue the red hot poker pain was back. It wasn't as painful as earlier but there nonetheless. The feeling in the room changed in a heart beat. From sitting and lolly gagging around, to urgency. Everyone put on a happy face though and Josh stood up.

"Well, enough about me. You have got to be getting hungry. Shane and you go, hunt. Ethan and I have this Popsicle stand." Josh bent down and kissed Shane. "Kera and Zachary will be safe," he said to me and started heading for the back door. "Y'all have a good time."

"Yes. Have fun, I guess. I've never went hunting with a vampire. You do have fun right?" Ethan said playing with Shane and leaned in to me. "Be careful. Don't think you're big enough to take on a task that Shane tells you not to. If you do, you have me to contend with when you do get home." Ethan winked at me. He stood up and headed for the kitchen. "By the way, the kids, Josh, and me are going to get your things out of the other house and move y'all in here. You have no say in it." He smiled that warm smile at me and my heart thumped. Damn it.

"Fine." I tried to sound mad but failed. "Well, if we're going to do this, now's the time," I said to Shane.

"Yup. Let's go." Shane flew to the front door and I followed. We hopped into their red Jeep and we took off down the road. She cranked the radio up, singing as we went. We hit the open highway and headed south. After a half an hour of listening to her singing to all the country tunes with a twang, I reached over and turned the radio off. I looked over at her and noticed her frowning. It really was an exaggerated one and I couldn't help but to laugh. She did too, pulling her bottom lip back in her mouth.

"Sorry. I couldn't take it anymore." I giggled and Shane joined in. A few miles of quiet was enjoyable. My mind could go into itself and process things. I was about to go on a hunt. What would we eat? Well that's not too hard to figure out, animals. I wonder what noises they would make. What kind of a fight would I be getting into? I am strong, but how strong? Who is stronger out of Shane and Josh? Which one was older? Better yet, who is the oldest vampires out there? Where do they live? Now I have gone and done it. Letting my mind go too far into itself is a bad thing. I looked at Shane. "I was thinking."

"Uh oh." Shane glanced at me shaking her pointer. "Not a good idea."

I ran my tongue over my teeth, out of habit, and cut the end of it on my now sharpened teeth. Note to self, do not do that again. My blood seeped out of the paper cut into my mouth. I pressed it on the roof to stop the bleeding. After a moment I let it loose and it wasn't bleeding any longer. "On a serious note, just out of curiosity, what's the history behind vampires? How did it start?"

"In the beginning, vampires were quite different from what we are now. They had no empathy, morals, conscious, or anything that people refer to as 'humanity'. They were repulsive. They had a retched pungency percolating from them. The secretion of death. Our bodies were not like this either." She looked down at her lap, "Their eyes were a deep red, the skin almost transparent and was stretched over their bones, and their veins were like blue green ropes showing through it. They were skinny and stealthy, sneaking into the open windows at wee hours of the morning. At this time, vampires slept in coffins that they emptied. It was the safest place, they thought, to hide during the daylight hours while their prey worked and ran about. In the earth six feet under, noise was muffled. Another good thing about locating themselves there was that living people didn't visit graves then like they do now. They thought if they went to the graves of their loved ones that they could possibly catch something someone had died from. The vampires only came out at night to feed. Then they would return to the cemetery during twilight to rest."

"They also ate differently. Every human on the planet has a life force. An 'aura.' Vampires, in their primitive form fed off of it. It was like eating only bread and butter. You know what the people looked like in the Nazi concentration camps? The death warmed over appearance." She looked over at me and I nodded, bringing forward the pictures I saw in text books in history class. "That is all they ate. I can't tell you of how the aura tasted or how it was eaten exactly. That was before my time," she smirked. "Back then, our venom sacs were almost non-existent but they were there. The mind of these first vampires were that of feeding and no real memories of their lives before being turned. Mindless eating machines. They were stronger than us too, if you can imagine being any stronger."

"We started out being called 'the plague' or something to that effect, if and when people caught on. At this time in history, people were becoming more and more superstitious and taking part in silly wive's tales. Putting knives under their pillows to cut out pain in their bodies, placing spider webs on wounds. For colds, they drank lambs tongue and whiskey tea. For cramps in their feet, they would turn their shoes upside down before going to bed. The list goes on and on." She started giggling and slapped the steering wheel. "Oh, my favorite one. Warts. There was this woman who had warts all over her face and body. She couldn't find a suitable suitor for herself, so she blamed the warts. She pricked them with a needle, and put a few drops of blood from each one on some fat meat. She then buried the meat and when it rotted, the warts were suppose to disappear." Her laughing subsided and the smile escaped her face. "If humans found where the vampires where dwelling, they came during the day and cut the vampires head off. They took out the heart and other organs and burned them. They also took garlic and stuffed it in the mouth. The part that killed the vampires was the decapitation."

A quiet pulse of sorrow filled the cab of the jeep. Shane stared out the window shield. I was certain she was reliving some deep painful memory that she witnessed while we drove in silence. I watched out my window following the wires on the telephone poles. Birds had camped out and broke the continuous rise and fall of the wire. I inhaled and decided to talk after the feelings lightened in the Jeep. "I wonder how we got to be this way?" I looked down at my hands and nails. My nails were thick and shiny like I had painted them with two coats of clear nail polish. I was still seeing tracers all around me but, they were fading just like Shane had told me they would.

She cleared her throat and started talking again. "The first of our kind to break the cycle of living that way was a very rich lord named Ishmael LeFlore. He was deeply and passionately in love with a woman named Lovidia Valbuena. They were to be married just months before he was attacked. The love he had for Lovidia was strong enough to withstand the grave. He evolved to drink the blood of his sept.

An endless buffet of food. He had a big family. He realized that drinking the blood, his vampire body got more from it. He was still a shadow of his former self and was terrifying to look at. Years had passed and he still longed for Lovidia."

"So the story goes that, one night he visited Lovidia to reconcile their relationship. You can only imagine how that went." She glanced at me with a sarcastic grin. "She screamed in horror and he had to silence her before someone from the dwelling house awoke. Noise in the old structures echoed and projected clearly even if they had the thickest tapestries. So, he put his hands over her mouth. He was so effected by the sight of her for the first time in years that he became aroused. With the closeness her body, the sound of her heart thrumming out of her chest, he exploded and bit her. He secreted his poison and she began to die her human death. He was so distraught because he thought he killed her. He stayed by her side through out the night and by the twilight hours she was a vampire. She stayed with him for several months. The tale gets fuzzy from being told for so many years by different people that the conclusion is iffy. One constant is Lovidia was not happy with the change and turned on Ishmael."

"So what happened to her?"

"I'm not sure." Shane was quick to answer like she knew I would ask.

"And him? Did Lovidia kill him?"

"Let's just leave sleeping dogs lie." She cracked a smile. "Wouldn't want to stir up the past too much." Shane once again peered out the windshield and the sense of apprehensiveness littered the air. It was faint, as though trying to hide at the top of the cab. I caught it, the anxiety drifting in small waves off of Shane.

I saw a sign for the Texas border out of my window. There was a small town coming up but before we entered the 25 mile an hour zone, we stopped for gas. An old, rusty Phillips 66 sign shifted in the light breeze. Cracked, chipping paint clung to the small building. Bald and blown tires were lined up along the side. Only one pump stood outside in front.

An irritant twinged my abdomen. My guts began to twist in pain. I rubbed the lower half of my stomach to try to ease the knife pain while Shane paid for gas. I closed my eyes tight trying to mentally remove the demanding emptiness inside. Shane, out of nowhere, opened her door and placed her purse on her seat. "You alright?"

I tried to smile. "Yeah. Just hungry I guess." This pain was stronger than before, yet different. The first time I felt this I had no idea what it was. It hammered the insides of me, ricocheting around dropping me to my knees. This time it was subtle, creeping, but ever so damaging.

"Lets do it here then. I'll pull over on the side of the road and we'll just walk okay?" She winked and shut her door. She finished pumping and got in. I was intoxicated with the gasoline smell. I was woozy. Sickly. After we drove for a minute, I started getting better with the fresh air. I took long breaths of clean air that filtered in through my cracked window. I caught a whiff of something different in the air. "Stop." I whispered to Shane.

"Oh. Nice." She nodded her head up and down. She pulled over and turned the engine off. We both stealthily got out of the Jeep through the sun roof. The doors would make a sound and possibly make whatever it was run. I zeroed in on the smell. It was a buck. An eight pointer and his heart was weak. That is what I smelled. Weakness. I was crouched on the ground slinking to it. Shane was two steps behind me. I openly ran at the buck catching it quickly. It had no fight in it. Well, not against me, a vampire. I wrapped my mouth around it's neck. Fur and skin were the only thing keeping me from its life source. I sunk my teeth in with accurate precision, its tendons snapped and popped against my bite.

Flashes of trees, rocks, creeks, and grass flew before my eyes. Shane said it would be like this. I was now on my knees placing the buck's head to the ground. Shane and I took turns on draining the wildlife from the woods. After we had our fill, we walked back to the Jeep. When we got back in, we both started to groom ourselves and pulled the visors down with the mirrors on the back. I wiped the blood off of my mouth and chin. Shane pulled leaves and twigs out of her hair and I looked at the mirror intensely. My eyes were a dark blue almost purple color. "Look at my eyes!"

She just smiled at me. "Yes. That is the color of a well fed vampire." She turned the engine over and put it in gear. "You ready to go home?"

"Yes let's."

We drove down the road and I could tell Shane was itching to turn her radio back on. No way. I wasn't going to put my ears through that again. Shane was a talker so what would I ask her that would keep her mouth occupied? Ethan's wife. That's a good topic. Plus, I was insanely curious about my predecessor. I would need details that would not be told by Ethan. "Tell me about Ethan's wife."

Shane chuckled. "Um, okay. Where do I start?"

"At the beginning would be best I think." Anything to keep that radio off.

"Alright. Let me see . . . She worked at the hospital. She was a therapeutic nurse. Lots of hours. She had Zachary and then went back to work after her maternity leave was over. They began building that house Ethan lives in now. She knew what Ethan was. When Zachary was born he had the mark too."

"What mark?" I interrupted.

"All transbears have a crescent moon shaped birthmark on their chests." she drew an imaginary moon on her shirt, "Anyway, Evelyn, that was her name, was driving home on that road the houses are on. It was raining pretty good and Ethan in bear skin was walking around the property and was in the road. She swerved to miss him and ran into a tree. One of the limbs broke off and went through her chest. Ethan returned to his human form and tried to save her. He gave her mouth to mouth for hours. He couldn't save her. He was so upset that him and Zachary moved into the new house within a week. It wasn't done at all. Josh and I helped him get the rest of the building done. He had been selling us furniture forever and I felt horrible for him to lose his wife like that. Josh and I decided to help him build the rest of the house and we have been good friends ever since."

"Is that why he's so upset about not getting to me in time?"

"Yes. You also have to understand that you're the first woman in years to turn his head. You and him have chemistry. Like I needed to tell you that!" Shane laughed. "How about you? Did you ever get married or just have a steady beau? I mean boyfriend?"

"Steady beau? Wow! Umm, no. I never had anything promising if that's what you mean. Some flings here and there. No one struck my 'fancy'." I giggled smiling at Shane. "Well, I have trust issues. My father was a pervert that had the hots for little ones." I stopped talking because I couldn't believe I was telling her about him. What is wrong with me? I have built walls to keep this sort of thing from getting out. I quickly changed the subject. "Do you get angry at the people you feed on? I mean, don't you get the memories of them hurting their wives and stuff?"

"I do. I just keep telling myself I'm ridding the world of their sick presence."

"I would like to aim my sights on pedophiles." I told Shane in a flat tone staring out the windshield. My memories of my father seem to want to stay in the forefront of my thoughts.

"I don't think that's such a good idea. I hunted down a known wife beater one time. When I found him and bit him, it turned out that he was also hurting their four year old daughter that way. I ripped his head off. Straight off his shoulders." Shane jerked her hand upwards. "Now, we have told you about your new vampire emotions. I strongly suggest you start out small. Just until you can get a handle on yourself."

I recognized the landscaping now. We were just about to Ruth's Place. We went down the gray shale road to Ethan's house. I was still toying with the idea of hunting a pedophile. I just wished I could get around the fact Shane told me I couldn't. Ethan was very specific with his 'orders.' I was not to take on any tasks she thought were too big. If I did I would have to deal with him. After Shane pulled in and turned the Jeep off, I knew what I was going to do.

"Shane, can I ask a favor of you?" I pivoted in my seat to lock eyes on hers. I caressed my voice softly to her.

"Sure. What?" She looked straight into my eyes.

"Don't tell Ethan or Josh about telling me to stay away from pedophiles. We never discussed them okay?"

Her eyes glazed over. "Okay."

"You won't feel or remember my bespelling either." I quickly added.

"No. I won't." She responded like a robot.

I turned my face to my window breaking my gaze and waited.

"Oh, sorry. I must have been thinking of something. I drifted away. You ready to get out?" Shane asked me.

"Yeah." I was dumbfounded. It worked. What a gift I have. Now I can go kill those bottom feeders and no one will try and stop me. Later tonight I will jump at any opportunity I find. Shane and I walked though the foyer and Josh was standing on the top step with an ill-favored look on his face.

"What is it babe?" Shane asked in a whisper.

"Ivy and I have to talk." Josh opened his eyes after he passed Shane on the step.

"Okay." She slowly said. Shane walked through the living room with glances over her shoulder. She went through the kitchen and out the back door.

Josh stepped eye to eye with me. His breath hit my face with a voice almost audible, "You need to remember that you are in the company of other vampires with the same hearing you have." I stepped back one step due to his tone and domineer. Josh stepped up again. "If you ever do that to my wife again, you will be dealing with me. I have had years of dealing with, and killing vampires that had gotten out of line. I have given up the practice thanks to my wife. But, it's like riding a bicycle. You never forget."

"I'm sorry." It was the only thing that came to mind to say. Then it hit me. I wonder if I can do that to him? I felt cornered as I reacted. I began, not thinking of the consequences. "Josh?" I caressed my voice to his ears.

"No." Josh forced out of his mouth quickly. "Like I said, I'm a little smarter than you. I will chalk this up to a learning experience for you, because I don't think you're stupid. It would be stupid of you if you were trying that on me. Even after I have already warned you about using it on my wife." Josh stood staring me down for a moment. Then his cocky little grin cracked his straight mouth and he shut his eyes. "Let me let you in on a secret. I would have taken you on your little errand . . . later."

I felt really stupid now. I should have guessed. He was the type to break a few rules. Well, if he thought he could get away with it. "I am sorry." I repeated with more sincerity. Josh stood there for a few more moments and then backed up to the top step.

"I won't tell Shane about this. I will take you out tonight. This is why we are talking now if she asks. We are planning tonight's rendezvous. Ethan is out on the patio with Kera." His voice was dismissive.

"Thanks," I said while he turned his back to me. I waited until Josh was a few steps ahead and continued to the kitchen after him.

We went out to the backyard where Kera and Zachary were rolling around on the ground wrestling with Ethan's dogs. Isis was on top of Zachary and Blue was pinned down to the grass by Kera. Sampson was wiggling on his back. He was going after his own tail. Nomad was sitting on the side lines watching. I couldn't help but laugh at Sampson. Ethan was chuckling next to Nomad.

"Everything all right, you two?" Shane asked from the seat over by the table.

"Yeah." Josh looked back at me and smiled. "We're going hunting tonight. I wanna show her some tricks."

"I don't know about that, Josh. I know some of your tricks. She doesn't need to be tainted by you." Shane was giggling.

"You are going to have to go hunt again? I was kind of hoping you would have had enough with Shane that we could spend some time together." Ethan said.

The sound of spending time with Ethan sounded so enticing. "I did have enough to drink, I think. Could we do it tomorrow?" I asked Josh.

"Not a problem. Tomorrow at noon. That will work out better for me too."

I strolled over to Ethan and leaned into his ear. "Sounds like we're not the only ones wanting time alone." I ran my tongue over his earlobe. He shivered ever so slightly. I smiled at my little accomplishment and pulled my face to his. "If that was what a little lick can do, you're in trouble." The smile on my face grew larger. "Are you going to show me a bear tonight?"

"I hadn't planned on it. I had had other plans for the main attraction." Ethan winked.

We continued to play with the dogs for another hour or so when Shane and Josh decided they wanted to go home. Josh promised to come back in the morning close to ten so we could go hunting. We said our goodbyes and they left. Ethan and I were alone at last. Well, we weren't counting the kids. Ethan asked for my help in the kitchen around dinner time. He was making his famous meatballs that Zachary loved. He swore that Kera would love them too. The kids went into Kera's room. They said they wanted to build a fort. I think it was secretly Zachary's way of playing with Kera's toys. He kept rambling on and on about what kind of toys he thought were cool. Ethan and I prepared dinner.

We stood around the island in the kitchen across from one another. He was making the beef into meatball shapes. I was peeling the potatoes. The meat Ethan was fondling had an appealing smell. I took a deep inhale savoring it sitting on one of the bar stools. I dismissed the feeling of hunger stirring in my gut and looked at the potatoes. The knife in my hand felt as light as a feather. I held it long ways in the palm of my hand, the blade facing out of my finger tips. I flicked my thumb on the side of the handle. It spun on the palm of my hand. It went round and round for a few seconds. I could feel Ethan's eyes on me. I glanced up at his yellow-green eyes and my heart beat, startling me.

The knife flew off of my hand and dropped. It fell with the blade down, of course, landing in my foot. I sat there shocked. I felt no pain. How weird was that. This four inch knife just went through my foot. Blood began rolling down the top of my foot, where it stuck out, to the floor. I'm glad I took my shoes off outside while we played with the dogs. I really liked those sandals. Ethan put his thumb on the top of my foot, pinching the blood flow. I must have been in shock because I just kept staring at the blade in my foot.

Zachary called out from Kera's room. "Everything alright Dad?" There was no way that little boy could smell the blood. He was too tiny and all the way into the other room!

"Yeah, everything is fine. Just keep playing. Dinner will be ready in a little while." Ethan's eyes had a proud twinkle. "His nose is already very good."

"Can he turn into a bear this young?"

"Not yet. He will be able to when the dormant gene awakens. When he is about 14 or 15 years old." Ethan had grabbed the knife handle and wiggled it out of the top of my foot. It came out with a wet suction sound. "Does that hurt?"

"Yes it does now! When it went in I didn't even feel it. Now that your moving it around, I really feel it." I had both of my hands on my shin looking at the blood dripping off my toes now. The droplets were making perfect round dots on the floor. The outside edges were beginning to serrate all around from the blood in the center flattening with gravity.

"Now it's all up to you." Ethan said shrugging. He put the knife in the island's sink, plugged it, and opened the cabinet door from under it. He retrieved a bottle of bleach and poured it on the blade. Oh how that bleach burned my nose! He took a wash cloth from off of the faucet, wet it, doused it with bleach and placed it on the floor underneath my foot.

"I don't . . . How do I do it?" I was lost. Shane wasn't here. Now I felt incompetent.

"Shane said you could heal yourself. Think about it. Make your body do it." Ethan shrugged again.

I focused in on my foot. I could feel the hole from the inside. I felt flesh separated and throbbing. Veins sliced and muscles torn. Mend. It was the only word I could think of to try and fix the cut. Mend. I thought again. The center of my wound began to move in a snail-like pace, fusing back together. I was excited and pushed my blood harder through my body and it mended quicker. My heartbeat thudded in my ears at a fast rhythm. Little by little, the wound sealed shut and the only thing left of the incision was the blood that remained on the skin. I glanced up at Ethan, showing off my foot.

"See, I knew you could do it." Ethan smiled with confidence.

"That was easier than I thought. Wow! That's awesome." I took my foot and rotated it in a circular motion and looked at it from various angles.

"We gonna finish cooking or just starve the kids?" Ethan joked. He walked over to the stove and put his meatballs in a pan. He had a nice butt. I can't believe I had never noticed it before. Very bite-able. No pun intended.

An audible 'Mmmm' slipped out. Ethan didn't hear me or just ignored my yummy sound. Well, back to work or I will bite him. I finished cutting the potatoes and placed them in a big pot on a burner for them to boil. Ethan and I were standing side by side at the oven. I felt a static charge beginning to build up between him and I. He felt it too because he looked at the hairs on his arms. They were on end. I stepped away slightly and they went down some. I stepped back into him and they raised again.

I giggled out loud and asked Ethan, "Are you cold?"

"No . . ." He began to say and then he grabbed me up and pressed his lips to mine. They were warm. My heart sped up and then his lips were melting into mine. He let out a sigh and his hands wrapped tighter around the small of my back. Our tongues danced their familiar tango and then he pulled away. "We will continue this later." He said with a confident smirk. I heard foot fall in the hallway. It was Kera and she ran through the house squealing a high pitched scream. She ran out the back door, passing us with Zachary in pursuit. Damn it. Later. I told myself.

We all ate supper. Yes. We ALL ate, me included. I could make the acid in my stomach digest the food. It was delicious. Kera had two plates full. Ethan dried while I washed and the kids walked around the kitchen putting them in the right spots.

We had played family for the night and we got along. I liked that part better than the food itself. That's saying a lot. We watched some TV in the basement. The basement was the game room. It had a pool table, a Wii, X-box, Playstation 3, all the games children liked to play. There were two couches and a coffee table. The table had coasters imbedded in the wood.

Ethan kicked my butt at bowling and a fighting game. The kids took turns playing when Ethan and I were finished and the time was quickly approaching for them to go to bed. Ethan tucked Zachary in and said his prayers. I did the same for Kera. She was so exhausted, I gave her five minutes before she's out. The night was mine. No interruptions. I grinned.

I went looking for Ethan and found his scent the strongest outside by the fountain. Where could he be? I felt breathing on my neck and I didn't move. It was Ethan. I could smell him. He smelled of earth. Dirt and the outside breeze. It was nice.

He draped his hand around my chin from behind, and put his mouth on my neck. He pulled slightly on my skin with his teeth. He pressed his body to mine. I could feel the warmth of his body penetrating my skin. He whipped me around to face him. I threw my arms around his neck and stood on my toes. His eyes were that yellow color once more. They pushed into my soul. He put his hands under my arms and lifted me up. He held me in the air. Eye to eye. I smashed my lips to his. We had the same idea. Hard passionate sparks flew into the air. Ethan carried me to the bedroom and placed me on the bed. His passion written all over his face. This was about to be a euphoric night.

CHAPTER 12

The morning sun poured into the windows of the house illuminating them. I didn't sleep. Ethan did for a couple hours. I spent most of my night, after leaving Ethan's room, in the backyard. I have never felt that intense bonding before. Ethan and I were inseparable all night. The vampire emotions I now feel were so profound that it was almost painful. I stood out on the patio staring off in the trees and looking at all the different animals forage.

Raccoons, possums, owls, snakes, and the most interesting were the spiders. They weave the most intricate webs. The silk itself has spots that aren't sticky and they remember where they are. The spiders creep around their temporary homes and trap the moths or other bugs, wrapping them into these blankets of satin. They are so careful while they do it. Slowly spinning their food around in circles covering all of their bodies, legs and all.

It reminds me of how we wrap our baby's in the hospital and in their first year of life. Wrapping them in a fleece or soft blanket, tucking in their little hands and feet.

The spiders have sly tricks they use. The one I enjoyed watching the most was a Garden spider. They perch themselves in the very middle of their webs. When a cricket or grasshopper comes close enough to their trap, they bounce it. The movement of the web makes the grasshopper jump. The bugs really have no control on where they land. The web embraces the bug and the spider waits, for the bug will squirm and fight. The spider will pull on the support strands of the web to help this along.

Time is on the spider's side. It's not long before the grasshopper tires and gives in to the inevitable. The spider will stealthily move in and deliver it's toxic bite. As the spider does this, it's so sweetly done. Like you were watching it kiss the bug ever so gently. They would spin it a few times wrapping it up and then bite in the same spot. Each kiss sealing the bugs doom deeper.

Each and every creature was fascinating to watch. After it was close to the sun rising, I went back into the house and sat in the living room. Isis, Sampson, and Blue were sleeping all over the floor. With my vampire ears I could hear each person in the house breathing.

I started thinking of the outing I was going to have with Josh today. How do we find one of those evil people? Do they smell different than an average human? Or do we do it the human way and get on some computer and look them up in the data bank for known sex offenders? That sounded like a good idea. I really was bored counting heartbeats and snoring.

I think I saw a computer down in the game room in the corner. I went down to check it out. When I got the computer going, it automatically went to a password box. Damn it. I sat there guessing all the words I thought Ethan would use. Isis, Nomad, Blue, Zachary, I even tried Evelyn. I got tired of trying. I really have no patience when it comes to inanimate objects.

I heard Ethan get out of bed and whisper my name. "Down in the game room," I said. He made his way down to me and I had moved over to one of the couches.

"Good morning. Have a good night?" I asked.

He rubbed his eyes and wiped the sleep out. He had that warm smile on his face and it quickly turned to a bigger one, when I assumed last night played in his head.

"Yes. Last night was great. You're stuck now."

I smiled back at him. "Stuck?"

"Yeah. You're stuck with me now."

"I wouldn't have it any other way. What time is it?" I asked. "The sun has been up for awhile."

"It's time to start breakfast. Boo Boo will be getting up here in a minute." Ethan put his foot on the bottom step.

"Boo Boo?"

"Yes, sorry, it's my nickname for Zachary."

"Oh, adorable. But about the time, do you ever answer questions right?" I laughed.

"I did. If you want to know what hour it is, it's 8:30 am." Ethan said sarcastically.

"You really are something else." I replied.

"I know. I'm a bear. By the way, you never got to see that part. You wore me out. You know it's really not fair that you're a vampire and all that. Y'all don't get tired. I do." He started to go up the steps.

"Ethan?"

"What?" he said as he turned around.

"Can I try something on you?" I sheepishly asked.

"Sure."

"Anything?"

"There really is nothing you can try that I can get hurt on. You won't hurt me and you know what I am so, go ahead," he grinned.

I made my voice caress his hearing and started. "What is the password to your computer?"

"Ivy," he answered.

"Was it me you were thinking about last night and not your wife?" I slowly asked.

"Yes. Why would you question that?" He scrunched his eyebrows together. He walked over to me and put his hands on my face and my heart began to beat. "Your bespelling doesn't work on me. I have a block to ya'lls powers. Besides, you can ask me anything and I will answer you straight. If it's something you won't like, I'm sorry but, I'm not going to candy coat anything for ya. You're a big girl and you know how the world works. If I lie to you, it will bite me in the ass sooner or later. It's not worth it."

My face filled with blood. I shouldn't have asked that second question. I do appreciate the honesty part. "Okay."

"Let's go wake the kids and get them going." He kissed my nose and walked up the stairs again. I sat on the couch and processed that conversation. Did he say that the password to his computer was my name? I never would have thought of that. Well, I guess I'll go get Kera up and join the land of the living.

I walked through to the kitchen where Zachary and Kera were already eating bowls of cereal. How long had I been downstairs thinking? I better get a grip on that. I did the morning routine of kissing Kera on the head and saying good morning to Boo Boo. I was now calling Zachary that too. So was Kera. I heard the tires on the road turning off the highway and hitting our road. I said "wow" out loud. Ethan grinned and winked at me. Shortly after, I heard the very loud honk of a horn in front of the house. I guess I'm just going to hop in the car and go. I looked at Ethan standing in the kitchen drinking a cup of coffee.

"See ya later."

"Thanks." I walked over to him and gave him a bear hug and a kiss on the cheek. There were giggles from the peanut gallery behind us. I kissed Kera on the top of her head. I told her I would be back and to listen to Ethan.

I threw on my sunglasses and looked in the mirror on the wall by the front door, how convenient. My hair was shiny with the spiral curls perfect. My shirt and shorts were picked out just for this occasion. I didn't care if blood poured all over them. They were headed for the trash anyway. My shorts were cut off jeans with bleach spots on them. My shirt was a thin fabric with the collar stretched from Kera wearing it to watch TV. She would pull her knees to her chest and force the shirt over them. I also wore socks and a pair of old sneakers. I pulled the door open and I was off. Outside was bright even with the sunglasses on. The many smells pulled and tugged at me with so many fighting for my attention. I ignored them to reach the Jeep. It was pulled up with the passenger door facing me. It was Josh and he was alone. I got in the Jeep and said hello to him.

"Hi. You ready?" Josh was wearing sunglasses too. I was in shock that he was driving, being blind and all.

"Yeah. I have been thinking of how to find one. I tried to . . . Never mind. How do you go about it?"

"We go to a park. There will be kids playing and where there are kids . . ." Josh responded with a growl. This made me sick as well. You can't even take your kids to a park without a predator watching and getting his jollies off.

"How far away is a park? Or just the one we're going to?"

"It's not far. Over by where I live. Shane doesn't like me to be gone to long. She doesn't trust herself. She wants a child. She told me you made her tell you about that. She's practicing on her levitating right now. It keeps her mind busy."

"Levitating! How cool. Is that her gift?" I was excited. I can't wait to see.

"That really was a stupid question." Josh's laugh filled the Jeep.

"Uh. Yeah. Sorry." I giggled too.

We drove for about a half an hour before he pointed to a road and said that was the road he lived off of. It was another back road like mine was. We went another ten minutes until we turned off the road by a gas station and followed the road until we saw a brick building. It was an elementary school and it had all the toys a child would love to play on. Teeter totters, swings, jungle gyms, slides, all of it. We pulled up and parked facing the playground.

"Now, crack your window." I did. "Smell. You are seeking a strong smell. Not necessary a bad one, just strong. They are good at manipulating their prey. They lie and abuse trust." He pointed out his windshield. I took long inhales of air. I looked with my vampire eyes and scanned every smell placing it with the person I was looking at.

I found him. He was sitting on a bench talking to a mother. He was laughing and joking with her. The mother's daughter came up and got a drink of water. That pile of snot was watching her as she went to go play some more.

"Got it. Now what?" I hissed, gritting my teeth.

"Now we need to get him alone."

"Something just came to mind. Wanna follow my lead?" I had my hand gripped on the handle of the door.

"Sure. What do you want me to do?"

I pointed to the trees over to the right. "Wait there." I didn't give him a chance to answer. I got out of the car and step by step I walked over to the play ground. I put a concerned look on my face and made a 'B' line straight to him. My stomach started hurting as I walked closer to him. This creature that would crush a little girls hopes and dreams. Destroy her whole life because he's evil. Not anymore. Not after I'm done with him.

I reached the lady and man sitting on the bench. "Have you seen my daughter? She was with her friend at their house and they decided to walk here. Her friend is home but mine never came back. She's seven years old. She has blue eyes and blonde hair. She was wearing a dress with flowers on it and ribbons in her hair."

The lady responded, "No. I haven't. I've been here an hour or two and haven't seen any little girl like that." She looked over at the man. "You have been here longer than me, have you seen her?"

The man shook his head and said no.

"Well do you think you could help me out?"

"Oh, well my daughter is playing over there by the slides and it is about time I take her home. I'm sorry." She placed a hand on my shoulder, picked up her pocketbook and walked away.

The man stood up. "I'll help you. Which way was she walking from?" He was wearing a pocket blue t-shirt and a pair of pants. He was slightly taller than me and my intensity was growing from all the hatred running wild within me.

"Her friend lives that way and we live this way. Maybe she took a short cut through the trees." He followed me and we walked away from the playground. "I'm so scared for her. She's so little and anyone could just grab her up." I kept on.

"Yeah the world we live in sucks." His voice was rough and he followed close behind.

"Do you live around here?" I asked him as I stopped walking. We were just inches away from the tree line. I was acting like I was frantically looking for my daughter over the school grounds. I was really checking to see if anyone had noticed us walk here. The lady was gone and so was her daughter. She must have been alarmed that a child was missing and left to the protection of her home. What she doesn't understand is these people, monsters, are in your home, your schools, your playgrounds, you're around them constantly and you don't even know it. It's the partner of yours tucking them in at night at your side. It's the teacher that teaches them, helps them pull up their pull-ups in kindergarten, the coach that hits their butts when they have done a good job at practice. I have heard that the average pedophile will have molested or raped ten children before they are caught the first time.

"Not here but close by."

"I don't see her. Hopefully she went this way." I turned and continued into the trees. The realization that

I hadn't told Josh anything sprung to mind. I mumbled, "Stay where you are. Not yet."

The man behind me asked, "What? I couldn't hear you?"

I pivoted and looked at him with a puzzling look on my face. "Do you use the lost puppy ploy?"

"What?" His face froze.

"Well, I've made the decision to use a ploy of my own. The, I have lost my daughter can you help me, ploy." I stepped into his space.

"Really woman, I have no idea what you're talking about. You must have gotten me confused with someone else." He began to back away with his hands up like I had a gun. I don't need one. I grabbed his finger tips and forced them back and twisted his wrists upward. He began to scream in pain. I let one hand free and punched him in the neck crushing his voice box.

I leaned into his face. "I wouldn't want you to draw attention to us." I grinned venomously at him. "Besides all your going to do is lie to me. I'll find out the truth my own way!" I hissed. I grabbed the free hand by the wrist, and bit off his pointer. Memories flooded my eyes. Pain, shame, distrust, were written in all the little girls' faces I saw. I spit the finger in his face. Rage was fueling me now. I kicked his knee caps and shattered them with one swipe. He let out a silent gust of air dropping to the ground. His face was twisting in pain. His head was now at neck level to me. "That's better. Now your smaller than me. How does it feel to be dominated? Feel small don't you?! You have spent your whole life raping, hurting and destroying innocent children. How pathetic! Can't do it with a real woman? Do they laugh at you and your tiny digit?" He just poured tears out his eyes.

"How many girls cried for you to stop? How many girls have you hurt? Do you even know?" I was screeching at him. The rage in me wasn't letting me talk anymore. I was done with this puke in front of me. I let go of him and he sunk down on his butt. He grabbed his knees in pain. "Pathetic!" I hissed again. I took my right hand and put it on the bottom of his chin. I started to slowly push my nails up into his mouth. He grabbed my wrists with both hands. I just grinned at him. I took my other hand with his hand still firmly grasping my wrist and placed it on top of his head. I jammed my right hand inside his head until I felt brain matter. His heart was still beating. It just hadn't caught on to the fact he was dead. I took my hand out of his head. I flicked the blood and brains off of my fingers onto his face. He was still in a sitting position with his eyes still open. I kicked his chest and made him lay down.

Josh let out a breath of air. He stepped into the area I was standing in from the shadows of the tall trees.

"That was extraordinary! You must have been born to be a vampire." Josh studied the body in front of me.

"No. I just had one of those for a father." I was exhausted. The rage had left my body taking the fuel with it and I wanted to go.

"Oh." He didn't know that's what this was all about. That man wasn't a stranger to me. He was my father in theory. I stood there while Josh pulled the man into thicker trees. I was shocked perhaps. Was this really a deep seated fear of mine? To face my father for all he had done? Or did I wish for revenge so deeply it was hidden even from me, from my own conscious thoughts?

"There." He said when he returned to my side ripping me from my thoughts. "The coyotes will get to him before anyone finds him." Josh brushed his hands together smearing the blood on them. He pulled a handkerchief out of the back pocket of his pants. "Are you alright?" He tried to reach for my hand. I pulled away. The last thing I want is for him to have pity on me, to think of me as a victim. I was anything but that. I survived hell and then some. I am past that place where someone has that much control over me and that much power. Never again! "Ivy?"

"Yes. I'm fine." I wiped my cheeks, seems fluid was leaking from somewhere. They couldn't be tears, I have cried enough over that lost childhood.

"Would you like to go to the jeep now?" Josh's voice was tender and soothing.

"I'm fine really. Yes let's go." If we stand around here and he continues to play gentle with me, I'll lose it. I began to walk to the Jeep pushing off of the ground with my back foot. I was going to the Jeep but felt the air whistling through my hair. Standing by Josh at the Jeep I knew I moved in mach mode. "Did I . . ."

"Like a vampire." He smiled opening the passenger door for me.

I pulled the visor down and saw there was a little blood coming out of the corner of my mouth and dribbling down my neck. I wiped it away with a tissue from the glove compartment. I didn't want any of that repulsive human on me.

"So, you are alright?" Josh was sitting looking out the window of his side of the car.

"Yes. I am fine."

"Understood. How did you like our little outing?"

"Not sure. It was a new thing for me. The low life's blood was so coppery. It was so bitter." I tried to forget the taste screaming in my mouth.

"I think it's the imprint of evil flowing through their veins. You needed to feed. It was really a waste that you didn't." He was still looking out of his window. "Drink him that is."

"I think I can do it next time. I know what to expect. I just have to get a better grip of my emotions. Practice makes perfect, right?" I laughed and Josh smiled at me.

"Tell you what. Let's go see Shane. She is at the house and is probably worried or bored by now."

"Yes, let's." I agreed.

Josh turned the engine over and we headed for his house. His road was just dirt, no gravel. We went down and up little hills all the way to his place. The road stopped abruptly after he turned a sharp corner, and there his house was. It was a brick, ranch style house. Green awnings and shutters framed the windows. The trees around his house were thinner than at Ethan's. They were sporadically placed throughout his yard. He had peach trees, cherry trees and apple trees surrounding the walk way to the front door. The smells tingled my nose. I would smell peaches, then cherries, and then apples. They were all fighting for my attention. Tidal waves of scents crashing over me, all the way to the house.

A large, Calico cat was sleeping with one eye open on a chair on the porch. They had wooden furniture. Ethan probably made them and they were beautiful. A rocking chair, a bench that sat three, a table, and a swing hanging from the porch roof.

Josh sniffed the air and breathed to me softly, "Around back. Let's try and sneak up on her." He grinned from ear to ear. We snuck around the side of the house and I followed Josh to the corner. He poked his head around and waved for me to look.

Shane had rocks lifted off of the ground in the back yard. Huge rocks, some where bigger than stoves. Big indents of dirt like scars in the ground, lay from where the rocks had been imbedded. Shane stood in the middle with her arms extended out to the sides of her. Her focus was broken and the rocks fell from the air to the ground with a slamming thud.

Shane whipped her head to us. "You guys suck! That was a record I was going for. I had seven rocks up and was attempting to make it eight." We stepped out from the side of the house.

"Oh my god. That was awesome! Do it again." I was so excited.

She faced me and my body felt different. A numbing feeling was invading my body. It started at my head and down through my torso. It went out my fingers and my feet. "You need to be perfectly still while I do it."

"You're lifting me?"

"Be still. That means your mouth too." She winked at me. Then she closed her eyes and inhaled. She held the breath in and I felt the pulling of my body upwards. I started to lift. Her arms lifted with me. Her palms were facing up to the sky. I kept as still as I could. After I was in the air for a moment, she flipped her hands over a quarter turn. My body jerked to a lying down position.

"Whoa." I said.

She pulled her hands together and I started to do flips over and over, head over feet. Slowly at first, then faster and faster. She started to hiss the air out of her lungs and pulled her hands apart. My flipping slowed and I stopped. I was upside down, unfortunately. I started to return to the ground.

"Shane. I have a problem with this." I giggled.

Shane's eyes popped open and as they did, I went colliding to the earth.

"Ouch!" I said to her. Josh was laughing his head off. He had his hands on his knees as if to not fall over.

"Liar-face. That didn't hurt." Shane laughed.

"I'm so glad my head broke my fall!" I was giggling again.

"I'm glad it was just your head. No damage done." Shane began laughing even harder.

We filled the yard with laughter in unison. It was so nice to laugh and feel carefree for a change. To not try and learn something, to not try and control yourself and above all, to not try and think that the entire world as you know it, has changed.

It wouldn't last though. Good things in your life are just flashes. They are wonderfully bright and profound. Then, they are gone before your eyes can blink. These are the times you grab with two hands and hold in a death grip. Never let them go. If you do, you will only remember the bad and evil things that have happened to you. They fester up inside you and kill you slowly. Don't hold on to them. I know. Your holding on to them will only make the memory worse and painfully stifling. The act done to you becomes a tragedy, ten fold, then it festers.

The fat, Calico cat that was sleeping on the porch chair came strutting around the side of the house. It's meow was short and squeaky. It rubbed it's body along Josh's calf. "Hi there, girl. How are you today?" Josh bent down and picked the cat up. "This is Esmeralda." He held her under his arm and stroked her jaw. Her purring got louder and louder. It was filling up my ears and soothing my thoughts. Weird. A peaceful feeling seeped into my body, just from the sound.

"You feel it don't you?" asked Shane. I found my eyes were shut and I was drifting off in time. A black, soft caress of nothingness passed around me, carrying me off. Shane's words were just whispers to me. The purring stopped. I returned back to the sunlight and grass opening my eyes. Josh and Shane were looking at me smiling.

"My god that was extraordinary." I blinked my eyes slowly and inhaled deeply trying to adjust to the loud light and buzzing world around me.

"They are very relaxing. You should get one. Ethan needs a cat over there at his place. It's gotta be hard for you to be there with all that panting and slobbering."

Josh smirked and Shane continued. "A cat is sort of like white noise to us. Esmeralda sleeps around my neck when I am watching TV in the recliner. It is as close to sleep you will come to as a vampire. It's trance like. Pulls your thoughts and soothes your mind. Well, I don't need to tell you, you just felt it." Shane pulled Esmeralda from Josh's arms and tried to hand her to me. Esmeralda put her ears back. A low growl emitted from her throat. She started licking the front of her mouth and the growl began to break up. It sounded like the cat was talking to me. Shane pulled her away and looked at Josh.

"You took her to feed on one of those didn't you!" Shane placed the cat on the ground and it scurried off to the front of the house. "How bad was it?" She asked him without waiting for a response to the first question. She put her hands on her hips.

"Baby," Josh tried to explain.

"No way. You know how dangerous it is especially for her being new and all." Shane shook her head in disbelief.

"I was there to make sure it was all under control. She did fine. She started by getting him alone, all by herself. He fell right into her trap. I was right there when it all went down. She conducted herself like a very dignified vampire." Josh grinned snakelike.

"Well, we have different opinions on what dignifies vampires." Shane wasn't buying his lie.

"Shane," I started, "I didn't do a superb job of controlling my anger if that's what your getting at. I did lose it for a minute. I regained my composure and killed him. The only thing I didn't do, that I had to do, was feed off of him. I tasted his blood and it had an aire of poison and filth about it and the memories flooded me, god the memories, that's when the anger irrupted. I read his mind with my hand." I put my hand up to my chin and made a thrusting motion upwards. I couldn't help but to smile. Josh cocked the corner of his mouth up and let some air out of his nose.

"You two are disgusting you know that?" Shane shuttered.

"Oh babe, I'm sorry. She did well for her first kill. Next we just need to get her to feed off of them."

Shane sighed and dropped her shoulders. "I guess I trust you, dear." She walked over to Josh and lightly punched him on the shoulder grinning.

"Yeah, yeah," I said, "Next time I would enjoy you coming with, Shane."

"I would like that very much Ivy." Her voice immediately turned to a mothering tone. "Now to find my kitty."

"What was her problem?" I asked.

"She has a good nose for evil. I have figured that out the hard way." Shane smiled. "I told you that I fed off of a man that turned out to be a child rapist. When I came home that night, I grabbed Esmeralda up, like I usually do when I get back. I pulled her up to my face to kiss her and she took both of her paws, claws out, and dug them into my face. I had four claw marks on both sides." Shane was taking her hands and dragging her nails down the sides of her cheeks. "Cats are very complex creatures. I suppose they feel the evil in you, the blood, and they think it's from you. They know who you are but the scent you're oozing is not you. They get confused and that's what you get."

"So you don't feed on them and come straight home cuddling her anymore do you?" I grinned.

"No but I really don't have to go out and feed if I don't want to."

I was puzzled. "You don't have to drink blood? How's that?"

"My job provides me with all the blood I need." Shane and Josh looked at each other and they started for the back door. "Come on. I'll show you what I mean."

I followed them into their house. When I went into the house, the first thing I smelled was sage. A very calming affect to my vampire body. I was peaceful. The first room was the kitchen. It had decorations of grapes stenciled up along the walls by the ceiling. Green vines and purple grapes of all different shades. Her canisters rested on the counter, cups hung on hooks, place mats on the wooden table, everything had some sort of grape design on them. The walls were a bone white.

Black and white tiles ran the length of the room. The cabinet doors had glass framed by wood. I could see all the contents in them. They were neat and tidy, full of sparkling crystal cups, plates, and bowls. The sink was deep and silver with counter tops of purple marble. We walked into the next room.

The floors were covered with thick white carpet. Shane and Josh stopped in the entry to the living room to take off their shoes. The couch set was an off white and three large windows were covered with maroon colored curtains. The curtains were long and draped down to the floor. There were shelves all over the room on different levels filled with candles of all colors and sizes.

A wide variety of scents perfumed the air. I could smell vanilla, roses, cookies, cakes, flowers, fresh breezes, and many more. On one wall, there was an old cabinet of long, tall cylinders. The cabinet was shaped flat on the bottom, wide at the sides and quickly came to a point at the top. The doors were open to display them. I paused looking at them and I caught Josh's attention. He pulled one of them off of the shelf and handed it to me.

"It's a kaleidoscope. Point it to the window."

I held it to my eye and closed the other one. Holding it to the window, the light lit up the crystals inside the end of it. With my vampire eyes the kaleidoscope revealed all the usual colors a human would see, but I also saw all the rainbows that the new vision I had displayed. My brain was overwhelmed with all the colors. I pulled it away and looked at Shane, who was now standing in the opening to the hallway watching.

"Oh my." I couldn't put into words how to explain what I just saw.

"I know. There are fifty in there. I haven't been able to look in half of them," Shane said before she continued down the hall. Josh and I followed.

The hall had doors on both sides and all were open, except for one. It was located on the left, all the way at the end. We passed the bathroom and I peered in. I noticed a huge mirror with a vanity. The theme for the room was the beach. Shells on shelves, bottles of sand on the sky blue counter, the shower curtain painted with a beach scene, and the floor was done in slates of light brown rocks.

Going down the hallway, I looked in every door as we passed them. I guess the human nature to look into an opened room as you pass was still with me. A guest bedroom to the left and a room just for painting on the right. The room at the end of the hall to the right was an office with a computer desk and other office supplies in it.

We went into this room. Shane walked in first and stepped to the right. Josh stepped left. I walked in and stopped right in the middle of them. The back wall had a high, thick black table with some microscopes on it. Paper work in a pile, glass tubes in a wooden holder, and mason jars full of red liquid sealed with glass lids with clamps.

"I have a friend that works for the Center for Disease Control in Corpus Christi. We go way back. I study blood and the viruses it can contain. He contacted me a long time ago and asked if I was interested in helping him try and create synthetic blood. He was the one that first had the idea long before the technology was around. Of course he's a vampire and wanted to find another way to feed instead of killing people. So, I agreed and here I am. I get boxes full every week. Some synthetic blood that has been contaminated with viruses, some regular blood contaminated. Legitimately, I study the blood and incinerate it when I'm done. This is a government project, funded and all." Shane laughed. She pointed to a big metal door on another wall. "This leads to my stash. It's a walk-in cooler. I don't burn the blood. I keep it and violà.

I have plenty to eat." She lifted her hands and then let them drop to her sides.

"Wow! That is pretty neat. Do you drink the blood Josh?" I said jokingly. I had a feeling he didn't. He was too much of a stalker, a predator for that. Josh just glared at me.

"No. I prefer the real thing." Josh gritted his teeth. Then his expression changed quickly. "Change your clothes," he said to Shane. "Get some shorts on and show her your spin!" He tugged at the bottom of her dress. Adorable really. He was full of anticipation.

"Okay," she told Josh with a dirty look, swatting his hands off. Then said to me, "You'll love this but I don't like being a show off and he knows that." She went into the room next to this one. Josh and I went back through the house and out the back door. He took me through the yard and led me to a spot where a white speckled rock was in the middle of some trees. The rock was the size of a small car with moss growing under bottom of it. The trees that were engulfing the area were silver-leaf maple. Shane met us a couple minutes later.

She was wearing a pair of khaki Capri's and a red t-shirt with Betty Boop on it. "I think she's so hot!" Shane giggled at me as I looked at her shirt. Her hair was oddly slicked back and pulled into a pony tail and then twisted into a bun. She jumped up and landed on the rock gracefully.

"You ready?" She looked down at me and smiled really big.

"Ready." I gave her the thumbs up.

Shane took and extended her right hand and stood on her right foot. She lifted herself to her toes. She reminded me of a ballerina, pirouetting. She began to turn very slowly. One of the trees, the one closest to her hand, bent. The entire tree bowed and touched her hand like a kiss. She moved slowly around to the next tree with it responding the same as the first. She spun on her toes and picked up the pace. The trees magnetically dropped one after another to her hand. She went faster and faster until she looked like a spinning top. The trees came down to her, wave after wave. There was so much movement that it was creating wind around me and Josh. My thick curls were being pulled in all directions. Shane was just a blur she was turning so fast. The wind started to settle as Shane slowed down. She came to a stop facing me.

"How did you like that?!?" She glided down the side of the rock like it was ice, holding Josh's hand.

"That was, incredible!!!" I clapped loudly. I really wished I could do that. That really is something to see. "You have got to be dizzy."

"No, surprisingly." Josh escorted Shane towards the house smiling so proud. When we got back to their house, Shane got some of her fake blood and poured it into their beautiful crystal wine glasses. We sat in the kitchen at the table. Josh didn't participate in the drinking of course.

"So, when you break concentration, what would happen if it was a person and not a rock?" I asked her.

"I am moving the matter in one motion up, or whatever, and if I lose it, it would break or tear at it's weakest spot. I haven't done that to a person, yet. Josh here really loves me. He's my guinea pig. I have tried it with snakes and frogs before him. I messed up a few times in the beginning. Once I got it down, he volunteered. He was so brave, considering the pieces of the reptiles all over the ground from failed attempts." Shane shook her head.

"Eww. I can picture that. Gross." I scrunched my nose up.

"I can do it with my eyes open but that's like driving while your talking on the phone. You are aware of what you're doing but, not fully committed to either one." She finished her glass and looked at the blood that was still coating it. She swirled the last bit of the liquid around the bottom.

"Ethan is very happy. He was just plowing through his life taking care of his son. He worked and slept. That's about it." Josh told me softly.

"Well that was random," I said.

"Apologies. I was thinking of how he was before you came along. How lonely he was. He deserves to be happy."

"Y'all care for him very much. I can tell." I glanced at both of them. "Yes. We do. We consider them to be a part of our family," Shane said. "Now we just got another, a sister." I smiled sheepishly and looked at my glass. Empty.

"Looks like I don't need to go out and hunt. I'm stuffed." I rubbed my stomach and smiled. "Thank you."

"You're welcome. Not a problem." Shane placed her hand on mine.

"Do you want go back home?" Josh suggested.

Home. That was a wonderful word to hear. I had a home and a place. This will take some getting use to. I enjoyed Josh and Shane's company so much that I really wanted to stay longer. I did have to get back and be Mommy. Shane left the table and went down the hall and I could hear the metal door open in the far back room. Being able to hear all the things happening around me was pretty neat. She returned with a lunch box.

"Here. Now you can hunt if you want, but you won't have to. In here is a months worth. It's the least I can do. I hope you won't be a stranger and call me regularly." Her voice was sad talking of goodbyes.

"Hey, you are nuts if you think I am going to go a day without talking to you. You have no idea how much you have helped me. If I have it my way, I'll be seeing you everyday too." I hugged her tight. She smelled like orchids.

"Oh, well, that would be so nice." She sniffled.

I pulled away from her. The smell of orchids jogged my memory of Azrael. "Question before I go. What's with Azrael smelling like Vanilla? Do you know?" I babbled out.

"Vampires have pheromones they secrete. Whomever they are hunting, their bodies will put out the scent most likely to attract that person. You now do that." She smiled pushing some curls over my shoulder.

I picked up the lunch box and slung it over my shoulder putting the strap on. I wonder what smell I am. Shane and I walked outside and to the Jeep. Josh was behind us when his cell phone rang. He answered it and I could hear the other end of the conversation. It was Ethan. He was short and to the point. "Y'all need to get to the house. We need to talk. I just got off the phone with Jack. We have problems." Ethan spoke quickly.

"On our way." Josh hung up the phone and we all looked at each other for a split second. I remember Josh saying that I needed to remember that I was in the company of vampires and they have the same hearing as me. So I knew we all heard the conversation. Shane, Josh, and I got in the Jeep and flew down the road. Shane drove and I sat in the back seat pondering what else could happen to me in one week. I did a play by play of what has taken place in the few days leading up to now. Soccer moms got nothing on me.

CHAPTER 13

We pulled up to the house and the air was thick in the Jeep, full of anticipation. When we got into the house, the kids were playing down in the basement. I could hear the Playstation loudly. Ethan was sitting on the couch facing us with an ill favored look on his face. Shane and Josh took a seat on the other couch next to him. I immediately sat next to him.

"Well. What is it now?" I said laughing trying to make the room lighter.

"Azrael is starting to get his fiends together," Ethan said in a monotone voice. Silence filled the air, stolen glances throughout the room were evident.

Josh spoke up. "What was said? What did Jack have to say?"

"Jack told me he got a phone call from a source and they said Azrael was gathering favors others owed him. The source is reliable. It's a messenger." Ethan stopped talking. He could tell I had no idea what that was. Josh broke the silence again.

"A messenger of this sort, Ivy, is someone that knows about our secret and wants to be one. They prove they are worthy of becoming one by listening in on things normal, unsuspecting humans would miss. It helps on these situations," he explained.

Ethan continued. "However it is, Azrael is calling on all that is owed to him from other vampires. Jack said there is a lot of movement in Texas right now. Many vampires are taking up hotels and motels around Paris. There are a lot of them. He asked if we would need his help. I told him we would have to talk about the situation amongst ourselves. I told him we also have others here that could help that know what's going on." Ethan's eyes were on Josh's.

"I think not!" Josh snapped.

"What?" I was lost again.

"Now hear him out Babe," Shane said rubbing Josh's hand.

"Nope. I think that is a very bad idea Ethan. What if they turn on us?" Josh said leaning towards Ethan in his seat.

"They won't. Besides they hate the vampires just as much as we do. They will jump at the chance to kill them, especially Gabbi." Ethan grinned at Josh.

I was now in the loop with her name mentioned. Would Ben really risk his family to save ours? That is something very big to ask of someone.

"Would they do it?" I asked. I was timid while asking, half hopeful.

"I will call and find out. They need to know anyway you look at it Josh. Whether they are going to help us or not. If they won't then they'll need to get out of town. They would do the same for me and mine." Ethan stood up and went out back. I guess he wanted privacy. I went to the playroom to see the kids. I didn't want to wait in the quiet living room trying to hear anything I could from the conversation Ethan was having with Ben. I was better off hearing the whole thing in one piece from Ethan when he got off of the phone.

I walked down the stairs and the kids were still playing a fighting game on the Playstation. Kera was sitting on the couch with her arms folded, pouting. I guess by the looks of it she was losing.

"Momma!" she shouted. Kera came running around the couch and met me at the bottom of the stairs. She threw her arms around my waist and squeezed as tightly as she could.

"Wow! Did you miss me?" I smiled and tightened my arms around her too. She smelled wonderful. Her blood under her skin teased my nose. Her big, sapphire eyes twinkled up at me. She really was a beautiful girl. She missed me and that was a wonderful feeling. To be missed.

She was a light in my darkness for a long time. Now my life and loves have grown. How do I balance this new life? For starters, I'm a vampire that would love to bite my own flesh and blood. I wonder what her blood would taste like. What kind of memories would she remember in her life? I have been there from day one. Which ones would stand out to her? On the other hand I'm repulsed by those thoughts. This is my daughter we are talking about. I have been there since her first breath. How dare I think of those thoughts! I guess I'll battle with this for her life time and that sucks.

I have also found Ethan. He completes the circle I start. He is the punctuation to my sentences. The breath

I take to talk. The left to my right. I guess I won't ever really comprehend the importance he has on my life. I haven't ever felt this way about anyone before. This must be the right thing for me if I have never come close to feeling this before. Now with my life changing, my footing in the food chain, Ethan takes care of Kera while I am unable to. He is the father she never had.

Kera and I embraced for a while on the steps. I had sat down to cuddle with her better. Zachary was still playing the game and I smelled the lingering chocolate in the air. Zachary dropped his controller. "Yeah!" he yelled as he skipped around the couch. He squeezed past me and Kera still on the bottom step. I stood up and walked up the stairs to the front door. Zachary left it wide open after he had flown out of it. He was hugging Gabbi in the front yard. Her smell infected the entry way. I breathed the sweet smell into my lungs and closed my eyes. This was blood I would love to get my tongue on. When I opened my eyes, Gabbi cleared her throat. She locked eyes on me and I smiled at her. I smiled warmly at her to the best of my ability. I didn't want her to feel threatened, even though I wanted to jump on her and sink my teeth deep into her jugular vein and drink till my heart was content. I really was curious on why she was here and alone. I didn't see any vehicles, so she had to have walked.

She lifted one side of her mouth in a very good effort to smile back, considering both of our makeups. She smelled so edible. Gabbi stopped at the beginning of the bridge and placed Zachary in front of her.

"I need to talk to you." Her voice was shaky.

"Sure. You want to do this alone or with the kids?" I said softly to her. I could feel Kera on the landing.

"I would like to do this alone, but I really don't know if I can trust you. Have you already ate today?" She was eyeballing me hesitantly. She really was testing my patience. I hadn't attacked her yet. If I wanted to I cold have killed her already. I stood straight and answered her stupid question.

"Yes for your information, I have. Let's get the kids inside and we'll talk. Alright?" I extended my hand out for Zachary to grab. "Go inside and play with Kera."

Zachary met Kera inside and went back downstairs and I walked to Gabbi. She was letting go of ground, still not sure of me.

"I'll tell you again, I'm not going to hurt you. Let's take a walk down the road and pretend we like each other." I smiled as nicely as I could again. Gabbi turned around and walked next to me with a little reluctance. I peered over my shoulder back at the house and saw Josh standing in the long window by the door. He was grinning at me and nodded. I held my hand to the side of me opposite of Gabbi waving at Josh to stay.

We walked a little ways down the road until Ethan's house disappeared in the green trees surrounding the road. Gabbi stopped walking and turned to me.

"Do you really understand what has happened with your arrival?" Gabbi was whispering.

"I got the gist of it. I also understand you wanted to talk to me and no one else. Why?" I asked.

"I need to have you understand that if my family and Ethan's are no longer friends, we will perish." Gabbi was talking with a stronger voice. It was like the more she talked, the more she had to say.

"It seems to me like Ben jumped the gun on that one."

Gabbi straightened up and said, "He didn't have a choice. Ethan had Josh antagonizing him. You were changing when this all went down. That's besides the point of me being here. I came to see if you would reconsider living here near our town. All this evil you have brought here is going to bite you in your ass. Zachary is going to get hurt. Maybe even Kera. Have you thought of that? I'm not perfect and I have issues of my own but, people are going to die and it's all your fault." Gabbi pointed at me. She barely took the time to breath while she talked.

"Hold on just a minute!" I yelled at her. "I don't think Ethan would have Josh do that and even if he did, I didn't ask for this. Azrael chose to do this to me. I am worried about the kids just as much as anyone else here. Me moving is out of the question. Ethan can protect the kids and me better than if I was on my own trying to take care of Kera by myself don't you think? This evil will follow me wherever I go. Azrael is the monster here not me. This in no way is my fault!" I took a step in her direction. My rage was surfacing and I was trying my best to regain control. Gabbi took a fighting stance and put her hands up.

"Whoa. I'm not going to fight with you," Gabbi started out.

"You're right! You shouldn't! You'll lose! Don't test me." I said it without thinking. Great, just what I needed.

"This will not be good for anyone. If you think I am just going to sit idly by, you're wrong. I came here to try and talk to you. Something big is about to happen. People I care about are going to die. I can't allow this to take place." Gabbi's body was shaking.

"Why can't you help us," I just blurted out without thinking, again. "We could do more damage together then separated."

"Do you really think Josh is going to work with us? Get real. I really have a problem swallowing that one! Has he told you his favorite past-time?" She just looked at me. "No. I didn't think so. Let me tell you that I can't even count how many of my kind he has gorged himself on. He probably couldn't either." She stood there watching my response.

"If I told you that I could help with Josh, would you believe me?" I said softer. There really was no reason to yell or scream anymore.

"No"

"Well I think I can. Shane won't let anything happen to you if I tell her I brought you to help the kids. Josh will respect his wife's opinion. What do you think of that?" I asked her.

"I don't know. This requires me to trust you." Gabbi hesitated.

"Are you breathing?" I said with a smile.

"Yes. This is a first for me. Talking to a vamp-" Gabbi stopped talking and growled low and deep. Her eyes were looking over me to the trees. Her body started to shake violently. She was beginning to blur.

I heard the noise of foot fall behind me. When I felt something jumping from behind, I whipped around to face it. It was Josh and he was in the air ready to pounce on Gabbi. I reacted. I grabbed him by the throat. I dug my nails into his skin and pulled him into my face. He was stunned by my action. I took my other hand and squeezed his cheeks making his lips pucker out.

"What do you think you are doing?!" I yelled at him. Josh opened his eyes and smiled slyly at me. All of the sudden the air became thick. I couldn't breath. A ringing began to sound out of Joshes throat. It vibrated my hand until the vibration wiggled him out of my grip. The ringing continued in my ears, louder and louder. It was paralyzing me. I dropped to my knees. I grabbed my ears and the sound didn't change. It was going right through me to my bones. I collapsed on the ground. I was facing Gabbi, who had stopped shaking. She stood there looking at me and then turned her attention to Josh. He stood over my body, straddling me. Gabbi's mouth was moving, so I know she was talking to him. I just couldn't hear anything but that ringing. Gabbi was pointing at me and the veins were popping out on her forehead.

The ring ceased. All of the sudden my hearing started to return. It was like the volume was turned down and then slowly cranked up again. Gabbi knelt down next to my head.

"Are you okay?" She sounded concerned.

"Yeah. What was that Josh?" I hollered placing my hands on my temples. I stood to my feet and brushed the dirt off of my pants and hands. I felt like I had a hang over. My yelling at him made my head feel like it was about to pop off.

"I was making sure you were alright, so I followed behind a distance. I was down wind of the two of you. She smelled so good. I didn't want to fight it. Ethan said they would be fair game here." Josh just shrugged. "But . . . You seem to have persuasive ways to change my mind. Sorry about the hearing, I don't like my face being touched."

"Well, I think we need to get back to the house and let Ethan know that I have talked Gabbi into helping us. Ben and Abbi need to know too." I looked at Gabbi. "You should go, get them and bring them to the house. I'll let Ethan know." I turned to Josh, "Let's go. We need to talk and Shane needs to be present." I walked off and Josh followed. This is too much. I just stopped Josh from devouring Gabbi. I was quite proud of myself but, Josh did get me to the ground and kicked my ass. I was not in pain when I was laying on the ground but the ringing was very intense. Gabbi reacting the way she did was most promising. If she can talk the others into coming and helping us, we will have a good fighting chance. Josh and I walked back to the house quietly.

The air was light and cool. The evergreen trees perfumed the air with their unmistakable pine scent. The flowers pollinated the air as well. Dragonflies twirled in the air above our heads. Their wings buzzed lightly as they flapped them. Birds chirped and sang their endless songs. They were oblivious to the evil that was on the way here soon.

We approached the house. Shane was outside. I looked over at Josh and he had dried blood on his neck where my nails had penetrated.

"What happened?" Shane said floating over to Josh's side. She caressed his neck and tried to wipe it off.

"We had a disagreement, Ivy and me. I wanted a sweet snack and she stopped me." Josh smirked, looked over at me and then grinned.

"Gabbi? I smelled her on Zachary. Ivy, explain yourself." She turned to me and put her hands on her hips.

"I have talked Gabbi into helping us with our dilemma. She is going home right now and getting the others. Josh here, was going to eat her after we made the agreement. It was all I could do to keep my word. Then he opened his eyes and put me to the ground." I felt like a child tattling on a sibling. While I told on him, I even pointed at him.

"Well it's a good thing you talked to Gabbi. Ethan got off of the phone with Ben and they both were coming to a dead end on how to get Gabbi on board. You have solved a big problem and that has tilted the scales to our advantage, Ivy." Shane walked over to me while she talked and kissed my cheek. "Thank you. Ben is going to arrive tonight with the twins and we are all going to sit down and talk the strategies over."

"Well that's great." I was stunned. This could really work. I was very positive with the whole idea of evil vampires showing up now.

"We do need to get you up to date on the vampires we know will be here. Azrael will certainly be bringing the old rat pack with him. Ethan needs to hear this too. Let's go into the house and have something to drink. We are going to need all the strength we can get for this fight." Shane held hands with Josh and they lead the way to the front door.

"Hello gorgeous!" Ethan called from the dining room. He was sitting at the head of the table with his back to the window. He was watching me flow into the room. His eyes were vibrantly yellow. He grinned at me and held out his hand. I took it and he caressed his lips on the back of my hand. After he made a few passes, he kissed it.

"I think we should do this before the animals get here so Ivy has a grasp of the ones we are dealing with. I would like to talk in detail about them. A little more than with the others," Josh said cutting the romantic air in the room Ethan was creating.

"Kill joy," I mumbled under my breath.

"Okay. The first one I am sure will be there is Eadric. And of course, wherever he is, Tobias will be. Eadric and Tobias are very good, very close friends. Close enough that one never goes anywhere without the other." Josh stopped talking because Shane had returned from the kitchen with large, tall, crystal glasses filled with our drink. She placed one in front of me and took a seat next to Josh at the table. She also had a pitcher full. "Now, Eadric has the power to manipulate fire. He can will it into existence. He controls it in his hands and can throw it. You need to understand that our skin is not flammable but, our clothes are. The victims that fall prey to him are lit up until charred up. He is the reason for the term 'human combustion.' The doctors today can't even explain a human sitting in a chair burnt to a crisp with no point of origin. Arson is never to blame because there are no chemicals present. The hands, feet, and other parts of their extremities are intact due to the fire not spreading all over their bodies. Eadric's bite marks are burnt away. He is cannibalistic, Ivy. He takes bites of his prey in very fleshy areas. The thighs, the stomach, you get the picture. The problem I have with that is, they are still alive while he does it. When he has ate his fill, he will drain them and then burn them."

"Oh my God. How grotesque." I was appalled by this vampire and just wished Josh was pulling my leg. The faces around the table told me that was not the case. This was the truth and the world I now live in. I truly feared for my daughter.

"I know. I was an acquaintance of his for awhile until I learned of his favorite past-time. Now, on to the next, Tobias. He is the chameleon of the vampire world."

"Chameleon?" I interrupted.

"Yes. He can mimic the power of a vampire if he is close enough to them. For example if Tobias is near Shane, he will have her abilities and so on and so forth. The vampire he is mimicking can still use their own gifts but has to fight fire with fire, so to speak."

"That is a neat power to have. Why does he have such a disgusting choice of friends?"

"Make no mistake, he is just as evil. His ability to do what he does to a vampire differs with a human. He has the power to make a human go mad. The people that hear noises that no one else hears, he is creating. The noises you store in your head are recorded. For example, the sound of your child running down the hall. You would recall it if your eyes were closed right?"

"Yeah."

"Well, he pulls those sounds and plays them over and over in the humans head tormenting them. He finds this amusing. I am not sure of the other vampires Azrael will gather. I have been out of the loop for too long Ethan. I'm sorry."

While Josh talked and we listened, Shane filled up our glasses. By the time he stopped, I had drank six cups full. I was feeling stronger. Powerful. Ready to take these creatures to the ground where they belonged.

The children were in the game room playing when we all smelled the smell of death. That is really what us vampires smell like when we don't feed enough. All of us fled the room in unison. Shane and Josh left out the back door, Ethan and I ran out the front.

She was standing in the middle of the driveway. She had her hands out to the side of her in a non-threatening manner. She had long, brown, curly hair to the middle of her back. She was wearing jeans with a ruffled shirt and vest. The shirt was a dark purple. Her skin was pale and not so velvety looking. If I had to guess, she was sickly looking for vampire standards. I didn't care how she was standing or how she looked. She was here to hurt me and my family. I was not going to let her destroy anyone. I lunged at her from the bridge and landed on her chest. I placed my foot on her throat and pressed as hard as I could.

"What do you think you are doing here?" I growled.

"Ivy!" A voice called out at me from behind. I snapped my head towards the sound. It was Shane.

"What?" I spit at her.

"Look at her," she plainly said. I looked automatically down at the woman's face near my foot. She just stared at me. Her hands were out at the sides of her. It was then that I noticed she wasn't struggling under me. I let off of the pressure on her neck but didn't remove my foot.

"Why are you here?" I asked again.

"I wish to talk to you and your family." She spoke in an English accent.

"Talk," I said leaning on her neck a little more.

"My name is Creodra. I did not come here to harm any of you," she forced out of her neck. I could feel the vibration of her voice box through my boot. I took my foot off of her and bent down, leaning into her face.

"Be careful of what you do," I whispered to her and backed up two steps to let her stand.

"I have to say I understand why Azrael picked you."

"Not a good way to start woman." Josh said from behind me. Ethan was standing next to me and Josh and Shane where to our left behind us.

"Forgive me. I have come here to warn you about Azrael. He plans to come here to retrieve Ivy and her daughter. He is wanting to turn your daughter as well for the little stunt Ethan pulled." Shane gasped. "Yes. He is mad. Some of the others are behind him. Others not so much. The ones that won't have any part of this have left Paris and returned to their homes. I couldn't do that. I feel responsible for what happens to you if I didn't warn you. When, and I mean when, they get here you better have the children hidden well and don't fight here. There will be no containing this battle. Do you know somewhere else to go?" Creodra asked.

"The lake." Ethan spoke for me. "If you go east, the highway splits to the right and the left. Go left. There is a lake there about ten minutes further."

"I will return to my house and take a detour through Paris to tell Azrael. I will tell him I went spying on you. I'll tell him where to find you. I will be telling him of some crisis I need to tend to because if he does succeed in getting what he wants, I don't want to be exposed." She turned to leave and I jumped in front of her.

"Thank you so much. I really have no words to tell you what this means to us." I studied her face. I wanted to remember it so I could find her when this is all over with and thank her again.

"This is about what is right and what is wrong. Don't thank me," Creodra said placing her hand on my shoulder. She ran off. She was gone just as fast as she had appeared. I stood there looking at Ethan. Josh and Shane stared at me. This was turning out to be quite the mess.

∽○∽

CHAPTER 14

Silence. It is very peaceful at times. When your day has been stressful, when children have been running around all day screaming, work won't let up, or other things like that. On the other hand, it can be torture. The silence of news to come of a loved one's health for example. Doubt creeps into your mind. The death of hope comes swiftly in silence. Every scenario playing over and over in your head. Each ending more terrifying than the next. The unknown. Silence.

Josh and Shane kept to themselves and sat at the dining room table. Ethan and I were sitting on the couch in the living room. The children continued to play in the basement with the entertainment down there. Ethan lightly caressed my hands in his, telling me not to worry. The tightness in his voice told me he was unsure. I was really getting angrier as the moments passed. I had a life and a daughter that was taken care of before this crypt keeper came sniffing around. I came to the conclusion that they all must die. That was all there was to it. Anyone that would follow this vampire to the evil lengths he will take really are a waste of space.

"Josh, Shane, could you come in here for a minute?" I said after I decided to go through with my thoughts. Shane and Josh came into the room and sat on the couch with no questions. They were waiting to hear what I had to say. After all, this was my life and my daughter. "I think they should all be slaughtered. I want them all to die. I think we would be doing the world a great service. Are you all in? Do you think I am overreacting? What would you do in my shoes?" I looked at all the faces I was asking to fight a fight that was not necessarily theirs. Would they all come out on top. Which of us could perish? My thoughts were uncontainable. I rambled on and on in my head.

"I wholeheartedly believe that they all deserve to die. I think we need to evaluate how many we are dealing with when we get there. Let's not get ahead of ourselves and bite off more than we can chew," Josh softly said.

"Yes sweetie, we will be at your side. I'm sure you are thinking about that," Shane whispered across the room.

Shane was so insightful. She was someone that I was learning to care a lot about. Josh in his own way was a great vampire. He didn't take crap and protected his wife with his life. So what if he had bad habits? Killing and eating more than his fill of changelings really was a bad habit. Well, on the other hand I can say that I have never really tasted one. If they taste just as good as they smell, I really don't blame him. No one ever got in trouble for eating too many candy bars. We can't gain weight so that's off the table. If you could eat all the chocolate you wanted without the side effects, a lot more people would be eating them to no end.

"Ivy. I have been thinking. You are going to have to start getting stronger in your abilities as a new vampire. What would you say to sparring with me?" Ethan said smiling.

"I guess. Can I hurt you? You did say once that vampires have no effect on you." I was confused. I didn't want to hurt him. Even if it was to prepare for fighting these fiends.

"I'm not invincible but your mind games can't hurt me. I'll be fine. I just want to see if you are as strong as I think you are." Ethan squeezed my hand hard.

"I feel like that is a challenge." I took my hand out of his and stood up. "I accept." I smiled back. Ethan stood up and brushed his body against mine and headed for the back door.

"Play nice you two." Shane called from behind us, catching up.

"Nonsense. By all means fight. I have got to see this. Are you going to fight as yourself or human form Ethan?" Josh asked with delight. He was like a kid in a candy store. I stopped walking. I froze. What did I just get myself into. Can I really fight a bear? Damn it Ivy, you really need to know when to control your impulses. Now I'm going to get creamed by a grizzly.

We all were outside. Josh and Shane were on opposite sides of the yard. Shane was by the jungle gym and Josh by the patio table. Shane looked worried and Josh was giggling. Ethan stood in front of the water fountain, grinning from ear to ear.

"Do you know what I find so amazing about being with you, Ivy?" Ethan chuckled.

"What's that?" I was scared, excited, nervous, and antagonized all at the same time. He lunged at me and grabbed my throat and squeezed in a death grip. He licked my face and said, "We can wrestle and I can be rough with you, where a human woman would break."

I rolled to the right and broke his grip on me. I squatted down and ran through his stance, popping up behind him. I threw my arm around his neck and hopped on his back. I locked my hand in the crook of my other arm and had him in a rear naked choke. I was amazed. I did it.

"You were saying?" I slithered in his ear intertwining my legs around his stomach.

Ethan took his hands and grabbed me under my arms and yanked me off of his back with little effort. I went flying through the air. He tossed me into the direction of the wooden monkey bars. I dropped my feet through one of the slots, hooked my hands around the metal bar. I was like a boomerang. I placed my feet squarely on his chest and knocked him to the ground.

"Get up," I said to him waving my hands.

"Ethan, you be nice! It's just her vampire emotions fueling her now!" Shane shouted at him.

"Stay out of it Babe. Ethan's not going to hurt her," Josh said irritated.

A musky smell flowed around my body. Ethan's eyes turned from a greenish yellow to a neon, piercing yellow. His skin stretched over his muscles that were now growing. Long, black nails stabbed through finger tips and bare toes. His skin began to rip and tear allowing his body to expand. His skin peeling away, yielded jet black fur. His face slid off and a brownish tanned muzzle replaced it. His vibrant eyes jumping out at me from all that black. The hair on his chin was white. The hair on his neck and shoulders was thick and long like a lion's. On his chest was a white patch of fur in a crescent moon shape. His ears were large and set far apart on his rounded head. His skin was a pile around him. It began to darken until it was ash-like. The swirling wind broke it up and lifted it. It danced in the air for a moment before it blew away. He was standing on his back legs. He had to have weighed four hundred pounds and stood five foot three! He jerked his head towards me and let out a thunderous roar that blew my hair backwards. I was terrified.

"Now you did it." Josh breathed excitedly rubbing his hands together.

I took a step back and braced myself for his advance. He just stood there staring at me with those scary eyes. I took a hard swallow and moved forward. I stopped just at arms length from him and extended my hand out. He dropped his head a little and glared at me. At least I thought he was. I put my hand on his chest and felt his fur. My hand was quickly buried. Thick course hairs slid through my fingers. His body radiated heat from underneath all that fur. He fell forward to his front feet and was now standing on all fours. He swatted at my feet in a playful manner. One landed on my right foot and dang near knocked me over. He kept moving towards me trying to take my feet out from under me. I put my hands on his head and pushed with all I had, trying to stop him from moving forward. I just started to lose ground. With one slap he took both feet out from under me and I was flat on my back. Shane gasped. He walked over top of me to stop at my face. He snorted a few times then took his enormous tongue and ran it the entire length of my face, chin to forehead.

"Yuck! Cut that out," I said wiping his bear spit off of me. His breath smelled like blueberry muffins. I pulled my knees to my chest and pushed him as hard as I could off of me. I lifted his shoulders up and his front paws came up off of the ground. I rolled out from under him and stood up.

"Okay," I said backing up. "Be Ethan again. This is cheating. It's vampires I'm going up against, not bears." I was back-peddling trying to get him to stop.

Ethan stood on his back feet and snorted at me again and growled. He started to hunker over. The fur was not as full and the earthy smell I associated with him began to linger in the air. The jet black fur that covered his body was shrinking and sloughed off of him. It slid down his face, over his shoulders and down his legs. It was darkening the same way his skin had. It turned to ashes and floated away with the breeze. Ethan stood naked as a jay bird with his hands over the front of him. All he wore was a smile. The warm smile that melted my cold heart when we first met. I ran over to him, threw my arms around his neck and held on tight.

"You said you wanted to see." He spoke lightly in my ear.

"Yes, I did but not like that!" I stared into his eyes as they swirled with the green returning to linger on the edge of his iris. He left and went into the house while I stared at Josh and Shane. I was speechless. That was quite the stunt. He returned wearing a pair of faded jeans and a black t-shirt. He was smiling and seemed quite pleased with himself.

"My turn," Josh said as he crossed the yard to stand closer to me.

"Alright." I felt more confident fighting him than that bear. I took a fighting stance and Josh did the same.

"Ready?" Josh asked. He didn't wait for a response. He jumped at me and I dropped back. He was throwing punches, kicks, jumping and acting like a jack rabbit. Every time he would try to assault me, I defended myself by catching his hand or foot. I put him to the ground several times. He was attacking me from the front, the back, the sides and from every angle he could muster. I was quicker than him. I could tell he was getting frustrated. The smirk or grin that he always wore had disappeared. He was determined. He was grinding his teeth. They were loud and sounded similar to nails on a chalk board in my ears. Josh was opening his eyes. I cringed. I threw my hands up over my ears trying to stop the ringing from entering. That was a failed attempt. The sound bulldozed its way through my hands. My eyes rolled upwards. This was a more intense ringing that did hurt.

"That's enough Josh!" Shane yelled at him. The ringing stopped once more. I took a long deep breath in order to reset myself. "I want to see what she's got." Shane put her hand on his shoulder and put herself between us. Josh stood straight and backed off.

Shane squared off to me. I started circling her. Her hands were out to her sides. I tried to hit her and my arm stopped in mid swing. Shane smiled and slapped my cheek. When she dropped her arms my swing continued. Unfortunately she dodged it to smack me. We went round and round doing this. I started to swing or kick as fast as I could. My fists were flying at lightning speed but it made no difference. My cheeks were bright red and stinging by the time I surrendered. Josh thought this was hilarious. He was giggling the entire time. When she slapped me he lost control to where I thought he would pee himself. This infuriated me.

"Do you know what the definition of insanity is?" Shane laughed asking.

"What?" I growled at her.

"Doing the same action over and over again trying to get a different outcome. If you run into this problem when this all goes down, switch it up. Use your power and manipulate their minds. Make no mistake, they are not going to be fighting fair with us." She stopped talking and gave Josh a look. This glance they give one another is a silent conversation that I have honed in on.

I reacted and smelled the air.

"The animals," Josh mumbled.

"Okay. Let's be nice," I said and Shane grinned.

The loud sound of crunching rocks under tires came down the road. We all, Josh, Shane, and I went into the kitchen to sit and begin our planning.

Ethan let Ben and the twins into the house after one of them knocked on the front door. I thought it silly to knock and announce themselves. It's not like we can't smell them from miles away.

Ben entered the room first, of course. He was quite calm. Abbi followed behind. She looked around the room and her eyes stopped on me. Gabbi walked in with a smile. I had never seen her smile that way before. They must have had a long talk because they were not as tense as they usually are.

"Hi," I said welcoming them into the room.

"Hello. We are so glad to be here once more as guests." Ben announced. We all sat talking about the vampires that Josh knew would show up. He filled them in on the essentials and specifics. Josh did not tell them about his involvement with them or how he got his information. We told them about the visit from Creodra.

They agreed to take a stand against the vampires. Ben's take on all of this was, if we are not able to defeat them alone, his family would be next on the list. We were all in agreement that we would be a force to be reckoned with if united. Ethan told Ben and the twins about Jack being in Paris keeping his ear to the ground. He would get a heads up and arrive here before the vampires move in.

"The lake is a great place to do it at," Ethan began. "There are cabins located on the lake were we can stay in the first couple of hours before they strike. Jack is going to stay here with the children. I am going to install a steel door at the entryway to the basement. Luckily, Ruth can keep some cabins empty for us. With fall quickly approaching, there won't be too many visitors."

"Ruth? She owns the cabins on the lake?" I asked.

"Yes. She is a vampire too. She's a very strong vampire. She has healing powers and can read thoughts. Now, she won't fight with us and I wouldn't ask her too. Reasons I can't go into right now. If it gets too messy at the lake, she will have no problem with that. As long as we clean up after ourselves." Ethan laughed.

"That's good," Gabbi said smiling.

"Are you going to tell Kera about yourself?" Abbi asked me.

"Why should I?" I didn't see the relevance to her knowing.

"If she is brought into the loop, it would make her more aware of the people around her. I just don't want her to get derailed in school. When's it start Ethan?" Abbi asked, looking at Ethan.

"By the end of this month. I think that is something for you to think about Sweetie. They might show up there. The school she will attend is small and they combine grades. The teacher that will be teaching Zachary will be Kera's teacher as well. They are combining first through third. She is pretty safe there. I have other friends that work there that can keep a close eye on them," Ethan explained.

"Wow. That's a concept, to have such a small class together grade-wise," I said. I then thought of how to go about telling Kera what I have become. "How do you tell a six year old about vampires?" I wasn't so sure if that was a great idea. I just looked down at the table while playing with a piece of string on my pants.

"You would be surprised at how accepting children are," Ben told me. "I'm so glad we could work out our problems, everyone," Ben said to everyone at the table.

They stayed a little while longer. Zachary and Kera came up the stairs and Gabbi took them outside to play. Just before Gabbi went out the back door, she turned to me and said, "She knows about me. She didn't freak out when she saw me shift. Just think about it. She's stronger in more ways than you think." She flashed a smile and out the door she went. I was flabbergasted. I recalled the conversation Kera and I had in her room that night about Gabbi and raccoons swimming. I remembered she talked quite calmly about it.

Ethan and I decided to have the cookout that was interrupted awhile ago, when I first met all of them. We all ate hearty and laughed together. All of us seemed at ease with each others company. One big, happy, complex family.

Ben and the twins left and Ethan and I put the children to bed. Ethan fell asleep watching television while I took a shower. I went in the hall and pulled an afghan off the shelf and covered him up. I sat on the other couch so I wouldn't disturb him. He looked so peaceful. considering the mess we were nose deep in.

I stared at the television. It was on the history channel. People were reenacting the Civil War and talking about it. They had letters they were reading sent from Officers and such. Gettysburg, in particular, was the focus when I was watching. Photos of dead soldiers lying on the ground in trenches, fields, everywhere. Blood tainted the green grass around them. Some of them had their eyes open, fixated on the sky. Pain seared on their faces. Holes in their clothes. No shoes on most of them. In one, someone was lying on the ground with the confederate flag clenched in his dead hands. I could, on any other night, be able to watch this show intensely. Tonight it was hitting too close for comfort. That could be Shane on the ground dead. Even worse, Ethan.

I decided to go for a walk. The crescent moon was throwing cool rays on my body, I basked in the moonlight for a few minutes at the water fountain. Then I took off. I broke out in a fast paced jog. I had to think and being alone would help.

After just a few minutes I slowed down to a slow snail pace. I was inhaling the beauty of the evening. Ethan chose his home wonderfully. This wooded area on the side of the mountain ridge is sublime. The evening moon threw its silver light down to the earth, creating a platinum glaze everywhere.

Tall trees reaching for the stars clustered together. Pine trees tightly packed in the woods standing huddled with one another, as if they were whispering about the other trees around them. Oak tree trunks swerve their way to the black abyss above. A lot of them had vines intertwined around their trunks all the way to the ends of their branches. Twisting trees, bending trees, bowing trees, and dead trees inhabit his woods. So much character to all of them. They are alive and speak volumes silently. I passed over a dry creek bed. Earthy colored rocks lined the parched ground. Clumps of dead, dried grass and debris molded to the rocks. I picked up an oblong, dark gray one and threw it as hard as I could to the north. It took a good four or five minutes until I had heard the sound return of it hitting the ground.

I chose a grove of trees to saunter to. These were massively tall trees. They had bark like the rest of the trees, but it didn't cover them completely. Where their bark was missing, white limbs and branches grew out. Their white skin glowed in the moon light. I stepped up to one and ran my finger tips over it. The white was silky and smooth. I felt insignificant next to it. How funny. I am at the top of my food chain, yet something that has no protection or defense against me makes me feel this way.

I went into the heart of the trees and found the biggest one to climb. I climbed all the way to the top and perched on a limb. The sky was open to my eyes. Stars glittered and winked at me. A thick blanket of sparkling confetti. I felt as if I had never seen them before. What marvelous beauty. I sat still, stopped my heart, quit breathing, and became a spectator to the world around me. As my body cooled down the tree became warmer than me in my hands. Being a human, I would have never experienced this.

The normal critters foraged like the possums, the raccoons, and of course my favorite ones, the spiders in their silky homes biting and eating. This time I was further out in the woods and more animals came to my attention. Field mice scurried around sprinting like runners in the Olympics. Lightning fast, jetting from under a broken tree branch to the next bush. They were actually very noisy.

An armadillo came strolling around a clump of dead leaves. A walking armored tank with legs. He rooted and moseyed around the area and continued his journey off out of my sight. Very shortly after the armadillo came and left, a fat skunk came into my trees.

He was quite silly looking while he walked. No he didn't walk, he waddled. His thick black and white fur slid around side to side. I was trying very hard to not snicker at this animal. Up in my tree, I looked all around in the surrounding trees. I spotted an owl on a branch on another tree diagonal to me. Her enormous amber eyes fixed on the ground. She had a red-brown, almost rusty colored face with white covering her throat. She had horns on her head that were made by tufts of feathers. This owl was big.

It was amazing that this huge bird was as stealthy as it was when she came flying down the tree. She flapped her wings with a thrusting motion downward to get off the branch. Then, like the helicopter seeds, floated down to the earth, drifting silently and descending on the unsuspecting skunk. Even with my superb hearing I could not hear its wings flap. The air passed threw its feathers mimicking a breeze. She extended out her talons and the nails sparkled silver from the moon. The owl jabbed its razor sharp weapons into the back of the skunk. The black and white forager never knew it was coming. It screeched and growled as it sprayed the air. All of the animals in the area stood still. With little effort the owl toted the skunk up onto another branch further away than the tree it started its attack from.

I was very glad I had chose not to breath. I am quite sure that it was a repulsive atmosphere around me now.

The owl took its beak and tore the fur and skin off of a spot underneath the skunk's jaw. She began to pull flesh out of the opening. Long strips of pink meat stretched, snapping from deep inside of the skunk.

"Ivy." A murmur came from behind my left ear. It broke my concentration and startled me.

I whipped my head around. I breathed in deep, expanding my lungs to full capacity. I smelled no one.

"Ivy," it called out again. A giggling followed and rumbled through the trees all around.

"Who's there?" I called out loudly. Birds unaware of my presence flapped in retreat out of the trees from around me.

"Hello, Ivy," the voice whispered from the right.

"Who are you?" I snapped back more forcefully.

"You know," it whispered.

The voice was a woman's soft, fluttered voice. It called out to me quietly. The birds didn't fly away until I said something. Was this in my head?

"No. I don't know who you are," I protested.

"I am watching you." The words slowly called out from the left. It was all around me, taunting me.

"What for? Too chicken to show me your face?" I challenged her.

"All in good time," the whispering continued.

"When?" I yelled, throwing my arms up. I had let go of the tree and fell towards the ground. I pushed my feet under me and landed on them. I felt better equipped to fight on the ground. Giggling sounded out again through the woods.

"Come on!" I screamed. "Where are you?" I scanned the surrounding woods. There was nothing but trees and more trees. I let out a low hiss at the emptiness.

"It's our secret, meeting like this," she whispered even softer. "Keep it that way. If not, Ethan will perish quicker than his expiration date." I stood dumbfounded. Who was this person? I knew that was a promise and not a threat.

"Hello?" I whispered. There was no response. Did she know Ethan? Why would she want me to keep this a secret? I didn't even know to whom I'm to keep it with? What do I owe her? Ethan? What about him? I needed to keep this to myself until I can figure this out. I knew that for sure. I didn't want Ethan hurt, even if I thought she would not follow through. I quickly dismissed that thought. She meant it. I could feel it in my bones. I stood in the woods for a few hours like a statue. My thoughts ran rapid through my mind. I couldn't get a grip on them. I closed my eyes and made a humming sound. I slowly calmed myself and my thoughts.

I caught the smell of orchids and knew Shane was near. I relaxed my body language by smiling. I didn't need for her to start thinking I was crazy. Imagine that, a crazy vampire.

"Hello Shane," I said in her direction.

"Hi. Beautiful night, huh?" she responded.

"It has got to be impossible to sneak up on us," I remarked when I saw her pretty face lit up by the moonlight.

"Almost," she giggled.

"Whatcha doing?" I asked her.

"Same as you probably. Thinking."

"Yes. Good night for that."

"What's on your mind?" Shane sat on a big rock.

"Ethan," I sighed.

"What about him or do I want to know?" She was laughing and blushed a little.

"No. It's not like that." I smirked. "It's just, with his genetic make-up, does he live long?" I sat on a rock near her and pulled up a tall group of weeds. I began to dissect it piece by piece.

"Umm. He won't live forever. If that's what you're getting at. But, they live twenty or thirty years longer than an average human. Ethan is around thirty in human years but biologically he is in his teens."

"Oh." I looked down at the grass now demolished in my palms. I blew them off and wiped my hands on my pants. "So I will lose him."

"Eventually. But not today." She placed her hand on mine. "Ethan loves you and you two need to live it up. You also have to know that when he does go, he will probably ask you to take care of Zachary."

I was shocked. I don't want to lose Ethan. How do I go on without what I just took a lifetime to find? Zachary? How do I take care of him? Once again, I had thoughts tearing through my mind. Shane started to sing a lullaby I didn't recognize. It was beautiful. Soothing. She always knows just what to do.

We sat on the rocks in the middle of the forest until the sun began to heat up the air and break over the mountain ridge. Crows called out, flying high up in the air gathering warmth. Their calls were obnoxious and sort of laughing in nature. Squirrels stretched and emerged from their nests up high on the trees. With our presence being so close, they began to screech and create a ruckus. They were very persistent. Shane and I decided to head back to the house before the whole forest made up it's mind to begin a full frontal assault on us.

∽o∽

CHAPTER 15

The world of color now lingered out the back door. It had been a month since I heard that strange voice in my head in the tree that night. It has not returned. The green trees outside transformed themselves. They displayed their colorful dying leaves on the ground. Like a child, the breeze scoops them up the tosses them around. They twirl and dance to an untamed number, twisting to the sky and rustling back to the earth.

The bugs are far and few between now. The sound of the country with it's unending chirping of crickets and locusts were gone. Animals were going into hibernation mode. Squirrels burying nuts trying to fake out their hiding places only to forget where they actually hid them. Cool sweeping breezes caress the ridge.

Kera is now in school and loves the attention she gets from all the one on one. The smaller classes provide a feeling of an extended family watching over her. She is doing well and getting good grades. Her and Zachary are inseparable. They do homework together, play together, and act like biological brother and sister.

Gabbi is a constant here at the house. She loves spending time with the kids and I have grown to like her company. Josh hasn't changed much and still picks on her. Shane pulls on his leash if he gets too out of hand. Ben and Abbi visit regularly. We have cookouts that last all weekend. Shane and I are drinking her stash dry though. It won't be long before we will have to drink the real thing. That bothers Shane.

I am growing to like Gabbi more and more. One thing does stand out about her. She dropped a bombshell on me a little while ago. We were walking around the property late one night. She was telling me about Ethan's wife. "He loved her," she started. "They were living in the house over there."

"My old house?" I asked.

"Yes. She was a nurse and Ethan was wood working, which you probably know." She walked around three huge oak trees. Walking further down a hill from the gray shale road was another oak tree. It was black and dingy gray. No green leaves clung to the limbs or branches. The side of the tree was dented in and scarred. "Ethan had several clients of a blood sucking nature." Gabbi continued, "One wasn't happy with Ethan's work. Actually, it was a device a vampire wanted built and he refused." Gabbi walked around the tree caressing the trunk. Thick, light green ivy was growing from the ground and encased the trunk up to the thick branches. It covered almost all of the trunk, except the blow to its side. "Ethan called me one night crying, telling me he was scared of the rain storm rolling through so he shifted. He was out patrolling the ridge." She stopped at the hole in the tree and knelt down. She grabbed a handful of grass and began tearing blades apart. "His wife was driving in the storm up the road and he was in the middle." She stopped talking.

I walked to the tree and ran my fingertips over the coarse ripples in the bark. They were thicker than sandpaper. I softly pet the tree over to the scar which was smooth and lighter in color. "And?" I asked.

Gabbi tore two more handfuls up as she said, "He was giving her mouth to mouth for two hours before he got her to the house." She shuttered. "He called me to come and read her."

"Read her? Like what Josh said? You can read minds." I stooped next to her, gazing into her eyes. They were light blue. Like mine when I haven't ate enough. She had deep red hair with strands clinging to the breeze. Her sweet blood tingled my nose. It was harder to control in this close proximity.

Gabbi sighed, "Yes I can read minds but here lately I have read the dead's thoughts." She smirked.

"So, that's why he called you. To read her last thoughts?" I was engrossed.

"I suppose. There were many weird things that happened that night. Ethan's concern at the time was what she went through before she died." She tossed the grass on the ground, took deep breaths, and continued. "His wife was driving down the road in the rain. The rain had made this road slick and unpredictable. Ethan was in his bear body and she swerved to miss him. She was thrown off the road and collided with this oak tree." She placed her hand on the scar. "A branch from up there," she pointed to a severed stump, "busted through her window, through her chest, and fused her to her seat. She inhaled for several minutes before she drowned in her own blood. Ethan couldn't get her out quick enough." She stood toe to toe with me now. "He feels responsible for her death. No one can tell him otherwise. Then you come along. You get attacked and he takes you in." She shrugged.

That changed everything for me. I was understanding Ethan better now. He believes she died because of him. He feels guilty about it. Maybe everything I'm feeling is one-sided. On the other hand, Ethan and I are so close. I never would have expected two people to be so, one. If that's a good word for us. All but the ring on my finger, we are living like there would never be another for either of us. I love him. I have not said it to him yet. I am scared if I do, I will lose him. It will be the final scene for us. I am immortal but he is not. If I let my guard down, something will get into my head again, and could find out how I feel and destroy him. He is so important to my existence. I will never live without Ethan. I have never been married and probably never will be. As close as I am to Ethan, the harsh reality is, he still loves his wife. She has been dead for sometime, but not long enough. This is an obstacle, I believe, that will never go away. If I do tell him that I love him, what would he say? Would he say it back? Or worse, reject me? I tip toe around the feelings he has for his wife. He talks in his sleep and calls her name. Her ghost will not leave him be.

It stinks to be this vampire that can defeat practically anything and I am powerless to help the man that I love. The irony of it is, he will die and I will shortly follow. Prickly pain jets through my body at the thought of eternity without him. Kera, Zachary, and Ethan are my life.

I am growing to love Zachary like a son as well. I would have told you that you needed to pick up one of those 'I love me' jackets they hand out at the insane asylums if you had told me I was capable of loving before all this started. I was poison. No one loved me. Then my eyes were opened to this beautiful, complex world of love. I don't know what the limits are. I have no rules, regulations to abide by. I can kill anyone I want and have no repercussions. If you are really good, the conscience you are born with shuts up after awhile. I have done one thing I don't want Ethan or Shane to find out about.

This was a week ago. Josh was with me and has kept my secret so far. We were going for a jog and came across some deer hunters. Josh and I swept up into the tree tops and peered down at them.

"You get the smaller one and I'll take the bigger one," Josh started out whispering.

"What? Shane asked us not to. You know she'll be quite mad if she finds out," I protested through my clamped jaws.

I looked down at the hunters on the ground. They were sound shooting. Retarded really. A hunting technique for amateurs. I really did want to feed on them. My intuition overrode my feelings of what Shane or Ethan would think of me. They were almost passing our tree. *"A few more steps guys,"* I said softly. Then, to my surprise, they robotically did. I was bespelling them. How cool. I floated down to the earth and stood face to face with them. Josh jumped, not so gracefully, down.

"Tell them to pull their sleeves up," Josh said excited.

"Pull up your sleeves boys." I said and they did. They stood there frozen in time. I had them in a trance. They were my puppets. I smirked and took the smaller one's wrist. I bit him and sucked his blood into my mouth. The photos ran through my mind. A gun collection in a thick heavy green safe, an old yellow Chevy truck, a bear

skinned rug, a deer head with enormous antlers, a woman in a bed on monitors, just random snap shots flashing before my eyes.

His heart was beating so hard. It was music to my ears. His life slowly ebbed out of his eyes while I watched. He had deep brown eyes with, what I thought was, a twinkle in them. When I gulped the last of his precious blood, the twinkle dimmed and slowly faded away. His body dropped to the ground as Josh finished his meal.

I was alive inside. I felt the predator in me rejoicing. Josh knew it because he grinned the entire way home. We have not spoke of this detour, ever. Shane and Ethan would disapprove. Kill joys. I can't wait until the next opportunity arrives.

Today is an important day. Jack has been in contact with us all month. He seems to think we have days left before the bomb goes off. Ethan and I are going to speak to Ruth about getting the cabins ready. We were almost at the end of our shale road.

"You think she can read all of your thoughts?" I asked Ethan.

"Sweetie. Don't worry. You are no different than anyone else. Your thoughts won't shock her. Don't do that to yourself." Ethan looked at me and caressed my cheek. He took my hands out of the death grip I had them in, kissed my finger tips and smiled.

"I just love when you do that," I told him exhaling.

"Do what?"

"You know. Reading my thoughts. Maybe you're a vampire and don't even know it." I laughed.

"Nope. Pretty sure I'm not," He said laughing loudly.

We pulled up out front of Ruth's Place and there were two other vehicles parked outside. One was a sports car that was a pale lilac color. The other one was a periwinkle four door coupe. The two contrasting colors hurt my vampire eyes. The sun was bright and beating through my bug shades. Ethan put the car in park and looked over at me holding my head.

"You alright?" He placed his hands on both sides of my face. "Is it the sun? Too bright?"

"Yeah. Let's hurry up and get inside before my head explodes."

Ethan opened the door to the store and held it open for me, such the gentleman. Ringing from the bells tied onto the handle of the door startled me. I stepped into the room and the pine scent lingering in the air burnt my nose. I stopped breathing and looked around. The white lights that lined the ceiling sparkled and glowed, throwing streams of light down to the floor. Several people were sitting at the table eating sandwiches and drinking sodas. One lady sitting at the head of the table in the far corner was very beautiful. Her bright brown eyes twinkled underneath her long blonde bangs that were pulled to one side. She was wearing a black shirt and silver bracelets that reflected the lights from the ceiling. Her teeth were white, pointy, and shiny. They showed off their splendor from between her crimson lips. I broke our gaze and continued to move forward.

Ruth was behind the wooden counter, cashing someone out. It was a man around twenty-two, twenty-three. He was wearing glasses and a button up striped shirt. He also wore blue jeans with black boots. He politely said to Ruth, thank you, and passed by us. His heart was beating slow and strong. I wonder what his blood would taste like. He walked out the front door and made those bells ring out.

"Damn it. That's annoying." I thought in my mind. "How does Ruth stand that noise?"

"Takes some getting use to," Ruth said, smiling from behind the counter.

"I . . . You . . . Never mind." I sulked.

Ethan thought this was funny. He was a by-stander in all this. "Hey, we have something to talk about. Got a minute?" he said to her.

"Sure. Come in the cooler. I need some help with the cases of beer anyway," Ruth said with a hearty country draw. She lead the way to the cooler door and opened it.

The cooler was neat and tidy. There was no trash lying about. The floor was gray and freshly mopped. It gave off the aroma of fresh flowers.

"I'm not a slob, if that's what you're getting at," Ruth interrupted my thoughts laughing.

"Could you please not do that?" I blurted out. Her demeanor changed dramatically. She no longer had a smile on her face and her hands found her hips.

"It's a little bit impossible Honey," she said defending herself. "Stop talking in your head." She paused. "See that's not probable." She laughed.

"Stay out of my head. Ethan doesn't need to know all of my thoughts. We are here because my family is in danger. Please don't think I'm being rude. I'm just on edge," I said her to her in my head.

Ruth winked at me and smiled returning her hands to the sides of her. "Ethan. What's wrong? Not too much detail because Marishka and her family are here. She is the woman in the corner." Ruth put her finger on her mouth as to say 'shh.' "How about Ivy tells me what's wrong? Marishka's thoughts are wondering to us. She's listening." Ruth took her eyes off of Ethan and looked at me.

"Um . . ." I began to say.

"Here Honey." Ruth pointed to her head and laughed.

"Now don't I feel stupid," I began in my mind. "Azrael is bringing some of his fiends out to play. Long story short, they are going to come from Paris with the intent to kill me and turn Kera. Something like that. They think we are at the lake. Ethan thought it would be better to be there instead of here. Can we get two of the cabins for a little while?"

"Wow. Making friends already?" She slapped my shoulder and laughed again. "Not a problem."

"Thank you Ruth. You have always been so kind." Ethan leaned in and kissed her cheek.

"Now get outta here." Ruth wiped her face and opened the door to the cooler. "Cabin four and five are open and out of the way. You two love birds have fun," she announced through the store and walked us to the front door. I placed my sunglasses back on.

"Thank you from the bottom of my heart," I thought to her. Ruth smiled bigger and scrunched her nose in response to me.

Out the door we went and back to the house. I had my eyes shut tight while he drove. The sun was piercing my sight. It was very painful. My head felt like it was being squeezed in a vise. I was nauseous. Ethan could tell and sped up the road. When we reached the house, Ethan called out for Shane. She was at my door seconds later.

"What's wrong?" she started.

"Ivy," he said worried.

"It's the sun and Ruth's power. Both within the same intervals is not good." She yelled to the house, "Josh, get Ivy a drink and set it up down in the basement." Shane helped me into the house and down to the entertainment room.

"Wow. This is horrible. My head hurts so much." I was lying on the couch now in agony. My skin was being prickled by thousands of pins. Josh breezed into the room and handed me a glass of blood. I chugged it. He refilled it and I kept drinking glasses full of blood until the pain was a distant memory. Luckily, Josh brought a pitcher full with him. It was empty by the time I was done. My eyes slowly became focused and no longer burned.

"I thought you said we couldn't be harmed by the sun?" I turned to Shane questioning her.

"It is different for everyone. The sun hurts some. I really just gave you a crash course of my world. You were an unexpected but wonderful surprise." Shane caressed my hair as she softly reassured me.

"So now the sun can harm me?" I was confused. "It never did before."

"Some vampires are harmed by the sun because they are becoming stronger than they were." Shane scrunched her eyebrows together. "Don't worry. We will figure this out." "Josh." She turned to him. He was leaning on the wall rubbing his chin near one of the corners in the room. "More drink please."

"Sure." He left the room swiftly.

Ethan sat on the end of the couch by my knees. He picked up my legs by the ankles and nuzzled them on his lap. He pet my leg and smiled at me.

"What?" I asked him.

"Nothing. I just think you're making this all up so I can't kick your ass at the sparing match later. I think you are getting tired of me beating you. This will be what, the whole month, of me doing it?" He laughed and was sweet about his teasing. I didn't get mad, just annoyed that I couldn't beat him. I stuck my tongue out at him and blew him a raspberry. He giggled.

"Now that was immature." That woman's voice rang in my ears. I scanned Ethan's face and Shane's. There was no change. I was the only one able to hear it.

"Of course you are." She playfully answered my mind.

"What do you want?" I spit in my head.

"Now be nice," she said in a whisper. "Have you tasted your daughter? I can't seem to access her in your memories."

"NO!" I screamed out loud and sat up. Shane bounced to her feet and Ethan jerked back on the couch.

"What? What is it?" Ethan grabbed my hand.

"Nothing," I said after I gained control over my emotions. Shane looked into my eyes and frowned.

"No. It's not nothing. Your eyes are darker. What's wrong?" Shane asked sounding alarmed.

"Ivy . . ." the voice slithered in my mind. "Not a word. Leave the room. Now! You don't want me to kill all of them do you?" she threatened in her sickly sweet voice.

"Hey, you know what? I just remembered that I wanted to go pick some flowers for Kera. I would feel better taking a walk and clearing my mind. I'll come right back." I didn't wait for a response. I left the house as quickly as my vampire feet could take me. I flew up a tree on the side of the highway after I stopped running. I had a feeling that the woman in my head was Ruth. How freaking stupid of her. I will tear her limbs off and drink her blood. The lilac colored sports car was still in the parking lot.

"I know you can hear me. Get rid of her. We need to talk." There was no doubt she heard me. I screamed it in my mind. She was the only one that's been in my head and we both knew it.

CHAPTER 16

Ethan looked down at his hands. "How am I ever to understand what is going on with her?" he asked aloud. She just left the room and didn't answer any of my questions. He shook his head and placed his face in his hands. I wish she would tell me what is going on. After all, we are in this together. Does she not know that? He looked over the top of his fingertips at the long faces in the room with him. Josh was still standing leaning against the wall, quiet and reserved as always. Shane, of course, was sitting on the couch by him, worried.

"Don't take it too personally Ethan. Ivy is still trying to settle into her new life," Shane said.

"How long will it take Shane? How much do I need to do, to prove to her that I am in this for the long haul?"

"I don't know. Just hang in there. I am sure she will come around and talk to you about all of it. She just needs time."

He just sat there with his stomach in knots. He knew she was slipping away from him. Was it because he hadn't told her how deeply he cared for her? Would that make her open up more to him? He just couldn't do it. He had to find the right time, the right place to tell her. Being with a vampire is wonderful, but all the same very hard. He didn't want to know about her outings with Josh and hunting episodes that are a necessity for what she is. He couldn't lose her, just couldn't. So what was the 'no' for like that out of the blue? "What was that all about then?" He didn't know where to go anymore.

"I'm not sure." Shane shrugged and looked to the floor. "Maybe she is changing more."

"Changing more? What do you mean? Is there more to being what you guys are?"

"I think, and remember I am saying I think, Ivy is making a change within herself to a darker part of being." Shane's voice wavered.

He dropped his hands to his lap and looked at Josh. He was now making eye contact with him. His white eyes were vacant and had no sort of comfort or aggression in them. "You want to run that by me again?" he asked Shane.

"They are called Dark Angels. Well, that's what we, vampires, call them. They are stronger than us and are harder to kill. If she is, then this fight will be easy for us. But-" She stopped talking and looked to Josh.

"But?" Ethan spoke louder than intended.

Josh crossed the room and sat on the other couch leaning forward. "But if she is changing, she will begin to lose her humanity."

"What does that mean exactly?"

"They no longer will try and make good choices. The human feelings of right and wrong can be turned off like a switch. They can rationalize anything they do. In short they become-" Josh stopped talking.

"Those that are coming here?" Ethan asked. He just had to know. If she is in some sort of danger, he had to save her even if it's from herself.

Shane spoke up, "Worse. I'm sorry. The ones that are coming here are not as strong or talented. Dark Angels are very different. They start out using their gifts unchecked. Murdering people, many people, without remorse is a surefire way down that path. It could take months to complete the change, or even years. Depends on how strong it is within themselves to be one. It is hard to explain it to someone that's not a vampire." Shane looked at the wall, as if looking for the words. "You know, both of you love each other. That's the only card we can play. Using her feelings for you to keep her stable and not let her off on her own. Thank God she has only been on the blood I have brought." Shane sounded solaced.

"Well . . ." Josh interrupted.

Ethan glanced at Josh. "You didn't." Josh just sat there. "Really? You took her out on a hunt? Why didn't I know about this?" He was raising his voice. He couldn't believe what he was hearing. What else did he not know about? "Shane does that make this worse?"

"I don't know for sure," Shane sighed. "Josh, how did it happen? Did she display any kind of out of the ordinary aggression?"

"No. We fed on some wildlife when we went for a stroll one time," Josh explained.

"So that's good right?" Ethan asked Shane.

"Yes, at least I think so. Look, I'm not an expert on them, I just ran into a few in my life time." Shane dropped off and closed her eyes tight.

Ethan shifted in his seat from talking to Shane. "What? What is it?"

"God, all this makes sense now. Azrael. He picked Ivy for a reason," Shane continued. "She has the inside strength and potential to become this. Ethan, she still has a choice though, don't forget. It's not etched in stone. Until, well, there's always one thing that makes these vampires snap. They can't come back. I have never heard of one coming back. Anyway, Azrael has a grudge with the only Dark Angel Josh and I know of personally. She beat him in hand to hand combat crushing his sensitive ego. Her name was Lovidia. Now we think she's dead. We haven't heard about her in sometime. A couple of decades as a matter of fact. She was the worse vampire ever made. Lovidia drank the vampires around her arid. She got more powerful. She also had a taste for innocence. She had, at one time, five or six Pure Angels with her at her mansion."

"Pure what?" Ethan interrupted. All this is unreal.

"Pure Angels are children vampires. They are under the age of ten. It is immorally wrong. Plus vampires need to be able to hunt on their own. Pure Angels can't. So you see, with Dark Angels they have no conception of what they do is wrong. They cannot control their impulses. I really don't think Lovidia is involved but, we need to keep Ivy thinking with a conscious. We need to keep her tapped in with right and wrong. Kera, and everyone here for that matter, needs her to. Let's not go into the discussion about what it would mean for the animals." Shane looked down and was silent for a moment.

"Great," Ethan said in a muffled voice. "What do I do now?" He really didn't mean to speak the last part aloud. He was just stunned, shocked. What else could be used to describe everything you love and want in life being capable of destroying itself and everything you hold dear?

"We need to go to our place and pick up some things, Josh." Shane stood. "Do you want to go Ethan?"

"Sure. Fresh air might help me think." Ethan shook the thoughts from his mind. One thing at a time and then he could pick apart everything and make it all make sense. He could find a solution to all the problems. He had to.

Shane and Josh led the way up the stairs and to the front door quietly. They all piled into the Jeep and began the trip to Josh's house.

The telephone began to ring while they all drove down the highway. They did not stop. None of them could have heard it.

CHAPTER 17

The tree was a great hiding place from humans but, the woman that left Ruth's Place was quite aware of my presence. She looked in my direction briefly before she got into her fancy lilac car and sped off.

"Are we alone now?" I thought.

Ruth's voice called from her store, "Yes."

I drifted down the trunk of the tree and dropped to the ground from five feet up. I barely hit the ground before I bounced to the front of her store.

"I'm not the one you're lookin' for darlin'," Ruth said as she opened the door.

"Playing more games are we?" I sauntered into her store pushing her with my shoulder as I passed.

"Open your mind to me and I'll tell ya what I can see." Ruth sat in one of her wooden chairs.

"Open my mind? What? So you can access the thoughts of my daughter? That is what you want isn't it?" I hissed at her.

"No Honey. I haven't been doing this to ya. Sit. Please." She extended out her hand and gestured to the chair in front of me. I scanned her and pushed my intuition farther than I ever had. What was it telling me? No harm here. I felt at ease, my muscles less tight.

"See. I'm not gonna hurt ya. Cop a squat will ya?"

I took the seat across the table from her and breathed in deep. "How do I open my mind up?" I felt strange. I was here to kick her ass and it turns out she only wants to help me. There is no way she didn't know what my intentions were. I had been running different scenarios over and over in my head in the tree top. None of them were beneficial for her.

"I knew. I just knew ya would listen too. Now then, think about the first time you were bothered by the voice." Ruth spoke and her words embraced my ears. Her voice sang lightly in my ears as it flew inside my head and gracefully caressed itself in my mind.

Imagine a book dropped on the ground outside with a rush of wind. The pages are violently flapped through. My memories were the pages of that book and they flew through my mind playing at lightning speed. A projector, if you will, of my life. The pages began before I could recall memories. My mother holding me and kissing my head while she handed me to another woman. My first birthday with strangers around me. Losing my first tooth and getting nothing from the tooth fairy. All the melancholy with the recalling of my adoptive father and the living hell I endured. I tried to ignore those flipping pages. Jumping to my daughter being born and the many homes we resided in. The men in and out of my life. Jack's memories pulled forward. The strange things beginning to torment and disturb me in Paris. The move to here and then at long last, Ethan and my change. She looked through them until she had the memory of me in the thick white trees and hearing the woman's voice that late night. She opened her eyes looking at me while she read my mind. There was no pain involved. I was shocked by that. As fast as she was scanning through them, surely there should have been some pain involved.

"What?" I blurted out prematurely. She was still processing the memories. "Who was that? Do you know?"

"Just a minute." Ruth closed her eyes once more. She sat quiet for a few seconds and she smiled slightly. "The woman's name is Lovidia. She is a Dark Angel, Ivy. She is very dangerous. She wants ya to be shaken up because then she might have the upper hand when she decides to show up. Not gonna happen." She laughed out loud. "You are very special darlin'. You have a lot of power within ya. Everything you have endured in your life has prepared ya for this one. Be careful. Remember to always keep this little girl inside ya alive. The one that tells ya to stop and enjoy the scenery. You have a wonderful mind and don't waste it." She walked over to her front door and opened it. The sign in the screen door was what she was after. She flipped it to read 'closed.'

"Honey. We're about to get a lot closer. In order for ya to win the fight out there on the lake, you're gonna need some extra oomph." She winked. "Any other circumstance I would tell ya never do this." Ruth walked over to behind the counter and returned with a small white box that fit in her hand. It was an ivory box with ebony colored roses engraved on it. The roses entangled among one another and wrapped the sides and top along with two rounded buttons on each side. I couldn't see the underneath, for it was sat on the table too quickly.

"This was a gift to me from my maker. It is very old. It was used to bleed people when they were sick." Ruth took her fingertips and gently caressed the roses tracing them. "He loved the roses on it and his master gave it to him. I keep it here because it makes me feel closer to em." She stopped talking and drifted off in thought.

"I'm sorry." I broke the silence. I knew she missed him for the air became melancholy.

"Well, anyways Honey. You're gonna have to drink some of my blood. It'll make ya stronger then you've ever felt. You'll be able to defend your family better. There will be side effects though. You may become a Dark Angel yourself. Transforming to this is detrimental. I know your strong enough to fight it off though. You know what I'm talkin' about, right? Those dark closets inside your mind. Those poisonous tendencies as ya put it in your thoughts. You will need to fight them off even harder then before. I don't have to give ya my blood but, I believe ya have the ability to keep yourself in check."

I did know the feelings she was describing. When I killed that hunter and the pedophile I felt invincible. The blood in the basement was not enough to satisfy my thirst. The sun searing through my eyes today. I do have darkness in my mind that I have always bolted behind steel doors. The fear of releasing it would be equivalent to the downpour of acid rain around me. Would I be able to stop it? Would I go mad crossing some imaginary line that would damn me forever?

"Ivy," Ruth whispered. "Those thoughts right there are the reason I truly have faith in ya to return from the darkness after you unleash it on Azrael."

"What if you're wrong?" I felt despair.

"I rarely am." She smiled at me and winked. Ruth picked up her little trinket and placed it on her wrist. She then pushed the buttons on the side and the box made a slight 'snap' followed by a popping sound.

"I'll try and make this as painless as I can." She placed the box back on the table in front of me and I realized the blood streaming off of her wrist and dripping on the checkered table cloth. "Drink," she said.

Her blood, I could tell from all the way in my seat, was warm and intoxicating. The aroma from it twisted my stomach, begging me to drink. I took her hand in mine and brought her wrist to my mouth. I looked into Ruth's eyes for any change on her face, but saw none.

Placing my lips around the three thin slices the blades of her device made, the blood pushed into my mouth and to the back of my throat. I took the first gulp of forbidden blood and a fire broke out inside and all the way down. No! A dragon's fire erupted. An acid liquefying my insides. Down my throat to my stomach, scraping the outer lining of it. The filling of my stomach was next. The accumulation of blue flames being contained, it was almost unbearable. Surprisingly, it was quenching my thirst. Any parched thirst anyone had ever experienced in their entire life.

All the while, I was not seeing her life story before my eyes in a photo array. I was seeing me through her eyes. Bent over the table drinking her blood from her wrist. A mirror, if you will, of me at an angle that I would never gaze upon. My stomach was full and could hold no more. I threw my head back and inhaled deep, quickly trying to cool off my throat. The heat from my stomach radiated warmth all over my body. A cocoon of sunshine, wrapping and cradling me. After a few deep inhales of pine scented air, the fire inside started to simmer down.

"Ya felling better Honey?" Ruth asked, returning to the table. I didn't even notice her leave. She had gone to put her heirloom back behind her counter. Her wrist had already healed but I could still smell it. My eyes felt more open and awake. I could hear something rustling outside digging in the dirt. I could hear its tiny heartbeat racing and it breathing quickly.

"Yes. I think so." I responded to her.

"You'll be stronger now and you're senses heightened even more. I know that seems impossible but you'll understand soon. Honey, remember why I did this and why you need to stay in the right mind frame. Ethan, Kera, Zachary, and the others are trusting ya. They will not have any defenses to ya now that you've drank my blood. Keep that evil inside until the right moment. When it comes you will know. Lovidia will be showing up now that you're stronger. She will feel the change in ya. She is beautiful and vicious. She'll kill ya, if ya give her half a chance. Be on guard at all times. She can't take a vampire being able to beat her. She has to be the top vamp. She won't be able to get in your head now. Throw steel doors up all over your mind so she can't. You'll do just fine. Now, you and Ethan will be goin' to my cabins on the lake. There is a woman that works for me cleaning and such. Her name is Catherine. She goes by Cathy. She knows nothing of vampires, but the cabins ya'll be in are always rented to my guests. Be kind to her. Ethan and the kids are probably waiting for you to come home by now. Walk home and take your time. Get use to the changes in your body and the way ya see. I'll be here if ya have any questions, but I am pretty sure Shane and Josh can fill ya in. They know who she is."

"Alright. I guess a thank you is in order." I smiled. "Thank you."

"You're welcome. I wished I could be there when ya take down Azrael. That would be great to watch." Ruth chuckled her rolling, contagious laugh and opened the door for me. "Just a little secret, the animal ya heard digging in the dirt, is half way up your road I suspect. Even I can't hear it." Ruth smiled and closed the door behind me.

The air all around me was filled with all kinds of smells. The smell of blood. Bird blood, raccoon blood, deer blood, and the lingering smell of human blood from customers that came in and out of the store. Smell of the trees too. Pine, oak, weeping willows, and too many more to name. The smell of car exhaust, snack cakes, BBQ sandwiches, and fire place fumes were all in the crisp cool air. My smell was so acute. Even better than Ruth said it would. My sight was better as well. I could see an airplane flying over head and I could pick out the individual windows. I could hear the low murmurings of the pilot over his radio and the passengers talking to one another if I concentrated hard enough.

I glanced over the terrain and the night was still and quiet. The animals were very easily locatable. I took a couple of steps and I felt it like I was floating. I wasn't. I was flowing and barley thinking of my motions. I was walking down the street gliding. After a few minutes I was almost to the road I lived off of when I saw a car coming around the bend on the highway. I stopped and watched it pass and then slow down. I could hear the heat beat of the driver and smell his blood. He was a young man in his twenties. He drove a blue hybrid car. It was quiet compared to the old Chevy truck I owned. The man pulled over to the side of the road a couple of feet away from me. I stood still hoping to keep my feet planted and not move. His blood was enticing me. He ate a lot of fruit. His blood was sweet smelling like a platter of apples, pears, bananas, and kiwi. He stepped out of his car.

"Do you need a ride?" he called out to me in the dark. He was wearing a blue and green plaid shirt and jeans. He began walking to me.

"No. I live right up the hill," I said quietly and tried even harder to stay put. His heart was beating faster because he was walking up hill to me. I began to feel my head swirling to the beat of it. My mouth was watering. I clamped my jaws tighter. He was almost to me and I took a step back.

"I'm not going to hurt you. I just don't think it's right for a woman to walk home in the dark, especially on the highway. My name is Kent. Let me drive you there." He held his hand out towards me.

His pulse throbbed inside the veins in his wrist. He smelled sweeter the closer he came to me. Everything in my body wanted to devour him and suck him dry of that sweet blood. Ruth's words rang in my mind about everyone trusting me and to not give in to the thoughts of killing and rage. Surely she didn't mean eating? I need to eat to survive.

I took his hand in mine and started to shake it. Automatically, he let out this high pitch scream. I was unknowingly crushing the bones in his hand. They snapped and twisted. Serrated ends of the bones tore through his skin and blood began to pour out. I had lost all the control I had and grabbed him up. I put my hand over his mouth and pulled my face to his throat. His jugular vein was jumping out at my face as if it were begging me to bite it. A big 'x' marks the spot, begging. I obliged it, sunk my canines into it, and his blood invaded my mouth. I was right, he tasted of sweet fruit. His heart was sputtering and beating irregularly. The rhythm was so wonderful, I felt like dancing to it and slowly swayed to the rhythm. I drained him and his heart gave in and stopped. I held his lifeless body upright and stood there for a moment. I didn't have the flashes of his memories. Any other time I had.

"That's because you are becoming a Dark Angel," Ruth said standing at the end of the man's car. I dropped him where we stood. "I told ya you would have to control your impulses better. You didn't need to eat. I just fed ya enough to last ya a week or so." She sounded disappointed. "Help me get him into his car."

"I'm sorry. I really don't know what came over me. I tried to keep a distance but he just kept walking up to me."

"Ya need to try harder. Ya should've ran up your road. Well, no use crying over spilt milk. You'll get the hang of it." Ruth grabbed his shoulders and I grabbed his legs. We put him in his car and Ruth got into the driver's seat. "Go home and don't stop until ya get there. Everything will be fine Honey. Ethan just called and I told em you were on your way. I'll take care of this guy. Don't worry," Ruth said with a wink and she was off.

I wasn't upset about killing that man. I felt nothing towards him at all. I wanted to feed off of him and I did. That's all there was to it. Is that what Ruth meant by needing to keep in mind that I would turn to a Dark Angel if I don't feel anything at all? Well, I don't. That is comforting, yet scary. Perhaps I shouldn't be reading into this that much. Why in the world did I not see his life photos? Everyone else, even animals show me something. Does that mean I really don't care about that human? I need to talk to Shane. She knows what's wrong with me. I started walking up our shale road and I picked up the pace this time.

Walking back to my house there was nothing eventful to talk about. I walked up to the fairy-tale home of mine and Isis and Blue were spread all on the bridge. They were snoring and deep in sleep. Funny how I just snuck up on them. They normally hear my approach. I called out their names so I wouldn't startle them stepping over them. When they jerked awake from my voice, they locked eyes on me and pulled their big lips back to snarl showing their teeth. The front door opened abruptly and Ethan stepped out.

"Hey. Where have you been? You left hours-" Ethan stopped talking and just stared at me walking up to the door. "Shane. I need you," he said after a minute of looking at me like I was some alien.

"Ivy? Is that you?" Shane's face was white.

"Yes, of course. Who did you expect?" I tried to make my voice light and soft.

"What happened to you?" Ethan asked me.

"Nothing much. I went to visit Ruth. Sorry I was gone so long." I stepped into the house and I smelled someone new. It had to be Jack. I could smell his cologne. I remembered him wearing it from when I was a human, but he really was wearing too much for my vampire nose. It was then I noticed Josh on the landing and Shane by my side reaching out to take my hand. I defensively pulled it away. "Why are you all looking at me like that? As if purple dots had broke out all over my face." I laughed. All of their faces were long and confused. Ethan was standing behind me and I suddenly felt the need to move. I bolted into the living room gracefully. Jack was standing at the bottom of the staircase to the loft with a surprised look on his face.

"Jack!" I screeched. Oh I was so happy to see him! I ran over to him and threw my arms around his chest.

"Whoa whoa whoa there tiger. You're a mess. Going to get it all over my clothes." He chuckled pulling me off of him. He looked into my eyes and I was home again. He was as strong as ever and missed me just as much. So much has happened since I first moved here. Talking on the phone with him was nothing like showing him.

"Ivy. What have you done?" Shane spoke up.

"What do you mean?" I asked turning to face her.

"Well, your face has blood on it and your eye color has changed for starters," Josh said dryly.

"I had a snack on the way home and that explains the eyes," I shrugged.

"No. Ivy. They are almost black. What did you feed on?" Shane was argumentative.

"A man named Kent. He was human."

"Ivy, please. Tell me what happened at Ruth's," Ethan softly said. His face cleared of worry and was now looking curious.

"Ruth came up with a solution to our problem with Azrael and the others," I said.

"No." Shane gasped. "You didn't."

"Yes." I admitted. I knew exactly what she was referring to. "I drank her blood and now I can take care of them myself."

"Then who was the guy Kent?" asked Ethan.

"Just a man that stopped on the side of the road trying to give me a lift," I muttered as I walked to the kitchen. I was being followed by all of them. I took a paper towel off the dispenser and wet it at the sink. I wiped off my chin and lips. There was a lot of blood on me. "I need to get all of this off. I'm going to the bathroom. I doubt everyone will fit in there comfortably. I'll be right back," I said trying to sound playful, but it might have sounded bitchy. I ran into the bathroom and shut the door. Nothing like feeling like a bug in a jar to make you go mad. I stood in front of the mirror before I turned on the light. I had to prepare myself before I flipped the switch.

I turned on the light and jumped at the sight of my eyes. They were midnight blue and glaring back at me. They were nothing like the eyes of a hungry or full vampire. They were not pale or saturated with color. They were deep and endless. They frightened me. I also had blood splatter all around my face. The man's jugular must have sprayed me when I bit into it. My skin was lighter and the veins under my skin were thicker, protruded slightly like when you work out and they pop out. I could see them clearly. In my forehead, my temples, my neck, all over myself. I inspected my arms and neck running my fingertips over them. This was strange to say the least. I sighed, "Well, what's done is done." I splashed warm water on my face and cleaned up.

Now what do I say to these people that are my family and friends? They all seemed to me, to be judging me and being confrontational. I must be paranoid. How to do this? I guess the best thing to do is meet them head on. If they don't like my decisions, then they can all go to hell. I took one more long look at my eyes and left the bathroom. There was no one in the hallway, that's a good sign. Short lived though. They had all clustered in the living room waiting for some explanation from me.

"You look better." Josh grinned. I walked into the living room and sat on the couch. Ethan sat next to me and Shane and Josh took the other couch. Jack stood leaning against the mantle over the fireplace.

"Okay. Ruth had me feed off of her so I would be strong enough to defeat the bad guys." I took my fingers and gestured the word 'bad' in quotations. "She told me what I might become and had all kinds of faith in me to not dive off the deep end."

"We are your strength Ivy," said Shane leaning forward in her seat.

"I know. I just don't feel right with all of you fighting my fight." I crossed my arms in protest.

"Haven't you learned anything yet? We are your family. Someone picks a fight with you, they are picking one with us," Ethan said as he caressed my cheek with the back of his fingers.

"I do know that. It's just, well, I'm not used to this." I was feeling ashamed of the thoughts I had in the bathroom now. They really do accept me as family. I should have never felt that way. They are still here, even with my decision to cross the line, drink Ruth's blood, and possibly become a Dark Angel. None of them left. They were still here supporting me. Josh was smiling his smirking little grin. He was enjoying this. I'm not surprised.

Shane spoke up and asked, "Ivy, how do you feel? What changes are there?"

"Umm, there is one thing I have noticed that never happened before. When I fed off of Kent, I didn't get a photo array of his life," I answered.

"That's a new one." She pondered that for a minute and continued, "Is there anything else?"

"My senses are very acute. I heard a pilot and the passengers talking on an airplane at 30,000 feet. That was weird. I can't hear the kids' heart beats though. Where are they?"

"Ben's," Ethan answered.

"Go on," Josh said impatiently.

I smiled slightly at Josh. "I can also smell the blood of all living things in the air. Doesn't matter how long it has been since they have been in a certain area. At Ruth's I could smell the customers that had been and gone through out the day lingering in the air." I paused. How much more could I tell them? "I had a hard time stopping myself from killing that man Kent. When he got within touching distance, I bit him. Well, I shook his hand and crushed his bones. I forgot to say that part. I am way stronger than before. His blood oozed out of his hand and I lost it." I looked at all of their faces and nothing had changed. They were listening to me talk and soaking it in.

"Off of the subject, I have to admit you are very stunning in your new skin Ivy." Jack said to me smiling warmly. He looked the same as when I left him in Paris. The salt and pepper goatee, mustache, and hair with that wise owl look about him. Big brown eyes that would never pass judgment. A voice that always had a soft but strong tone to it. With my vampire eyes I could now see his age. The crow's feet tracks under and around the eyes. Laugh lines framing his mouth from his wonderful warming smile. I wonder why, when I was human, I didn't see that.

He was patient during the whole conversation. A father figure to me while I lived near him. That is a big thing for me. I never wanted to answer my phone or door bell if we needed to 'talk.' I wanted him to be proud of me, always. If we needed to talk, it was about something he didn't approve of or didn't agree with. He was kind and gentle. I think now, that I have met Ethan, it is a bear thing. I also think humans are not capable of this kindness. Well, not anyone I have met.

"Thank you Jack." I felt the the blushing of my cheeks. He was after all my adopted dad that I had chose.

"Not a life I would have chosen for you but, given the circumstances, you make the best vampire I know." He made his way across the room and put his arms out for a hug. I got to my feet and embraced him. "Ivy. You're gonna break me. Little looser if you would please," Jack said, gasping for air. Giggling broke out in the room. I loosened my grip on him some but didn't want to let go all together. The hug and the laughter was wonderful. As if all the evil had escaped out of our lives through the cracks of the doors and widows abruptly. A family gathering, sharing a happy moment.

"I have missed you," I confessed.

"I have missed you too," Jack responded and kissed my forehead. "Cold. Guess I'll have to get used to that now." While he held me I jerked my blood threw my body rapidly and warmed up. "Never mind," he laughed. I let him go as the reality of why he would be here crept into my thoughts.

"Are they coming now?" My voice was a little shaky.

"Yes. They will be here tomorrow night. They all believed Creodra when she said everyone is at the lake," Jack said.

"When will the kids be coming home?" I asked Ethan.

"In the morning. Ben and the twins are coming too. They are going to stay with us at the lake. Shane, Josh and Ben are going to the smaller cottage. Gabbi and Abbi will be with us. Jack and the kids will stay here. We are leaving tonight to get our scent good and strong at the lake." Ethan stood up while he talked. Jack sat down in our chair by the fireplace.

"Are we leaving now?" I asked.

"Yes. We don't want you to get caught in the sun again. With this new change the sun will hurt you a lot more," Shane said. Ethan went into our bedroom and returned with two bags. Shane went into the kitchen and grabbed a cooler and went out the front door. The door opening let the evening's cool air into our house and I could smell the changelings' blood. They must be close. I could unfortunately smell Kera as well. My daughter and my weakness. Josh came over to my side and nudged me with his elbow.

"Ready? I can't wait to see what you can do now." There was excitement in his voice.

"Yup." I winked. I walked to Jack still sitting in the chair. I leaned down and kissed his warm cheek. I could smell his musky weapon hiding somewhere in his blood and hear his strong heart beating. "I will see you later old friend." I whispered in his ear, "Take good care of the little ones."

"No worries sweetheart." His voice was calm and comforting. He looked up into my eyes and I knew he would protect them with his life if need be. I had no doubt of that.

Ethan and I rode in his truck and Shane and Josh were in their Jeep. We left the house first with them following. I was staring out the window with my eyes gazing on the infinite stars glimmering on the black velvet sky. Down the highway we passed the mustang carrying our prized possessions. They were at the fork in the road that leads to their house. We continued to the left and didn't stop. We were headed to the lake. We were on a collision course for the biggest brawl any of us had ever been in. I was excited. The blood flowed quickly through my veins on its own, my heart racing. My muscles tensed up at the thoughts of swinging my arms and decapitating one of them. The speed I would have. The hissing, the scratching, the anger irrupting, the blood. Oh yes, all the blood that would be spilled. Yes, I was very excited. I was ready. Bring it on!

CHAPTER 18

The ride to the lake was a long blink for me. My mind was racing and wrestling with the thoughts of killing. This is what I was born to do. The battle, the blood, the rage. We arrived at the lake and we turned off of the highway. The main entrance was right in front of us, but we took a road off to the left. The back way I assumed. Pine trees lined the black topped road. As we drove, the ground to our left rose up and three cabins were placed on the hill side. They were spread out nicely. They were dark brown in color with a thin layer of gray chink in-between the logs. The cabins were no bigger than that of a large living room.

Driving a little ways down the road we crossed over a concrete bridge. Well, it was over a creek, not very high. Water had flowed over the top about two inches. There was no sides or top, just the concrete bottom. I was looking over my shoulder to the right and I caught my first glimpse of the lake. The creek we were crossing over fed right into it. White rocks littered the bank around the lake. Trees of orange and brown, colored the back ground.

The trees around the edges were beaten and worn from the rain and weather. The ones behind them were undamaged and protected by them. There was a mountain that stood here and the lake cuddled up against it. The evergreens lined up in rows and the colored, dying, leaved trees lined up under and above them. They created a wonderful pattern all over the side of the mountain. We were now climbing up hill to the cabins.

"They are just up this hill," Ethan said pointing to the right. "Shane and Josh will be staying in the one we come to first. Then ours is right around the corner."

I didn't respond. I was still looking at the beautiful colors. Fall has got to be the prettiest season to experience. I am sure when the sun comes up that this place will come alive with even more color.

My mind wandered off to the kids. They would be safe I'm sure. If I kept telling myself that, then I wouldn't keep them in my thoughts and give it away tomorrow night. Jack was there to protect them. I wanted to at least call, tell him we got here, and say good-night to Kera.

"Do we get phone service here?" I asked Ethan.

"Nope. We would have to go five miles further to get a signal." Ethan smiled. "They'll be fine. Anyway, there is a phone in the cabin."

"Good," I told him. I can call when we got inside. I just wanted to hear her voice. I wanted to tell her I loved her. If I don't come back then she would have, at least, that phone call to hold on to.

We began to slow down and pull into a clearing in front of a larger cabin that was the same style and color. There were big, flat, earth-toned stones on the ground leading up to the brick red front door. Bushes lined the outside of the cabin. They were sleeping now with their leaves and flowers all gone. Inside a light lit up the living room. An old oil lamp. Shane and Josh pulled up beside us and turned their Jeep off. They got out of their vehicle and came over to my window. I pushed the button to roll it down.

"We will stay here until first light and then come to your cabin. We are going to have to run around rubbing our scent all over the place to make it seem like we have been here awhile," Josh said to us.

"Okay. See you then," said Ethan. We pulled out of the parking space and followed the road to our cabin.

The cabin was further up the hill and around the bend. The driveway was a circular one. It looped wide, around a thicket of pine trees and back down the hill to Shane's cabin. Their cabin was longer than ours. Our cabin was square shaped. The logs were the same dark brown as all the other ones were. Ethan parked outside the front of the cabin. A light was on in our living room as well. I was sitting in the car looking at the landscape when Ethan opened my door.

"Ready?" he asked me.

"Yes. It is very beautiful here. We have an overlook of the entire lake." I was standing in front of the truck and peering down at the lake. It was an odd shape, like all lakes are, oblong with the river we drove over to my right. Ethan opened the front door to the cabin and held it open for me.

"Shall we?"

I, walking through the front door and the living room, was lit up by windmill lights on end tables. There were paintings and snap shots of windmills on the walls. The living room had dark blue carpet laid down with the walls of a lighter blue. A sectional beige couch set in a shape of an 'L' separated the one huge room into two. The kitchen was behind the couch. A kitchen table with four chairs sat in the middle while strawberries decorated the counters and outlined the ceiling. This house was equipped with all the essentials. There was a strainer, pot holders, glasses and food in the fridge. The cabin had a wall through the center and split itself almost in half. There were two doors. The right door was to the master bedroom and the left door was a child's bedroom. The master bedroom was decorated with a rack of quilts layered on the wall, a rocking chair, a king sized sled bed, and a closet. A big, comfy, green and white comforter and matching pillow cases dressed the bed. The walls were a pale green, with white trim around the two windows and doors. The windows let you gaze out down the hill and onto the lake. I stood in front of a rectangle quilt in a picture frame that read in blocked hearts, "Love is patient, Love is kind, Love does not envy, Love does not boast, Love is not proud, Love is not rude, Love always trusts, Love always helps, Love never fails. 1 Corinthians 13:7" I found that warming. The bathroom door was located next to the closet. The floor was made of circular, black and white tiles. The cloth shower curtain was black with white circles. An oval mirror was placed above sink with a black counter top. The finishing touch was the black and white overlapping hand towels and a matching towel rack. On the counter, there was a chrome tooth brush holder and a soap lather brush and bowl set. The bathroom had a door that led to the child's room.

The kid's room walls were painted like a jungle scene that wrapped all the way around. Tall grass, trees, vines, and animals peeking at you. It was incredible. The bed had a canopy that had leaves and camouflage draping down to cover the whole bed and was made out of a net.

A small table and two chairs were tucked in the corner made of untreated wood. It blended in well.

Ethan had stayed in the living room while I investigated the cabin. He was watching the television and drinking sweet tea. He seemed right at home. As I walked up behind him, I slid my hands over his shoulders and down his chest. He was tense.

"You alright?" I asked. It really was a stupid question but I asked anyway.

"Sure," he mumbled. I jumped in the air and landed softly on his lap sideways.

"It'll be okay, baby." I looked straight into his eyes and I could tell the strain on him was draining, slowly suffocating him.

"Maybe," he said and looked away. After a moment, he looked back. "Ivy, I can't lose you. I lost everything when I lost my wife years ago. I was lost and I just focused on Zachary to get through it. If I lose you, I don't think my heart would allow me to continue." He caressed my cheek with the back of his fingers as he always did when talking from his soul. "You need to promise me you will not do anything risky. All of us here will be able to help. Don't do anything that would take you away from me or the kids."

"I don't plan to." I smiled. "Besides, I'm stronger than I ever was and they aren't expecting that I am what I am."

"I know you think you're stronger and you very well might be, but, please be careful. I love you and if it was up to me, you wouldn't even be in this fight."

"Well, I guess I'm glad it's not up to you." I smiled.

"I would miss my cinnamon apples." He grinned at me.

"Your what?" I was lost.

"I haven't told you? You smell like cinnamon apples. That's my favorite smell." He slid his hand around the back of my neck and pressed his lips to mine. I wrapped my arms around him and the passion for him started in my toes. It rolled up my legs and lingered in my abdomen. Everything was going exotically wonderful until the smell of sweet chocolate slipped under the crack of the cabin door. I pulled away from Ethan sighing. "What? What is it?" he asked.

"Gabbi's coming. We'd better get ourselves together."

It took everything I had to get off of his lap and walk into the kitchen. I stood staring out the window overseeing the lake. Ethan went to take a cold shower. The cool air from the bathroom crept into the living room and kitchen. It danced around my feet on the floor, cooling them off. Ethan had made my body fire-like while his hands were exploring me.

The Mustang came purring up the drive. It wasn't long before there was a knock on the door. Ethan was dressing in the bedroom and I went to answer it.

"Hi. What happened to you?" Gabbi asked at the door, simultaneously backing up.

"Long story. Come in." I walked to the back of the couch giving Gabbi room to come in the door. She was scared of my appearance I assume. "I have drank some real strong blood. Very good year." I grinned. She didn't find that very funny. So, I continued. "That's why my eyes look like this. I'm stronger now. The way I look at it, the fight is now rigged in our favor."

"Good I guess." She slowly walked to the kitchen table and sat her back pack down. "Shane wants you to have this stuff."

"What's in it?" I stepped next to her and grabbed her around the shoulders like a sister and squeezed. She tensed up. "Abbi, I'm still Ivy. I'm fine. You're just as safe now as before. I just drank some potent stuff. I'm not any different than before." She relaxed after a little while. I opened the sack, discovering that it was filled with blood and weapons. Small hand knives with curved blades. They really were medieval looking. I loved them. I picked up the bags of blood, sat them on the table, and went for one of the knives. It cuddled my hand like it was happy to see me. Gabbi picked another one.

"Wow. I like this one." Her knife had brass knuckles on the handle and the blade was serrated and long.

"Too bad you'll be an animal," I mocked. She just stuck her tongue out at me. As we dug through the bag of a dozen knives, Ethan came out of the bedroom with another one of his black, ribbed muscle shirts and a pair of blue jeans. His arms and smile made me pause on what I was doing. He really was handsome.

"What kind of toys are those?" he asked, moving to the table.

"Shane's knives. Aren't they awesome?!?" Gabbi exclaimed.

"Yeah." He thumbed through them and picked out the coolest ones, of course. Ethan and I fought over a few of them and we were almost done when the phone rang. I answered it after knocking Ethan out of the way racing to it.

"Hello." I giggled. It was Shane.

"Hey just calling to let you know that the sun will be up in the next half-hour."

"Okay. You wanna meet us here?" I asked her.

"Doesn't matter. That will be fine. Until then, drink."

"I know. I know."

"Seriously."

"I know. Always worrying. Take a day off." I joked.

"Only when it's not an important day!" Shane said sarcastically.

"Touché. See you in twenty?"

"Okay. Also, I called Jack and told him we were here. You and Ethan get caught up? Never mind. Don't answer that."

"I'll call them in a minute. Bye." I hung up the phone. Damn. She always thinks of everything. Even when I think of doing it, she beats me to it. "Babe. Shane and the others will be here in twenty minutes. The sun's coming up in a half an hour. She called Jack already."

"Just go and make your phone call. It doesn't matter if she already did. Kera and Zachary will be happy to hear from you," he said in a soothing voice. He always takes her side. I picked up the phone and dialed the home number.

"Hello?" Jack answered.

"Hey. It's me. Can I talk to Kera?"

"Sure." Jack tried to cover the phone with his chest but between him yelling for her and his heart beating it was loud.

"Hello," my baby girl said.

"Hi sweetie. How are you?"

"I'm fine."

"Of course you are. Jack playing with you?"

"Yup. He built a fort with blankets and threw them over my bed and we got the flash lights out of the kitchen drawer, but not the ones you told us we couldn't play with, and . . ." she took a breath. "And we're reading 'The Cat and the Hat' . . . Momma why don't their Mom let them play out in the rain? You and Dad let us. And the cat . . ."

"Sweetie, slow down. We'll talk about the book when I get home. Make sure you brush your teeth and hair after you have breakfast. Did you sleep good? Doesn't look like you could stay asleep too long with Jack there."

"Nope. He snores really loud." She began to babble again.

"Hey, I called to tell you that I love you baby girl."

"Love you too, Momma. Wanna talk to Zachary?" The phone clicked and fuzzed like it was switching hands.

Zachary's voice came over the receiver. "Hi. You and Dad coming home tomorrow still?"

"Yes. Take good care of your sister and Jack. I love you."

"Okay. I love you too. Tell Dad I love him." Zachary started giggling and I heard Jack making bear noises. Kera had her high pitch scream going and the phone went dead.

I guess they will be having a lot of fun while we are fighting for our lives. Oh, to be a child again. To be oblivious to the world we live in. To have no cares and the only thing that could become a life-threatening problem would be a sibling taking your toy and not giving it back. The world is good and bad guys always get taken down. Dad or Mom are superheroes and if your drink or snack runs out they will fill it up. To have innocence again. To have a clean slate. To believe in people. To not feel deep rage, remorse, hatred, regret, revenge, or have a wounded soul. So wounded that breathing or living cuts so deep it hurts in the depths of your being to simply exist.

"How are they doing?" Ethan asked interrupting my thoughts. He's very good at doing that.

"Good," I said, clearing my throat and mind. "Jack is spoiling them. No surprise there." I half smiled at him.

Gabbi was still playing with the knives. She now had them all lined up, displaying off their shiny blades. Shane takes very good care of her things.

Ethan watched television and Gabbi paced while they were waiting for the others to arrive. I drank the four bags of blood while I waited. I felt full and recharged. Shane might be right, most of the time. I could smell Ben and Abbi as they left their cabin. The cool breeze outside brought their scent right up here. The feeling of 'it's time' riddled through me. Ethan led the way out the front door followed by me. Gabbi followed with a jump in her step. Josh and Shane were standing by our truck. Josh, of course, with a big grin on his face. This was just up his alley. He will be able to unleash his naughty side without disappointing Shane. He was an acquired taste as far as people, and even vampires, go. He had a dry sense of humor that I found wonderful. He loved Shane with all his heart and she kept him solid and true.

Shane was still as pretty as the first time I saw her at the cook-out. Pin up girl is the only way to describe her. She likes the girly clothes and the pretty sun dresses. Her blonde hair had natural highlights and her vibrant blue eyes spoke volumes of compassion.

Ben and Abbi were standing behind the truck some, waiting for Gabbi to join them. Ben was as strong as ever as he stood with his chest out and shoulders back. He was the protector of his family and wanted nothing more than to live in peace. Abbi was his go to 'guy.' She was his equivalent in mind as anyone were to get. She was always taking care of Gabbi and loved the family with all she had. Gabbi was the outspoken one that blended in with my family best. Her and Josh had this antagonizing relationship and she loved every minute of it. And then there's my big strong Ethan. He would defend me to the end. He would orphan his child for me. I love all of them deeply. They are my family and that's a lot to say coming from me. I have had no one my whole life and then these newly acquired strangers would die for me. That's what my family does. I am blessed to have them. I would die for them in return.

"We're going to shift and run around," Ben started out.

"Alright," Shane said. "Ethan can you and I go around. Josh and Ivy can go together. I want Ivy's scent and your scent the strongest. With you being a couple, you're scents blend together."

I looked at Ethan and nodded at Shane. We split up and went different directions. While Josh and I went walking I could hear the changelings shifting. I couldn't resist looking over my shoulder. There stood three felines I had never seen before. One stood in the forefront, the others to his flanks. The male, in front, was a golden brown that had horizontal black stripes on his forehead. He wore a light gold mane that framed his face and faded to a dark brown which covered his shoulders, tapering under his ribcage ending at the stomach area. The rest of his body was also golden brown with thick black stripes. His tail was like that of a tiger. The front feet were like a lion in color and the hind ones were striped like a tiger. The two females were similar in color at his sides. I jerked my face to Josh and he grinned at me from a few steps ahead.

"What are those?" I pointed at them.

"They are Ligers."

"Oh my God, they are beautiful." I looked back at them. They were now strolling into the woods from off the black topped road. Their stripes helped them blend in to the trees and they disappeared. I could, if I wanted to, focus in and scan for them, but I didn't want to. I could still smell them. That sweet chocolate blood. It really takes a lot of control to not give in and eat them.

I went to catch up with Josh after I followed the Ligers disappearing into the trees with my eyes. The night sky, with all its glitter, began to retreat from above and give way for the new turquoise morning. The mountain ridge to the east blocked the sun rays from flooding the lake and us. The light had nonetheless started to penetrate my eyes painfully. It began to hurt my head like an intense, crippling migraine. I took some long blinks to try to adjust to the new brightness. I found myself looking for Josh harder. I needed to tell him I really need to go inside until tonight. Something, anything to help me get this pain to stop. I found him at the edge of the lake. He had paused there looking into the water at his reflection.

"Here. Shane thought you might need these," Josh said as he held a pair of sunglasses up high enough that I could see them over his shoulder. I walked over to him and he didn't even turn around. I grabbed them and threw them on quickly. After a moment of my eyes focusing again, I could see better and the pain lingered. Only another second and it was gone. Thank goodness for Shane.

"Are you ready?" There was no rudeness in his voice, no joking, and no movement from his body. He just continued to have his head held down facing the still water.

"Yes. Are you?" I deflected. I was excited about this fight. I was also afraid for everyone else. Their deaths, if it comes to it, would be my fault.

"I sure hope so. I haven't really talked to you about how I feel." He looked away from the water and squared off to me. "I am happy you met Ethan. I'm happy you are the one that pulled our misfit family together. But there's a risk that some of us might fail tonight. Please, take care of Shane if something happens to me. I will take any risk to protect her." He paused. "You know what I'm trying to say. The same way you feel about Ethan getting hurt is how I feel about her. So would you do that for me?" He spoke to me softly and walked to me in a snail-like fashion. He stopped very close to my body, breathing my scent in. His eyes were opening and I tensed up. "No. Don't be defensive. Relax. I'm not going to hurt you. I just want to feel the promise. Not just hear it. It will be imprinted onto your soul if you say it. If it's not kept you will be restless. This is the only way, in my mind, I will feel totally fine with fighting this fight."

"I um . . . of course I will take care of her. She has taught me everything I know about this life. I will. I promise." I could feel a bond intertwining between him and I. An unseen presence connecting the two of us. The feeling, I guess you could say of a promise, that comes from your soul and is speaking silently to the other soul. I would only imagine that this feeling is only experienced by a vampire. Our emotions are on a bigger scale than humans.

"Thank you," Josh said to me in a relieved tone. "Let's go. We need to cover more ground." We walked away from the water's edge and onto a path in the dirt around it. As we walked, he and I were now side by side acting like children shoving and pushing each other. Out of the blue, Shane was giggling at us and Ethan was too. Josh and I had walked half way around the lake and met up with them in an area that was a spillway which was not in use. It was concrete. The rim of it was a half-moon shape and it sloped down. At the bottom, there was grass growing over dark brown bricks layered on the ground. I jumped down on the spillway floor.

"He started it," I joked as I pointed up to Josh.

"No I didn't!" exclaimed Josh, laughing.

"Okay you two, do I need to separate you?" Shane asked as she floated down onto the bricks.

"You told us to walk together," I smirked. Ethan dropped down next. He was not as graceful as Shane. Josh jumped off the rim and landed in front of Shane. He threw his arms around her shoulders and kissed her cheek softly. Ethan had made it to me by the time Josh kissed her.

"Hi."

"Hello to you. Did you miss me?" I asked.

"A little," he said as he frowned and tilted his head.

I socked his chest and it made a loud 'thud.' He was solid through and through. Shane and Josh led the way down the thick path of bricks until it dropped off. The bricks were laid down like a street on concrete. Now in front of us were enormous rocks. Oval, rectangle, circles, all shapes and sizes. Some stood tall while others drunkenly leaned on flatter ones on the ground. Some were bigger than me and others were the size of pebbles. Moss spattered over the tops of some of them. Water once ran between and over the rocks flowing down over this break and disappeared within the white trees lining the outskirts of the forest.

I could smell the changelings aroma tantalizing the air in the trees down there. They were somewhere, poised and ready. I could feel their eyes on me and I knew without a doubt that they were ready for the fight. I turned and faced the rest of my family waiting to live or die in this unresolved dispute between Azrael and me. I was sorry they were here and glad all at the same time. I glanced at the sky through my shades. It was becoming a pretty day. How ironic.

We were walking to the concrete rim, Ethan's hand in mine and Josh in Shane's, when suddenly I felt faint. I was on shaky legs. Fear invaded my gut. I let out a breath of air from all the capacity my lungs held. Deep intense dieing, dread pushed me to my knees. Ethan said something I couldn't hear. Blasting of drum beats, the cadence my heart, was all I could hear. Prickling pain ran over every pore of my body. I jerked a breath in. I felt the approach of 'them' coming. I forced my body to submit to my control and fought with it for a couple of minutes. It felt like an eternity. When I did regain my composer, I forced the words out of my lips. It sounded like a mixture of a hiss and a growl.

"It's time." I made my body stand upright. Ethan looked deep into my eyes and winked. He took his warm loving hand and caressed my cheek. I instinctively knew the direction 'they' would appear. I pointed to the north. "That way." I was better now. I overturned the feelings and pushed them down deep into my guts and extinguished it. I had to do that before. It was when I first met Ethan after I was turned. The only difference between then and now is, this was death coming. Icy, ghostly spirits on swift heels creeping in to reap life away, bottle it up, and destroy it until all the joy and love is extinct from this world.

The Ligers behind us began to breath heavier and started panting. I stepped forward and was in the front of everyone.

Ethan grabbed my upper arm. "What are you doing?" Ethan snarled.

"Getting ready!" I loudly said as I pulled my arm away from his grip.

"You're behind me. How am I suppose to protect you there?"

"What?! I'm the one he wants."

"If I know anything about his type, his fight will be with me. You're a bonus. He is furious with me for stopping him when he was turning you."

"He's right Ivy." Josh jumped in, "I knew him fairly well. He will want to fight Ethan. You and Kera are merely trophies."

"Ivy, please." Shane pleaded, "Just for now. Okay?"

"Fine," I spit. I stepped back behind Ethan and to the right. I didn't want to argue with them but, do you blame me? The stirring of the icy cold in my gut rejuvenated itself. The feelings of 'them' arriving took over and now I could tell they were seconds away. The knowledge of how many rang in my head. The number nine. "Oh no! They're nine strong!!" I informed everyone. Josh and Shane took a fighting stance. Ethan began to ooze that musky smell. He had not changed but was very close.

Moisture lifted into the air and the clouds rolled in from the north like a storm at sea, out of nowhere. Thunder playfully wrestled in the clouds that were now forming. Lightning sparks flashed in them like veins feeding life to the clouds. The lake began crying mist up to the gray black blankets now etched in the atmosphere. Wind began to pick up around our bodies. Not a strong wind, just a slight breeze. Probably to smell how many we are. 'They' walked out of the dark shadows of the battered pines lining the edge of the lake. Their cold gray skin stood out against the fall colors displayed by the dieing leaves of the forest.

Azrael was in the front wearing a grin showing off his white sharp teeth. He was in the same, or similar, clothing as the night he visited me here and ended my human life. A long, black trench coat and pale t-shirt under it. His black pants and those green, hollow eyes. His hair was let down and was past his shoulders.

Several others stepped out from behind him, closely following in a 'v' pattern into the open space as if they were a flock of geese. The one to his right was a man around the same height as Azrael, 5'8", about 170 pounds. He was clothed in all white. A white ruffled shirt and vest with a white pair of slacks. His hair was white and cut feathered on the sides with eyes of dark blue. One of his eyes had a fascinating gray circle around the iris. I could feel in my gut he was the source of the weather change. My intuition was pushing further into their beings and I could also not only get the feel of their gifts, but their names as well. His name was Neitherwood.

To the left of Azrael was another man with dirty blonde hair that looked like he had never heard of shampoo. He had a grungy look about him, holes in the knees of his jeans, a dark green t-shirt with a dingy black button up shirt opened over top of it. A chain connected to his back pocket while dirty worn out sneakers covered his feet. I couldn't tell you his facial features due to his hair falling into it. The mimicking vampire. The thief of gifts Josh spoke of at the dinner table that night. Tobias.

The man behind Tobias was quite the opposite. He was short, around 5'6" and weighed about 130 pounds. He wore a dark blue, short-sleeved silk shirt with a black pair of dress pants. He had black hair cut short and combed down. He was clean cut, dark golden brown eyes, and had a nice smile. He was built nicely and was not too bad on the eyes. Quite tasty. Eadrick was his name. Josh said he would be here 'fired up' right along side his side kick Tobias.

Behind Neitherwood, the white one, was a tall bean pole of a man. Bartimas. His blue eyes vacant under his short military styled hair cut. He was dressed simply in a blue muscle shirt, even though he was scrawny, and a faded pair of blue jeans that were, thank goodness, held up by a belt. To top off his fashion statement, he wore big boots. I guess he's over compensating. He was a levitator like Shane.

Standing next to Eadrick, the fire-starter, was a black man in his thirties. He was bald, had a goatee, smoky gray eyes, leather pants, and was wearing a duster. I could tell he had a muscular build by the way it fell over his shoulders and arms. He was named Quinton.

The man next to skinny Bartimas, was a short, dark brown haired boy. Well, he was a man but something about him screamed childish. He was plain to look at, especially in jeans and a button up shirt. Nothing special there. He felt to me like a temper tantrum thrower when not getting his own way. Lucas was his name and he had no gifts to speak of. Just your average vampire.

Then I smirked at the first female walking out of the shadows. She stood next to the black man, Quinton. She had straight, reddish brown hair and was paler than the others. She had a pastel floral dress on. It came down to her feet. Did anyone really inform her on what's going to happen here today? Not what I would have worn to my funeral. Etched on her gravestone would be, 'Rosanna the Liar.' She could bespell humans like I can, but fortunately, she couldn't bespell vampires, like me.

Next to Lucas, the nothing special one, was a tall, fire engine haired man. He looked similar to a shorter Paul Bunyan but his name was Kaine. He was strapped across the chest and wore a tight yellow shirt to show it off. He had dark blue jeans on and a thick belt. His deep blue eyes screamed out in contrast to his hair.

They all had an egotistical aura about them and were repulsive to watch strutting their stuff. This made me mad, furious, and very irritated. Patience Ivy. Patience. We all stood on the bricks of the spillway waiting for them to come closer. They, one by one, jumped over the cove near the cabin Ethan and I were in. They were now standing on the same side of the lake as us.

Azrael was still in the front, smiling and looking me over up and down. He seemed quite pleased with himself. I felt like a bug in a jar being studied. I was so uncomfortable. It was that 'knew what I looked like naked' uncomfortable. I wanted to take my teeth and peel the skin of his face off layer by layer. I threw a hiss at him, anything to make him stop looking at me like that. He dramatically laughed, as if I had made a joke and was not threatened by me in the least.

"Miss me, my elusive minx?" He slithered through his snake lips. His focus shifted to Josh. "Josh, haven't seen you around in decades, thought you were dead but, now I see why. Who is this irresistible morsel there beside you?" He pointed at Shane with his boney finger and its long, glossy nail. He pulled his bottom lip in-between his teeth, bit it, and let it slide out slowly inhaling Shane's scent.

"Azrael," Josh said tipping his hand from his forehead, as if he was wearing a hat. I had a profile view of Josh from where I stood. He was grinning ear to ear.

"I see. Nothing like a good fight for you to let your nature take over and run awry. You always were one to enjoy inflicting pain on others." Josh's grin melted and faded from his face. Azrael snapped to Ethan. "Good morning. Do you think we could have a conversation, just you and I, like two intelligent beings?"

"I suppose. But you didn't come all this way and bring these vampires with you just to talk to me," Ethan said.

"Now you're being rude." Azrael stopped smiling and paused. Then he said, "Here I am, trying to do this the right way. Now you really should be thanking me. I haven't killed your little party yet. We out number you four to nine, in case you haven't noticed."

Was he serious? Could he not count, or is he not smelling the chocolate factory behind us? They were down wind and deep in the trees but still, they are mouth watering!!

"Believe what you want. You should be thanking me for not killing you when you attacked her." Ethan took a step forward and my heart thumped a beat. Ethan looked down to the ground and with his peripheral vision glanced at me. Did he hear that? I could feel all eyes on me. Azrael's demeanor changed from being cocky to a stone facade.

"That's why I'm here now. I want to fight you one on one. No surprises. No ambushes. You came out of nowhere the night I tasted and turned Ivy." His green, hollow eyes shot at me. "Scrumptious by the way." Then back to Ethan without skipping a beat. "You meddled in something that you had no REASON to be in!" His voice was growing louder and angrier. "Everyone here will make sure that happens. No interruptions! And I mean not in the slightest. If you accept, it will be to the death." My heart beat uncontrollable with the word death. Ethan stood silent for a moment and turned to face me.

"Ivy, it will be alright. Stay put and don't get involved. Alright?" He looked at me with those warm, loving, greenish-yellow eyes. How could I not get involved? I can't lose him, I won't. I can't tell him I won't either. My mind ran away taking all reason with it. I was enraged with the thought of losing Ethan. I impulsively jerked my eyes past Ethan to Azrael.

"You better be careful. I have no say in you and him fighting. But, I warn you now, you should pray for a death he will deliver to you." I showed off my canines with a low hiss. "Mine will be satisfying my appetite. You know what I'm capable of. You chose me, after all, above every human you have came across for a reason."

"I'm intrigued. If I win, on the other hand, you and I will make our own understanding with stakes of our choosing. But that is a conversation for after I kill your little teddy." He chuckled.

Azrael stepped away from his body guards, from the lake's edge, and onto the spillway rim. Ethan had begun secreting his musky earthy smell even heavier. He was expanding inside and tearing his skin. The Ethan I knew slid off of his body and dingy yellow white fur danced in the slight wind in the air. Tiny glass tubes, clear and hollow, reflected what little sun we were experiencing. His ash skin was twirling in the air and taken off with the breeze. He now had a large body, a long neck, short tail, and small ears. His nose and around his eyes were a deep black. His feet were massive and webbed. He was easily a 1600 pound polar bear, and stood 10 feet tall.

He dropped to all fours and began to pace back and forth in a small area in front of me. It was in a protective manor. I don't need protection I wanted to scream at him. My thoughts were interrupted by Azrael pushing off of the concrete rim and throwing a superman punch to the top of Ethan's head. His head jerked down and he immediately pulled it back up. He growled at him with a growl that ran through my bones, shaking them from the inside. The polar bear stood on his back feet and took his enormous claws and swiped Azrael's right arm. The nails dug deep into his bicep, flinging blood on my face from the force. I licked my lips gathering the splatter with my tongue. His blood was bitter and stale. His memories didn't come to me just like Ruth's. It must be the age.

Azrael thew an uppercut at Ethan and he lifted up into the air and landed, almost right on top of me. I jumped back, threw my hands into a claw like appearance, and hissed at Azrael.

"No." Shane called out in a growling whisper.

Ethan sprinted forward and tackled Azrael. Ethan was on top, trying to bite his face off while Azrael was blocking his attacks with his forearms. Ethan was tearing into them and shredding his meat between the two bones with every bite. I glanced up at the ones he brought with him trying to see if they were about to get involved. They had no intentions of breaking Azrael's pact with Ethan. A few of them looked really worried about how the brawl was turning out.

I shot my eyes back to the blood and gore on the ground in front of me. I could smell Azrael's blood fumigating the air and watched his futile attempts to stop

Ethan. The polar bear sprung up on his back feet only to come crashing down on Azrael's chest. His ribs broke, crunching under the weight. The bear stepped off of him and paused for a split second to look at Azrael's broken torso.

Azrael slowly sat up on his bottom and his body began to heal inside. We all could hear his ribs snapping back into the right shape. Ethan could too I guess, because he roared in his face. He stepped towards him only to meet Azrael's fist across his temple and Ethan flew to the left, past Shane, and slid a few feet. I looked for movement from Ethan and saw none. My blood boiled from my toes and flowed throughout my body until it reached my face. I wanted to explode.

I felt a strange feeling of something wrapping around my hips and legs keeping me from moving and immediately knew what it was. Shane. She was holding me in my place making it impossible to move.

"Let me go!!" I screamed at her.

"No. Let's see what happens. Don't underestimate Ethan and don't break the arrangement!" She yelled back but was not angry.

"I will kill you if you don't!" I hissed at her, dropping my head and keeping eye contact. I wanted to be let loose no matter what I had to say or what it took. Not even Shane was capable of stopping me and with a painful face, she let go of my body.

I looked towards Ethan on the ground. Azrael, completely healed, was strolling to him. I pushed off of the bricks with so much force I turned several of them into powder. In the air, I silently came down over Azrael only to have him turn around to meet my advance. He had a smirk on his face but didn't try to defend himself.

I landed a punch to his cheek bone that fractured on contact. The sound was that of ice cracking in a glass of warm water. The punch I threw slammed his head to the right. He staggered laughing.

"You know, you're right." He stood straight and leaned his face inches from mine. "I do know you." He raised his voice in a commanding tone. "Rosanna, go!"

I looked over to her and she turned around. She ran from the side of the lake and jumped over the cove. She was running to the north. "No!!!" I screamed. She was headed in the direction of our home. Azrael grabbed my wrist in a vise grip, shattering it. I wailed out in pain.

"You will kill all those you love. Haven't you gotten that through your thick skull yet? I'm disappointed in you for even thinking you could keep them, being the vampire you are." He began to laugh again.

A rippling vibration rolled over the bricks where we were standing. The Ligers had charged out of the trees. Ethan was standing up now, behind Azrael. I threw Azrael his way with a power kick to his gut. Ethan caught him, squeezing him between his arms constricting him.

I jumped my attention to the vampires now advancing on the bricks. Josh had engaged Tobias and they were punching and kicking each other. The bean pole of a man, Bartimas, was taking swings at Shane and she was side stepping them elegantly. Ben and the twins ran past me and tackled Lucas and Kaine in mid stride saving me. They began to brawl. I looked past them fighting and focused on the side of the lake.

Neitherwood was still standing over there, powering his gift. The wind was picking up quickly. It began to rain. The rain hitting the surface of the lake was loud and distracting until I muffled it out. It was then I saw Eadrick coming over to me fast. I was taller than him but, he was a man nonetheless. He would be stronger than me but my children are in danger. Mothers protecting their young are a force to be reckoned with. I took a stance ready for the contact. As he ran to me his body broke out with blue flames covering him completely. Under the flames his body was like a mirage. He plowed into me clothes-lining me with the force of a train. I flipped head over heels and landed face down. I pulled my head up stunned. I could see Shane in front of me, a few yards away, levitating Bartimas into the air through my foggy vision. She began to spin him like a top faster and faster.

I felt the pain of landing. The impact broke my legs above the knees. He was on me in no time. The heat from the flames was burning my backside. He wrapped his arm around my neck and locked it in. As I grabbed for his head, I could see Bartimas fly apart into jagged pieces, spraying blood and body parts all over the place. I dug my nails into Eadrick's face and found his jaw line. I dug deeper underneath it. I gripped it with all the strength I could and ripped it off. He let go of me screaming. I stood up fast, mending my legs on the way, and faced him. He was now kneeling on the ground holding his neck from bleeding. I punched the top of his head and it smashed in. His brain squeezed out of the broken bones like a wet sponge.

I could see Ethan was fighting with Azrael over at the end of the spillway where the huge rocks were. They were both bloody and I could hear the sound of breaking bones all around me. I looked at my hands and saw the damage to them. I had third degree burns all over me where Eadrick had touched. I mended myself as I looked behind me. Quinton was approaching a few feet away from me when Ben jumped on his back. Quinton shrugged Ben off, with trouble, and clawed right through his neck. Ben's body went rolling through the air and landed in the lake. Fragments of neck meat plopped on the bricks beside me. I ran to Quinton and tackled him full-force and we went skipping over the lake like a rock. I was on the top and he was grabbing me around the neck. I was stronger than him. I pushed my mouth to his neck and bit him. My teeth scraped the vertebrate in the back of his throat and I pulled. I spit his Adam's apple out of my mouth and ditched it in the lake as we passed over. We came to a quick halt. Quinton's head crumbled from the impact of the tree we hit. I tucked and rolled after we slammed into the tree and stood up.

I was on the other side of the lake now and I had to get back. Something in the water caught my eye before I could. Bubbles, big ones, were floating to the top of the lake. Suddenly, something burst out of it. It appeared in a brown blur, but I caught a glimpse of wings. It penetrated the thick gray black clouds punching a hole through them. I stood staring in wonder at the hole waiting for it to return down to the earth.

My thick, black spiral curls tainted with blood were whipping around from the gusts of wind. Water on the lake sprayed up into the air, feeding the rain from its choppy waves bouncing off of one another. Leaves tumbled and flew all around. The thin pine trees bent, bowing to the power of the wind.

I looked across the lake and saw Josh leaning forward, focusing on Kaine. The big man had his hands in a death grip on his own ears and screamed in a high pitched voice that pierced my ears. Then, he became silent and his head exploded. His headless, thick body crashed to the ground.

A high screeching came calling from the clouds and my focus shifted to above Neitherwood, who was looking straight up to the sky. Plummeting to the ground was a Griffin. I could not believe what I was seeing. His head was an eagle, his body a lion. His wings were tucked into his sides tight, and his sharp shiny claws on his front paws stretched out. Right before reaching Neitherwood, he broke out his wings, slowed his descent, and snatched Neitherwood up by the shoulders. His wing span was 18 feet easily. He took off over the lake and made a hard left in the air, throwing Neitherwood up over the mountain. The Griffin soared over Josh and Shane who were now watching Tobias run away. The clouds calmed down, dissipating to streaks of thin clouds. The lake quieted its waves. I bolted over the terrain to the other side of the lake, scanning while I ran. Who would be hurt? Who was dead? Where was Ethan?

CHAPTER 19

I was standing on the bricks in seconds, looking around for Ethan or Azrael. All I could see was blood, body parts, Josh and Shane. Ben and Gabbi emerged from the lake, calling out for Abbi. She was nowhere to be found. At the end of the spillway, I smelled musky earth. I ran to the huge rocks and saw Ethan coming out of the woods pretty banged up. He was limping and in human form. I was so relieved to see him, tears came forming on the bottom lids of my eyes. I called out to him with a lump in my throat.

"Hey. You miss me?" The tears fell out.

"A little," he responded. He had reached me and I threw my arms tight around his neck. I pressed my lips to his and he moaned in pain. "I still can break." He smiled at me and took a step back. "I got something for you." He held out his hand and opened it. There in the palm of his hand were canine teeth. "Trophies."

I took them and put them in my pocket and laughed. Ben and Gabbi were calling out for Abbi still.

"Ben. Gabbi. Abbi took off after Rosanna. We need to get back to the house. Let's track her on foot in case she killed her on the way," Ethan call to them. No one said anything out loud as we started running following Abbi's scent. I was quicker than everyone else, so I broke out in front a few paces.

"You know this is not the end of Tobias. He will undoubtedly be telling others of this fight and they will come for you," Josh said as we ran. "Then, we will get to meet other unpleasant family members of the vampire world. It's only a matter of time before the thin, icy layer over the existence of us is cracked open and the whole world's eyes will be opened." He stopped talking and laughed. He really is an unusual character.

The scent lead right up our gray road to the house and kept going. Along the way I could smell Jack's blood, Abbi's blood, and mingling of two other bloods. I feared the worst.

When we got to the house, our dogs had blood all over their muzzles and were happy to see us. They stayed outside while we went in.

The house reeked of sweet, musky blood. Jack was hunched over the couch in the living room not moving. I ran to his side. I placed my hands under his chin and noticed the feel of death cradling it. Cold to the touch. I lifted his face just enough to see that his salt and pepper hair was falling into his eyes. I brushed it back for him. His face had long nail scratches, imbedded deep to the bone. Some of his ribs were protruding out of his torso, touching the top of the couch. His eyes were slit open. Those wonderful brown eyes that I always ran to, to give me advice in the past, were gone. They were hollow and dark. The smile that warmed my being would never appear again. I didn't even get to tell him what an impact he had on me and my daughter. The saving of my soul he gave freely. He died because of me. He did this of his own free will and look what I did to him. This should be me slouched over a couch and him holding my lifeless body. Nothing will be the same with him gone. Why do I ever let people in? I am exactly what my name represents.

I stepped away from Jack and scanned the room for the kids. I couldn't smell blood from Zachary. I could smell Abbi. Her sweet blood danced in the air under my nose. Then I smelled Kera's. I screamed for her. Out of the silence, we heard panting coming from the basement.

Ben and Gabbi were next to the basement stairs and ran down them.

"Kera! Zachary! Are you alright?" I cried out. Ethan was in front of me going down the steps.

"Keep Ivy upstairs!" Ben screamed to Ethan.

"Why? What's wrong?!" I pushed up against Ethan's back, dropping my head to see under the dropped ceiling. Kera was bloody and sitting up pressed to the wall. Her eyes were flickering and Abbi was still in Liger form. She was stretched out at Kera's feet, bloody, with her head placed on Kera's legs. I couldn't hear a heart beat from Kera. The smell of sweet blood filled the air thicker and thicker.

"What's going on?!" I pushed on Ethan's back trying to get past him. "Let me down there!"

"Momma." A small scratchy voice whispered from behind me. It was Zachary. He had a concoction of Abby and Jack's blood on him.

"Oh baby, are you alright? What happened?" I moved to the top step and knelt down to one knee. I caressed his hair running my finger through the knots of blood and pet his face. I wiped away his tears, mixing with blood, while he talked.

"Jack was fighting with a lady vampire. She beat him up bad. Then she was looking for us. She came down stairs and we hid under the computer table. She grabbed Kera out . . . I tried screaming at her to stop and . . ." His tears choked him.

"Go on. It's okay." I reassured him kissing his cheek. The smell of chocolate was over powering now and I tried to concentrate. It didn't help that the blood on his cheek was on my lips. I licked them instinctively. It was too watered down to over take me. I pushed the thoughts out and focused on Zachary.

"She cut Kera on the neck and a lot of blood came out . . . then Abbi showed up and . . . the lady is outside by the water fountain. I tried Momma. I tried to help Kera." He was getting hysterical. I hugged him tight and looked at Ethan.

"You're safe now baby." I kissed his forehead. "Is she alright?" I forced out of my throat. I was squeezing the tears off. They would do Zachary no good to see me emotional. I heard Kera's heart began to sputter. It thumped and broke out into rhythm after a few moments. It got stronger and stronger. Ethan looked up at me with tears in his eyes.

"She'll be fine . . . but Ivy . . . Abbi had to take drastic measures to save her life . . ." He took two steps up and stopped.

The smell of chocolate and Kera's heart beating pushed it further up the stairs and into the living room.

"No . . ." I shook my head in disbelief. There was no stopping the tears now. They flooded down my face and I clung to Zachary. "No . . . what is . . . what do I . . . I can't have this . . . this is not how . . ." I couldn't talk any longer. I began to sob uncontrollably. Zachary grabbed me tighter and Ethan joined us on the top step.

"Baby, Don't cry," he softly whispered in my ear. "Come on. Get up." He helped me to my feet and got me to the couch in the living room. Zachary still at my side, hugging me gently. "It'll be alright," Ethan said.

"No it won't be alright." I shoved the tears off of my cheeks. "I could kill her being one of them." I held my voice down to not startle Zachary.

"No. You won't." Ethan argued. "I know you better than you know yourself. I say you will do fine with this new change."

"I wish . . . I don't know what I wish. I want this nightmare over with. I just want it to end." I sniffled.

"Ivy. This is not the end. This is just the beginning. Imagine all the wonderful things she will be able to change into. All the wonderful things you two will have to share of her new life. No Ivy. This is just the start of a new journey." He kissed my forehead and caressed the side of my face. "I love you," he whispered.

I hope he's right. God forbid he's not. He hasn't taken into consideration that I am poison to everything I touch. The only thing I can think of is, with Ethan by my side I can conquer anything. Even if my daughter is the most intriguing, edible meal I will ever taste. She is now my Hershey Kiss.

I sat on the couch with thoughts running through my head. I had no control over them and no direction for them. Ben, Abbi, and Gabbi stayed in the basement with Kera while she transformed to begin a new chapter in her life.

∽∘∾

CPSIA information can be obtained
at www.ICGtesting.com
Printed in the USA
FSHW010019090920
73642FS